THE POLITICS OF Love

A MARRIAGE OF CONVENIENCE ROM-COM BY
DREW TAYLOR

Taylor Made
PUBLISHING

Cover and Interior Design by Drew Taylor

Character/Object Art by Callie McLay

Edited by Leah Taylor

Proofread by Lindsay Rankin

To me (2023 version):
Look at how much you've healed. I'm proud of you.
Love, Me (2025 version)

To the women constantly healing...
I see you. You're not alone.

warning

What's In This Book?

If you like to fully experience a book for what it is, then skip this section

T POL is a political marriage of convenience romance. It has *Pride and Prejudice*-inspired vibes without being too on the nose. I sought to write Darcy's perspective as if I was in the brain of Jane Austen when writing this misunderstood, grumpy man. It definitely took a big swerve away from the classic novel, but I am so proud of this story.

TPOL is spice free. There are kisses, attraction, longing stares, and a truly closed door scene. While this is a VERY SLOW BURN, my characters experience plenty of sizzling attraction to one another. Attraction and lustful thoughts are a natural, human thing that we battle. I seek to showcase that while also having my characters learn to take their thoughts captive. There is one brief nudity scene, though nothing is described, as a hospital gown slip happens... (So sorry, my dude).

TPOL contains mentions of drinking. These are grown adult characters who can make their own decisions and know the consequences of their decisions.

TPOL is spice-free and written from a Christian perspective. I am a Christian, but I do not write explicitly Christian Fiction. I seek to write characters who are flawed and sinful, yet, they recognize their need for Christ and seek forgiveness, repentance, and redemption. I wanted to read a romance where faith wasn't the main storyline, yet the characters were Christian and operated from that worldview...so I wrote it.

Read at your own risk. And I pray you LOVE this story. Please leave a review if you do :)

Prologue

Darcy

"I forbid you from breaking off this engagement." My voice rumbles like a volcano on the verge of erupting. Priscilla Weatherby, my fiancée and lifelong friend, shudders, but continues to slip the ring off her finger, placing it gently onto the marbled kitchen counter.

"Darcy, I'm sorry. You don't get a say in this part of my life. I will reach out to you once I am ready." And with those final words she walks out of my house, taking my ambitions of the presidency with her. Muttering a string of curses, I fish my phone from my pocket to call the last person I want to call at this moment.

But it's a necessity, and regardless of my disdain for the personality of the flamboyant, young woman, I trust her. At least with campaign matters.

The phone rings.

And rings.

Then goes to voicemail.

Who does she think she is, ignoring my call? It's her job to answer me. I throw my phone across the room, not caring if it shatters.

That's a lie. I have to care.

I'm running for president of the United States and have to communicate with people.

Stomping across the kitchen and into the dining room, I swipe my phone off the floor and check for cracks. There is one running across the screen but everything works. I'll get a new one.

I flip to Hayden's contact—accurately labeled *Divine Princess* because she voices her opinions like she is entitled royalty—and hover over the "call now" button. The name is a moniker, but she would probably think it a compliment. If she ever saw it, that is, which isn't going to happen.

It's not like I hate her. She's just too...happy.

Colorful.

Alive.

With a grunt, I shove my phone into the pocket of my black slacks and run a hand through my blond waves. I let out a breath of air and pace back and forth between the kitchen and dining room, my thoughts twisting and turning in my head as I circle my table meant to sit fourteen. As if it's ever used for that.

I have to find someone to marry me, and fast. If I want to have any shot at the presidency, I need a wife. Two giants already stand in my way—I'm running on the Independent ticket, and I'm thirty-nine. Having a wife is a necessity if I want to bypass my lack of party affiliation and young nature. Then again, my former campaign manager, Stella Harper, put my young status on the market to attract eighteen-year-old first-time voters. Let the record show I was against the idea, but she insisted it would boost my ranking in the polls. It did. Stella is always right.

Stella is still technically my campaign manager, but she's marrying a man back in Mississippi and is staying there while transitioning and training Hayden Bennett to take the reins of the campaign. Hayden is her second in command and the very woman who knows where my buttons are and makes a game out of pushing them.

Mississippi. Wedding. What day is it?

I check the calendar on my phone and remember it's Stella's wedding day.

Shoot. I promised Hayden I would not bug her today.

But my life is falling apart around me, and I need her to fix this. She is the only one I trust—outside of Stella, who is probably saying 'I do'—to put the pieces back together in a way that won't muck the situation up more.

I'm not unaware. I know I'm a complicated man. A good-looking, attractive man. A wealthy man. A man of importance and prominence.

But completely thorny, prickly, and stubborn.

Once a woman gets to know me, they run. Just like Priscilla is doing. Apparently, friendship was the only companionship she was able to offer me, though we both knew growing up that we were to be wed in order to solidify familial connections.

Why did she change her mind all of a sudden? Arranged marriages are not my favorite, and I know many people are absolutely against them, but the security they provide is unmatched. Trust is better than love in any relationship. I trusted Priscilla. We share common interests, goals, and values. At least, I thought we did.

What am I going to do when news of the broken engagement reaches the press? Those vultures are going to eat it up like roadkill on a country road, chewing up then spitting out grotesque narratives. I can see the headline now: *DARCY KICKED TO THE CURB BY THOMAS WEATHERBY'S DAUGHTER.* That story will be told over and over by political news outlets. The pop culture news will probably put their own spin on the story, definitely referencing *Pride and Prejudice* somehow.

Have I mentioned how much I despise that movie? I can't go one day without someone attempting to joke with me; the jokes typically involve clenched fists, ladies named Elizabeth, and the stupid quote I've had the misfortune of hearing one too many times. Something about being bewitched.

My campaign team likes to joke that I'm just as grumpy, if not more than, the leading man himself. I like to fire those people. I'm not grumpy. At least not in my head. It's my autistic ways, though I don't make a point to tell others I have autism spectrum disorder.

I have not watched *Pride and Prejudice*, but I don't need to. Society has told me the story, and I unsubscribed.

My phone rings, stopping me in my tracks.

"Hayden," I breathe her name in relief. "I need your help."

"I'm at Stella's wedding," she says in that aggravating way that is technically respectful but oozes disdain under the surface.

"I know, and I'm sorry." I pause, still not believing this predicament I'm in. "Priscilla broke off the engagement."

She gasps before stuttering a word that sounds like "what."

I don't have time for this.

"I don't know what to do, Hayden, so," my voice elevates with each word, "tell me what to do. I am not losing this election because I am *wifeless.*" I grimace over the word like it's the bad leftover taste of a jalapeño popper. I'm spiraling, and I loathe losing control.

"Unbelievably stupid, having to go to Hayden for this," I mumble under my breath.

"Breathe, Mr. Marshall." The soft way she says my name ruffles me. How can she be calm in this situation? This can make or break my campaign! She continues, "I'll be back in New York in two days, and we will figure something out. For now, I'll call our social media team to stay on top of the stories and make sure everything looks good and is in your favor."

Not enough. "Just get here fast." I hang up the phone.

I make my way to my in-home office and slump into the black leather chair behind my desk. A stinging ache arises in my chest, and thoughts of childhood days with Priscilla infiltrate my mind. I don't have time to mourn the loss of her friendship, though. Leaning my elbows on the table, clasping my hands, and laying my chin on top of my fists, I try to think of eligible single women in my sphere.

Most of the women that come to mind only want me for two things: my money and status.

But I don't want to marry a woman who wants to use me to climb her own social ladder. Those women are often clingy and dimwitted. If they are smart, they are manipulative and nasty. I would be utterly vexed to the point I would snap and send them packing myself.

No, I need to find a classy, respectable woman to be my wife. Someone who understands the world I live in but does not necessarily want to be a part of it. A woman who is independent, loyal, and a true confidant. One who doesn't care about the name, money, and status of Darcy Marshall but will be my sidekick all the same. One who can handle me when I can't handle myself.

I don't need love, but I do need respect, loyalty, and trust.

How will I find a woman who checks all those boxes?

POP CULTURE NOW!

PRESIDENTIAL CANDIDATE DUMPED BY FIANCE
IS THIS A SIGN AMERICA WILL DUMP HIM, TOO?

By Krissy Towers

Word on the street is billionaire, businessman, and presidential candidate for the Independent Party, Darcy Marshall, was given back an expensive Roman Malakov engagement ring. His (former) fiancée, Priscilla Weatherby, daughter of Weatherby Enterprises' CEO Thomas Weatherby, was seen bolting from his house in tears yesterday during the late afternoon. The 14.18-carat diamond was noticeably absent from her left hand.

We are all speculating over what caused Priscilla, a cultural gem to high-fashion society, to race from Ophelia Estate. Whispers stated he was seeing another woman, following in the footsteps of his belated unfaithful father, Gerald Marshall. Some social media users are placing the blame on Priscilla, stating they've caught blurry pictures of her out with a man who was not her fiancé. Another birdie suggests something more sinister is at play. We have reached out to Priscilla and Weatherby Enterprises for comment.

Will America continue to look favorably upon America's young, rising political star, or will Darcy Marshall be booted back to the tech world to develop more social apps like his highly successful networking app COFFEE? We at *Pop Culture NOW!* will follow the trail and find the reason Priscilla took herself out of the race for potential First Lady. Stay tuned for all of the tea in conservative politics!

CHAPTER ONE

HAYDEN

This is so not in my job description. Sulking over mundane tasks is my favorite pastime as I stand—in my one pencil skirt because all my pants were crumpled in the laundry basket begging me to wash them—in line for coffee at Five Four Coffee in Times Square. New York City has an endless supply of lines, providing an endless supply of thinking time on my end.

And I'm thinking Darcy Marshall could get his own dang coffee. Or at least hire a young, ambitious, wide-eyed lackey for mundane, totally irrelevant tasks like this. Who cares if this is his favorite coffee shop and it's on my way to work, i.e., his house, where he has his own espresso machine and full coffee bar that sits as new and pristine as the day he bought it?

The hum of the machines, the chatter and energy of the people, and the modern vibe of the place energizes me, but the thought that I could be elbow-deep in campaign plans right now sours the atmosphere. Not even the lo-fi music smoothly playing in the background can perk my mood. It's the beginning of March, and

I have eight months left to get this man to 270 electoral votes. I should be working!

"Stella would have never put up with this," I grumble under my breath. I contemplate calling my best friend to vent, but I know she's in the midst of teaching her first class of the day at the University of Southern Mississippi.

Ugh.

I check my smartwatch, watching the seconds tick by on the analog clock. Seconds that could have been used on proofing speeches, checking website subscriptions, filtering donations from political action committees, or even making dreaded phone calls to news media outlets to schedule Darcy's next interviews. I tap my toe against the white, tiled floor.

"Next," the barista calls as unenthusiastically as I feel.

I approach the guy behind the sleek black counter, kind of digging his midnight-blue hair color. He must be new here because I haven't seen him before. I'd remember that hair; it's like he's stepped out of an anime show. *Hmm.* He's quite handsome with his sharp features and dull expression.

"One venti Americano with two espresso shots, a pump of sugar-free butterscotch, and a splash of cream, please." I mentally pat myself on the back for getting through the complete order without stumbling over my words.

"Hot or iced?" he asks. Shoot.

"Hot."

"Name?"

The fun part. I have never given my real name at this coffee shop before, and I know the regular employees enjoy my name creations. Let's do something special for the new anime-looking guy.

I bat my eyelashes and say in Japanese, *"Namie."*

"Spell it."

"N-A-M-I-E."

The cute barista—Kale, as his name tag reads—scribbles the romanized name on the cup and puts the order in. He takes the card I hand him, all without the slightest hint of a smile.

"Need a receipt?" he asks in the same monotone voice he's used this entire exchange. Just because I don't want to be here doesn't mean I can't try to make this man's day better.

"My boss might literally morph into a Nomu if I don't bring one back," I jest. Kale only blinks, the blank expression still coating his face. *"My Hero Academia?"* I question, stating the show's name the Nomu monster is from. He shakes his head slowly. At least I got some reaction out of him, even if he's slightly terrified of me now. I thought for sure this guy watched anime based on his cool and wild hair color. He hands me my card back with the receipt. "You should watch it!" I call over my shoulder as I move to wait in the new line to receive the beverage. Cute Kale has already begun boring the next customer.

My shoulders rise and fall with my sigh. I miss Stella. She didn't watch anime, but she played *Zelda: Breath of the Wild* with me and let me ramble on about fan theories surrounding my favorite anime—*My Hero Academia*. It's not cool for a woman of my caliber to be into that sort of stuff, but it's my escape, and it has been for a long time. Regardless, I learned another new language out of the obsession.

"*Namie*," another barista calls out, pronouncing it like nay-mee instead of the proper nah-mee. Walking up to the counter with my head held high, I pick up the coffee for Darcy. I borrow the pen on the counter to scribble the Japanese characters above the romanized name, always jumping at the chance to practice the characters.

I freeze in my tracks.

This. Is. For. Darcy.

Darn it all. I forgot this was his coffee, and the name on his cup in Japanese translates to "God's blessing."

Dear Lord, if Darcy understands Japanese, now would be the time to give him amnesia, I pray. Okay, it's not a great prayer, but the Lord already knows my heart.

Of all people, Darcy Marshall does not need an ego boost.

After trekking to the nearest parking garage, I hop into my car and begin navigating the morning traffic as I make my way to Darcy's house—er, mansion? His massive place is located on the Upper East Side of Manhattan, which is why I'm driving and honking my horn at people jaywalking instead of walking on the streets myself.

There's a part of me that wants to crank up J-Pop tunes and take my dear, sweet time, intentionally letting his coffee grow cold so that maybe he will quit sending me on this waste-of-time errand every morning. But then again, the man is running for president, and I need this to go well for the both of us. My student loans won't pay themselves off. Plus, if I get him elected, the door will open with countless opportunities for me. As a young, Black female in politics, I'm not incredibly liked or accepted. I get called every name in the book by the liberal media, many of them saying I am a disgrace to my people because of my conservative-leaning beliefs. The conservative media always tiptoes around me like they don't want to offend me by saying the wrong thing.

It's all unbelievably frustrating.

But if I can be the woman to get Darcy Marshall—tech guru, billionaire, inventor of the popular networking app COFFEE, and Independent candidate—elected to America's highest office, then maybe that'll shut everyone up and I can do my thing. Debt-free. My ultimate dream is not to be president, but to be Secretary of State. That's where the *real* action is.

I've clawed my way to where I am and won't let cold coffee ruin it for me. I put the pedal to the metal and book it to Darcy's place.

Arriving at the entrance, I reach through the window of my car and punch the code in to open the large, white monstrosity of a gate. The name "Ophelia" is crafted in a thick, straight font across the top of the gate. According to the news, he renamed the estate from Marshall Estate to Ophelia Estate after his father passed away. Ophelia was also the name of his younger sister who passed away, though eerily enough, there isn't much online about her passing considering the fame and prestige of the Marshall family. The bars swing wide, granting me access to the long, stone road leading to the house—er, mansion. I really need to quit referring to the giant place as a mere house.

Houses are for normal people, and Darcy is *not* normal.

Centennial Blush Magnolia trees line the way forward, and I long for April to arrive in order to see the trees blossom, creating a wall of pink to brighten this dreadful drive.

Okay, the drive isn't dreadful, but knowing it ends with me sitting in Darcy's *mansion* twists my stomach into knots, and not the good cinnamon pretzel kind. The man infuriates me. He's cold and stoic. Hard to understand at times. My issue is with his grumpy personality, not his work ethic or values. I respect him and support his vision for the country; I wouldn't take on this campaign if I didn't.

I park my car outside his garage, flip down the visor mirror, touch up my lipstick and make sure my hair is in place, then step out of the vehicle. Right as I click the button to lock the doors to the black Toyota Camry, I realize I forgot Darcy's coffee in the cup holder. Beeping my key fob and opening the door, I lean in to grab the cup.

"Finally."

Jerking upright at the sound of the deep voice, my head hits the roof of the car and the coffee slips out of my hand, falling onto my black leather seats and splashing on my body.

My torso and face burn with the contact of the hot liquid, and I let out something between a howl and screech. Jumping away from the crime scene, I trip over my heels and squeeze my eyes shut, preparing for a painful impact with the ground.

It never comes.

Instead, I fall into strong arms. While it's not the concrete I was expecting, this embrace is as solid as if it was sculpted out of marble.

I don't have to open my eyes to know Darcy Marshall is holding me up, my white blouse is now a cream color, and my face is so scalded that a pink color is probably showing through my hazelnut skin. As a matter of fact, I think I'll play dead. Like a opossum. It's better than facing my boss, the future president of this country, while in this unfavorable, painful condition.

"Are you okay?" His voice is gravelly, like he is unsure whether or not he should be concerned. Not a comforting feeling when you're pretty certain you have at least second-degree burns coating your face, chest, and stomach.

It stings like a million bees.

My only reply to his question is a whimpered grunt.

All of a sudden, the ground disappears beneath my feet, and I'm being carried bridal style. I should jump out of his arms and walk myself like the independent woman I've been my entire existence, but that's asking for a death wish in my current state. My stinging skin, the throbbing in my ankle, and the lightheadedness from the sheer embarrassment of the moment take over, and I surrender to Darcy's aid.

I squeeze my eyes closed and enjoy the gentle sway of his steps and the light breeze caressing my burning face. It's like I'm a child being rocked to sleep on a front porch, something I've only experienced in my dreams. My brain turns off, refusing to face the reality of this humiliating situation. *Dear God, I pray I'm not fired after this...*

Far too soon, the rocking stops and the breeze vanishes. I'm lowered onto something soft and warm, and I risk peeking through one eye.

A tall, white ceiling welcomes me back to the world of the living, and I blink a few times to make sure my eyes are working properly. With great effort and a tiny groan, I sit up, which is quite difficult since I'm sinking into...whatever I'm on. Once I'm fully up and my head is effectively pounding, I register the couch.

The yellowest couch I've ever seen. Like a ripened lemon.

I sweep my gaze around the room, cataloging it as a bedroom. Darcy's estate is huge, so it's not abnormal that I haven't been in this room before. Not that I would ever go into one of Darcy's bedrooms, though I don't think this one would be his.

It's too...*warm.*

The sheer curtains draping the large floor-to-ceiling windows are obviously there for decoration as the morning sunlight pours into the room. The furniture looks to be made of pine wood while the art decor and flowers of the room carry the same lemon-yellow tone of the couch. Hues of pastel colors are woven throughout, somehow tying everything together into a perfectly chaotic bow. A teddy bear with a yellow ribbon on one ear sits on the bed like it's waiting for its owner's return.

I love it.

"Good. You're sitting up." Darcy clears his throat as I slowly turn my head around to find him standing in the doorway with a bottle of water and a wet rag. "Lay this on your face. It will help the burn."

I hold out my hand to accept the rag, but instead of handing it to me, he tosses it. My reaction time is clearly hindered at the moment due to the injury, so the rag hits me in the face before I can get my hand raised to catch it.

"Thank you," I mumble from beneath the folded rag as I pull it off my face.

"Go to the hospital. You're off today."

I'm... "What?"

Darcy turns on his heel and walks out of the room, still holding the bottle of water I had assumed was for me. Thirst squeezes my throat at the sight of the disappearing water.

"I'll be okay," I shout hoarsely toward his retreating frame. As much as I'd love to take the day off, there's no need for a hospital visit. I'll pick up an over-the-counter cream later. But for now, I take his absence as a welcomed visitor and slump into the downy couch, unfolding the rag and placing it over my face. The cooling effect is immediate, and I sigh with relief.

"Take this water with you."

I scramble to sit up on the sinking couch and tug the rag from my face just in time for something hard to slam onto my thighs. The water bottle he only moments ago walked away with now sits in my lap. My jaw drops in lieu of words while he exits the room as if he didn't just toss a bottle of water at an injured woman. His own campaign manager, at that. And if I didn't want to guzzle down this water right now, I'd have half a mind to throw it at his retreating frame.

What. A. Grump.

But I guess you get to be whatever you want to be when you're a billionaire running for the nation's highest office. Slumping my shoulders, I take a much-needed sip of the water, pat the rag against my stinging face, pull myself out of the sinking lemon couch, and then try to find my way to the bathroom to check the burn on my chest and attempt to salvage my blouse. The hospital was not on the agenda for today, and I hate reworking schedules.

Time to take this crappy day and turn it around. If life has taught me one thing, it's to never wallow in sorrows and hardships when I can choose to overcome them.

CHAPTER TWO

DARCY

Hmph. I was highly anticipating chugging the coffee that now resides inside Hayden's car and on her body. *Note to future self: don't startle the woman bringing you coffee.*

I hope she makes it to the hospital. Maybe I should have ordered one of my drivers to take her. Why are my manners always an afterthought when it comes to my personal life, instead of second nature like when I'm wearing my political persona? I don't know why my masking tendencies short-circuit in Hayden's presence.

Hayden is technically not a part of my personal life, but we work so close together almost every day that it's like she's family. I've taught myself how to be charismatic and likable, but with the people I'm closest to, I revert to my natural enigmatic self. It's part of living with ASD, according to the therapist I used to see back in my twenties.

And I should take better care of the people carrying some of the weight of this campaign on their shoulders in order to take some of the burdens off of me.

"Mr. Marshall, are you ready to begin?"

Taking one last deep breath, I fix my facial features into my well-practiced media mask and walk to the open seat across from the petite, blonde reporter. After sitting down in the suede chair in my sitting room, I reach to shake the woman's outstretched hand. Her grip is firm, and when I meet her eyes, her smile reminds me of a Disney villain. Who let me make the decision to allow the media inside my home?

Oh. That's right.

Hayden.

"Because people will want to see who Darcy Marshall truly is." I fight to not roll my eyes at the memory. *"And this is a conservative-leaning column."*

"Krissy Towers with Pop Culture NOW!" The venom in her voice is camouflaged as honey. I try to remember she is just doing her job, and I need to give a good, honest, and worthy interview to whoever I speak to.

"You know who I am." The dead chuckle I give only elicits an icy smile from her. Pop culture interviews are worse than the political ones by a long shot. But Hayden said it's imperative that I do a few pop culture exchanges since I'm on the younger side at thirty-nine.

My age doesn't necessarily reflect my soul. And I'll be forty this year, which means I have no business caring about pop culture. I've told her that, but she doesn't listen.

"A person would have to be living under a rock to not know your face and name."

My gut clenches. "If someone is living under a rock, I would love to meet them and help them find a home." I fight to maintain the easy-going, inviting persona, but a certain iciness seeps through. I've always despised that idiom.

Krissy's smile falters, but then she shakes her head. "Such a giving person, I suppose. Are you ready for the interview? I sent your team a list of questions last week."

I nod, sitting back casually in the chair and crossing my legs. I place my folded hands on my lap. "I'm ready."

Her smile is like a predator preparing to strike. It's a shame how reporters act kind and like they have your best interest at heart before the camera rolls, but then they shed their skin and turn into the hissing snakes they are when the person behind the camera gives them the greenlight that the camera is rolling.

I'm sure she's a fine lady, but her profession makes me automatically dislike her.

The producer behind the camera begins a verbal countdown, ending with finger motions for three...two...one.

"Mr. Marshall," Krissy begins without missing a beat; she seems to be a true professional at what she does, which I can admire. "Thank you so much for joining our program today. More so, thank you for being a gracious host here at your home—Ophelia Estate."

"My pleasure."

Her eyes continually flick from the teleprompter to me.

"You had a sister named Ophelia. She died at the young age of eight when you were only nineteen."

My fingers press hard against my knuckles, but I keep my hands folded on my lap. Her words were statements posed as questions, ones she already knows the answers to. "Yes, Ophelia was the name of my little sister."

"What prompted you to name the estate after her once your father passed and you inherited it?" Krissy crosses her legs and places her hands on top of her knee.

I super glue a tight smile on my face and fight to remain calm. "To bring her the honor she deserves." I unfold my hands and rest them gently on top of each other on my lap while taking a deep breath through my nose. *Please. Change the subject.*

Krissy smiles politely and does the sympathetic head tilt. "It's strangely impossible to find information about her death. Could you tell us what—"

I cough loudly, tucking my face away in the bend of my arm. "Excuse me," I choke. "Bennie, do you mind bringing Ms. Towers and me lemon water to drink?" I turn to the reporter who's wearing a concerned look. That's nice of her, I guess. It's better than her slithering smile. "Do you like lemon water?"

She nods her head. I smile at her and pray my expression conveys that she needs to change the subject. Bennie, my personal secretary, brings out two glasses of water. After taking a sip, I motion for the reporter to continue.

"The latest controversy surrounding your campaign is that Ms. Priscilla Weatherby broke your engagement because you had an affair. Would you like to comment?"

This topic is only one notch better than discussing my dead sister.

"As I've said in past interviews and speeches, I never had an affair while dating and being engaged to Ms. Weatherby. We parted on mutual terms for the benefit of us both." Half a lie. The breakup was definitely one-sided (hers), but I refuse to let the press continue correlating my name to the word *affair*.

I am *not* my father.

"Ms. Weatherby has confirmed this as well," I add before the reporter moves forward with her incessant questioning.

"If you win this upcoming election, you'll be joining the ranks of James Buchanan, the only unmarried president in our nation's history. Not to mention you would be the youngest president ever elected. How does that feel?" Look at that. The reporter princess knows a bit of history.

"Like I'm making history again." I shrug like it's no big deal, though I'm beyond panicked. How will I garnish enough respect and rapport for my age and marital status from the older generation?

"Culture has changed, so we at Pop Culture NOW are rooting for you. It will be refreshing to have not only a third-party president, but one who could devote the totality of his time to this country." She pauses. "If you can convince us your policies are better than Republican candidate Richard Loveless."

"Of course." I smile, hiding the building stress. Culture may have changed, but to win over the conservative, rural vote, I need a wife. It is the one thing that shows that I can run a household and, therefore, a country in the eyes of many. My younger age could be excused if I had a wife. Don't ask me the logic behind that train of thought, but it does exist. That sector of the population can't be dismissed, something the media doesn't seem to understand.

And thinking of all that has my soul panicking. Are the chandelier lights getting brighter in this little room?

But still, I smile. I sweat and I smile. And I stretch it further across my face. "I'm with someone new, however. We are seeing how things go before becoming public." Something shatters in the background, but I keep my eyes trained on the reporter. Even a slight shift of the eyes and the world would know that Darcy Marshall is a big, fat liar.

Krissy leans in, and I mentally slap myself a million times over. I bite my tongue to not let the curses swirling through my mind slip out.

"Do tell us more, Mr. Marshall. Could this lady be the Elizabeth Bennet to your Mr. Darcy?" She wiggles her brows. I swallow the growl fighting to escape the back of my throat.

"Too soon to tell," I remark with a light, unconvincing chuckle. I finally let my eyes wander around the room as I contemplate my next words. The mosaic walls provide no assistance as they blend together. I've got to change the course of this interview. "Either way, wife or no wife, I am the best candidate for the office of president." I continue with my usual spiel on my stances surrounding important topics such as foster care reform, immigration reform, and election security, all the while not giving the reporter a chance to circle back to my love life.

Because it doesn't exist.

Once the interview concludes and Krissy and her crew leave, I briskly make my way to my campaign team who should be gathered in the meeting room to discuss the situation I managed to implode with an idiotic, unprompted response. The press will pester me like Donkey pesters Shrek to find out who my new woman is. I need to clean this up. Quickly.

"Who's the lady, and when do we get to meet her?" Micah, my social media coordinator, asks as I slip into the long meeting room and close the double doors. I meet the curious, waiting eyes of my twelve senior staffers. *Twelve?* I flick my eyes to the lady standing next to me. I almost didn't recognize her without her makeup and the blisters forming on her face.

"Hayden, what are you doing here?"

She tilts her head. "Am I not supposed to be here, sir?"

"As I've requested before, please do not call me sir. I told you to go to the hospital."

"There's no need. I'm fine."

"You're blistering," I say. One hand leaves the tablet she's holding and touches her face.

"I'll buy burn cream on the way home."

I pinch the bridge of my nose with a sigh. "Fine. Do what you want." Tiresome woman. She never listens, which sometimes benefits me in the long run, but still. I'm not used to people going against my requests.

"So..." Micah prompts.

"There's no woman."

"But you just said," Paul, the assistant campaign manager, begins before I silence him with a glare.

"Paul, can you run this morning's meeting without me and Hayden? I need to speak with her."

"Yes." He motions for everyone to take their seats at the long, sleek, wooden table. I walk out of the room but stop when I don't hear anyone following me.

"Hayden," I bark, dragging out her name like a reprimand.

"Coming," she squeaks, and then the only sound is her heels clicking across the hardwood floor, echoing off the walls. When we are far enough away from the meeting room, I stop and turn to face her, but her body slams into mine. My arms automatically extend to steady her from falling.

"How many times am I going to have to catch you today?"

She stares at me, then her eyes flick down to my hands, which are grasping her surprisingly firm biceps. In fact, one look over tells me that Hayden is in fantastic shape, her body perfectly proportioned—something I hadn't paid much attention to before. I like proportions.

What am I thinking?

I rip my hands away and cement them to my sides. I don't need to be noticing my female campaign manager's muscles—or body shape. That's a lawsuit begging to happen.

"Sir, why did you tell that woman you're seeing someone? You've been on three blind dates and have turned every woman down. Is there something you're not telling me?" Hayden's hands find their natural home on her hips as she continues on. "If you're seeing someone, I need to..."

I fold my arms over my chest. "Stop calling me sir. I'm not seeing anyone."

"Why did you say that? This has got to..."

The pitch of her voice continuously grows with each passing word, piercing profusely into my skin. Closing my eyes, I uncross one arm and lean my head into my hand, pressing my fingers to my right, aching temple. Tuning her out isn't working, no matter how hard I try.

"...making *me* look bad..."

"Hayden. I said stop." My voice is as sharp as a pin prick.

The silence is a welcome guest. I rub my temple one last time before opening my eyes. Her eyes—a rich shade of cocoa—sparkle like they're on the verge of dumping tears.

Why? Why do I always go one step too far and make her want to cry?

A deep sigh releases from my chest as I think over my next move and drop my arms to my sides once more. Hayden remains silent just as I asked.

No, *ordered.*

What's the harm in one more command? "Follow me."

The moment I begin walking away, I hear her heels in pursuit. She follows at a distance, probably to make sure she doesn't wind up in my arms again.

Good. Personal space is imperative.

I journey through my home, weaving around corridors and taking a set of stairs. Eventually, we arrive at the third floor sitting room, which is tucked away in a corner of the house. It's much different than the first floor sitting room where the interview was held. That room screams old money, and it's what everyone expects in a house like mine. I strictly reserve this third-floor room for one-on-one conferences that I need to make sure remain out of earshot. It's also cozy and comfortable and doesn't overwhelm the senses. Plus, the shorter walls are lined with eras of knowledge accumulated in the form of the written word.

A room more preferential to my tastes.

After opening the door and breathing in the smell of old books, I sweep my arm to motion for Hayden to enter first. Her brows knit and a crinkle forms just above the bridge of her nose.

"After you," she says, dropping her head.

I don't have time for this.

Her heels follow me into the little nook.

Taking a seat in one of the dark brown velvet armchairs, I motion for Hayden to do the same. She sits, smoothing her black skirt and tucking her legs off to the side. I catch a glimpse of white gauze on her hand as she reaches for a stray curl in her face.

"What happened this time?" I ask with a huff of annoyance. Is it too much to ask that my campaign manager remains whole and unbroken for the duration of this campaign?

Her face twists in confusion before her dark brown eyes bug out at the sight of her hand. She yanks the injured hand down to her lap, covering it with her other hand.

"A little scrape from cleaning up glass earlier, that's all. No biggie."

I briefly recall something shattering during the interview. "Who dropped the glass? Why couldn't one of the housekeepers clean it up?"

Her tawny cheeks flush as she looks down at her hands. "I dropped the cup I was holding when you mentioned a girlfriend."

She meets my gaze. "So, I guess it was technically your fault for lying to that interviewer. I mean, we haven't even discussed—"

"That's why I brought you here. Please, fix this."

She stares at me, mouth agape. A beat later, she erupts with laughter, jabbing her finger to her chest. "Me? Fix *your* lie?" She laughs more, and I grow on-edge with every cackle.

"Yes, you. You were already supposed to have someone lined up like I requested last month."

Hayden makes a sound somewhere between a snort and huff. Then she adopts a horrid impression of what I'm assuming to be my voice. "She's too tall. She's too short. She's cretinous. She's tiresome."

I glare at her. Hayden resumes in her normal voice, "Look, Mr. Marshall. With all due respect, you're too picky. I could go on and on listing reasons you've given me regarding the unsatisfactory qualities of some pretty amazing women. Any of them would make a fine wife and first lady. I can't do my job appropriately, which is to manage your campaign, because you have me on this hopeless task of finding a woman who meets your standards. Yes, I'm your campaign manager, but I am not your press secretary. I'm not here to fix your image."

"Miss Bennett." I tap my fingers on the arm rest, one by one, thinking through my next words. "The women you have set me up with are...chasers. They all chase money, titles, and social status."

"But—"

I hold one finger up. How do I explain to her, someone who is not concerned with chasing money and fame, that I need a woman who is just that—not a chaser?

"I need a wife I can fully trust. A woman who not only understands my world, but can also be of assistance. I don't need a trophy wife, and I do *not* need love. I need trust, skill, and intelligence." I pause, watching Hayden's wheels turn. "You have yet to deliver that woman to me. We are in a pickle, it seems."

She narrows her eyes. "You got yourself into this mess, and there are a million other things I need to be doing to get you successfully elected to office. You need to get yourself out of this pickle jar. I'm the fork who keeps missing the mark, apparently."

My head pounds with the beat of my heart. Hayden Bennett is as vexing as she is good at her job, which is the only reason she is still here. That, and I know Stella trained her. Stella Harper was a phenomenal human to have around.

"Two more weeks, Hayden. I'll double your pay this month for the extra work and the previous time you've put into this." I know she isn't after money, but money can still talk.

Her narrowed eyes snap open, and she straightens. "Fine. I'll scrounge the earth for a few more women. But that's it. If you still haven't chosen one by then, I can't help anymore, Mr. Marshall."

Finally.

I hold out my hand to shake hers before realizing the hand she would grab mine with is the cut one. Instead of switching, I nod, rise out of the chair, and take my leave. I need time away from the woman—and campaigning in general. Just a few minutes alone would be satisfying.

"Mr. Marshall, come quick. The Republican candidate said that you were..." Micah skids on his heels as he rounds the corner of the hallway.

A few minutes alone...

CHAPTER THREE

HAYDEN

I'm an orphan, a product of the broken foster care system in the United States, a Black woman in conservative politics, and a single twenty-nine-year-old.

Regardless of all that, nothing—let me repeat, NOTH-ING—makes my skin itch and crawl with irritation quite like Darcy Marshall. My mind seethes as I clench the steering wheel to my car. The horns of cars stuck in five o' clock traffic vibrate my soul.

It's in the way he saunters—a cheetah on the hunt for the gazelle. He never smiles, unless he's doing an interview or event. No, that's not true. He also smiles when leading a meeting or talking to strangers. But with me, he wears his permanent scowl like a badge of honor. The scowl is simply an outside manifestation of his foul, filthy soul. Granted, his mind is sharp as a whip, which annoys me because it makes me like him. Something else that annoys me? Darcy never slumps, but always sits as straight as the Space Needle in Seattle. His eyes, though one may mistake them for the heat of a blue-flamed fire on a chilly night, are as cold as an early spring snow. And he's too tall for his own good. Seriously, the man looms over everyone. He's not human.

But enough.

Darcy Marshall will NOT steal my joy. I'm better than throwing a mental tantrum like a hormonal middle school girl. Been there, done that. Bright side: my weekend has officially started.

Against my better judgment, I pull my hair free from its pony-tail holder and black coils spring loose. I don't have to check the mirror to know I look like a dark-haired lion with what's bound to become scars coating my face, but that's okay. Because I am happy, joyful, ecstatic, confident... All the things. I even crack my windows and let the cool March air kiss my cheeks.

My personal feelings toward Darcy aside, I'm ecstatic to be heading his campaign. He may not be a treat to deal with one-on-one, but his Christian morals, conservative ideals, and per-sonal freedom-centered philosophical outlooks are worth backing. Throughout college, I changed my major more than politicians change positions on important issues to appease the culture. You could say I'm a multi-passionate person. With each new elective class I took, I became infatuated with a new career option: becom-ing an FBI agent, a forensic scientist, and even a brain surgeon. But after my first political science class—a basic American government class—I knew I found my home. My calling.

As they say, the rest is history.

My best friend is awesome; I love her and would give her my kidney. But when she stepped down as Darcy's campaign manager and recommended I take her place, I was popping like marvelous

fireworks on the Fourth of July. Then, a thought drenched my
fuse: there's no way Darcy is going to let *me* manage his campaign.
I was done for. However, Stella Harper is a magical being, and in
her unknown ways, she convinced Darcy to let me take the reins.
Cue the fireworks again.

Personality-wise, he's the literal incarnate of the romance hero
he's named after, but he's also my ticket into the world I was born
to live in. I pull into the parking lot of my apartment, get out and
lock my car, and head toward the elevators to my eleventh-floor
room. Glancing at Stella's old apartment brings a flood of emotions, but I shake it off and unlock the door to 11H.

The rotten stench of an empty chicken package assaults my
nose, and I chastise myself for not taking the garbage out sooner.
Blankets are thrown haphazardly across my couch, used cups sit
on every coaster in my living area, and I know if I walked to the
kitchen, a pile of dirty dishes would beg me to wash them. I would
staunchly say no because I'm the girl who washes as she needs
a dish. Takeout is my go-to for the most part, so dishes aren't
required on the norm.

Once I'm in the bathroom and opening the burn cream I
stopped and bought right after leaving Darcy's, I dare a glance in
the mirror. My face is bubbled and blistered, and when I take my
shirt off, I realize my chest and parts of my stomach match my
face. I gently and lavishly apply the cream, wincing at every touch.
Baggy clothes it is for the foreseeable future.

With a sudden wave of exhaustion—eighty percent emotional,
twenty percent physical—I zombie-walk to my bedroom and collapse backside down on the queen size of downy softness, wincing

at the movement of the burns on my stomach. If I splurge on anything, it's my bath time needs and my bed. The moment my head hits the pillow, I close my eyes and let out a tired breath, followed by a sigh of contentment at ignoring my responsibilities in favor of sleep.

Make it stop, make it stop, make it stop! I jolt upright, chest heaving and breath heavy, as I desperately attempt to find her in the dark alley. My hands search my body, and I realize I'm in my bed, clothed in my pajamas, and wholly frazzled. The cold, haunted streets of my dream fade away with each breath in through the nose and out through the mouth.

A succession of knocks on the door startle me again. I check my phone for the time and realize I've only slept for forty-five minutes, though it feels like an eternity. Wrapping my robe tightly around me and snuggling into my house slippers, I head for the door.

"I'm sorry. I didn't mean to wake you, Miss Bennett." My landlady stands outside the doorway with a stack of papers in her hands and a timid smile. I've often wondered how she came to manage an apartment building. Deborah is a soft woman to say the least. Not only is she small in stature, but also in personality. She's quiet, shy, and introverted to the core.

"Not a problem, Deb. What do you have there?" I eye the papers in her hand. "A notice I can help you pass around to the other tenants?" I take a paper from the top of the stack just as Deb vehemently shakes her head.

"Deb, please." I close my eyes and take a breath. "Tell me this isn't true." I hold the notice up as if she didn't already know what was on it.

"I–I," Deb stutters. I open my eyes and watch a tear roll down Deb's cheek. I take the stack of papers from her hands, place them on the floor, and wrap her in an embrace. Whatever the reason is for this, I'm sure she isn't the cause.

"It's going to be okay. Do you have a place to go?"

"How can you be concerned about me when you're losing your home?" Deb's words are mumbled as she cries into my shoulder.

"Because I'm going to be okay," I say. *I'll be okay.* Maybe if I say it enough I'll believe it? I peek over Deb's head at the stack of notices.

One month.

I have one month to pack up my belongings and vacate the apartment.

"So, what brought this on?" I ask. Deb steps out of my embrace and picks up the stack of papers.

"The city keeps increasing the costs for the property, and I can't keep up without raising the rent exceptionally high." Deb sniffles and rubs her nose with the outside of her hand. I reach through my door and grab the box of tissues that sits on the counter. "The city is going to take over the building. I don't know what they have planned."

Deb looks away and crosses her arms, her shoulders tensing. It seems she doesn't want to talk about it anymore, so I offer to go with her to pass out the notices to everyone.

"That's why I came to you first." She smiles sheepishly.

"I've always got your back, Deb." I square my shoulders and take the papers from her hands. We begin going door to door, and I spew a monologue of explanation and apology on behalf of Deb. I give hugs where needed and step between Deb and irate tenants more often than I should have to. The entire time, panic is rising in my chest and a million questions swirl around my brain. Where will I go? When will I have time to find a place within a month between work and trying to find a woman for Darcy? Will I end up stuck on the streets again? What if I don't find an affordable place to live?

The anxiety presses down hard with each door I knock on. When we finally finish, I feel heavier than the loaded barbell dropped after the final rep at the gym. I hug Deb goodbye and tell her I will check on her tomorrow. Meanwhile, I lock myself in my apartment and make the phone call to the one person I need the most.

After two rings, she picks up.

"Hayden! Is everything okay?"

"Chill, Stells. We're good here in New York City," I say, needing to inform her it's not a life-or-death situation. Though honestly, it feels that way right now. She lets out a long-winded sigh.

"I'm in the car with Luca right now. Just so you're aware he can hear the conversation."

Silence ensues for a moment. The rumble of the road is loud in the background, and then I hear Lucas say, "Sorry, Hayden. I'm in the middle of seducing my wife. Can't talk."

Stella giggles, then squeals. "Stop, Lucas! Eyes on the road."

"Oh, I have my eyes on *something*," he responds, his voice clearer as if he is leaning toward Stella.

I attempt a laugh, but it falls short.

"Hey, Lucas. I really need your wife for like two minutes," I yell into the phone.

"Ouch," Stella's voice grows farther away as if she pulled the phone away from her ear. "Okay, Luca. Let me hear her out before she screams in my ear again." Then back to me, she says, "I'm all yours."

With mustered sarcasm, I say, "Aw. Thank you so much, *best friend.*" She scoffs on the other end of the line. "Okay, but seriously," I begin, feeling the panic rise as I prepare to tell her everything. "I'm getting kicked out of my apartment, Darcy still has me on a wild goose chase for the perfect wife, and I'M GETTING KICKED OUT OF MY APARTMENT."

"I think we should start with the apartment thing," Stella says. "Tell me what happened."

I recap the events while fighting back hysterical tears. This isn't like me. I face situations like this head-first and with a bold, lioness attitude. Not like a hopeless woman who has no fight left in her. Have I gotten too comfortable in life?

"There's got to be something available with a decent rent and within your travel range," Stella says after I finish. "The issue is going to be finding time to move."

"Exactly." I sob, no longer able to hold the deluge back. "Because Darcy still wants me to find the mythical holy grail: a wife he'll be satisfied with."

"Oh, Hayden," Stella sighs, and I can visualize her sad, gray eyes in my head. "I'm sending you hugs right now. Do you feel them?"

When was the last time I cried like this? I collapse onto my couch, shoving my head in my pillow while my phone falls to the floor. I hear Stella's breathing through the headphone in my ear and my body relaxes, sinking into the taupe cushions. The cool air from the open window kisses my skin, and I am comforted. Knowing I have someone in my corner who is simply willing to listen calms me. As the tears begin to fall slower and my breathing becomes more even, I tell Stella thank you.

"Let's make a game plan," she says. I grin through the salty tears still rolling down my face and sniffle.

"My favorite words."

An hour and a half, several Lucas interruptions, a few hundred "I miss you's", and one demolished pint of ice cream later, we hang up.

"She's right," I say while hoisting myself off the couch. "There's no sense in panicking. There's got to be something available for me in this big city that is reasonably priced and not too far a drive from work. If I tell Darcy I need a day or two off to move, I'm sure it won't be the end of the world."

The trash can lid pops open with the tap of my foot on the floor lever, and I toss the empty ice cream container in. The chicken stench is overwhelming, but I think I can survive with the smell for one more day before mustering up the motivation to take out the trash.

"Also, she's going to reach out to her contacts and give me names of women who might be suitable for Mr. Never Satisfied."

I pause in my tracks on my way back to the love of my life—my couch—as an uncomfortable realization hits: I'm going crazy. I've been talking aloud to myself more and more with each passing day. I haven't done that since I wandered the streets alone for days on end as a teenager.

Chapter Four

DARCY

Monday. It always arrives too soon.

That doesn't matter much because my life is a constant string of Mondays. Sunday through Saturday—it's all a blur. Interviews. Meet and greets. Dinners. Façades. Speeches.

I'm given a schedule by my campaign team, day after day, and I'm enslaved to it. A prisoner to the life I chose. The plan was never to run for president of the United States, but after the dumpster fire that was the last administration, I felt God calling me to run for office. I had the money, the connections, and the name, so it made sense to take the leap into the political arena, though I was not—and will never be—a people person. But I push through my introverted and autistic ways because I have something many politicians lack: selfless motivations and ambitions. I'm running for the homeless, for the orphaned, for the least of them, as Scripture says. Having my name attached to that type of reform is nothing short of spectacular. Okay, so my motivations are mostly selfless. We all have a bit of selfishness inside of us.

My phone buzzes on my wooden desk, and I shuffle through papers until I find it buried underneath the campaign budget report. A text from Ren Sato, my best friend, flashes across the screen.

> **Ren: Who's the new woman?**

I ignore him, directing my attention to the mountain of paperwork covering nearly every inch of my L-desk, but then another text comes through.

> **Ren: I want to meet her.**

I crumple the newspaper in my fists, unpleasant words roaring across my brain. The door opens, pushing the scent of cedar and musk from the candle burning in the front of the room over to me.

"Mr. Marshall," a too cheery voice calls. Hayden. The only reason I look up from my desk is to glare at her for having a sing-song voice that drives me crazy when I hear it in the mornings. How can a person be this happy in the midst of the political whirlwind every day? Seeing the burn marks still lingering on her face makes me feel a little bad for thinking negative thoughts about her. She does great things for me and this campaign.

She clears her throat. "I have your morning sched—"

"Leave it here." I don't want to hear the word "schedule" ever again at this point in time. I used to love planning and to-do lists, but only when I get to make them.

Hayden sets the horrid paper—that will only end up in the recycling bin—gently on the corner of my desk before turning to leave.

"Wait."

She stops in her tracks and abruptly turns. A single curl falls from her bun, and she reaches to tuck it back in. "Yes, sir?"

A smidge of frustration flares within me at the word. "I've asked you several times not to call me sir."

"Yes, sir," she stammers. "I mean, yes. Just yes."

"Do you have the next candidate lined up?" Her brows pinch together, and she cocks her head to the side. The coiled, black strand falls out again.

"Candidate?"

"For my wife," I clarify. Her shoulders tense. The strand still cups her face, falling right over her temple.

"I've contacted a few women," she begins, tucking the curl behind her ear, averting her eyes. Why am I fascinated with a ridiculous, unruly strand of hair? "I should receive answers by the end of the two-week period you allotted me."

"Two weeks." The words taste sour on my tongue. I groan. "That will be too late."

"Too late for what, s—"

The piercing darts of death I throw her way with my eyes cuts off the attempted title. It makes me feel like I'm my father, which I most certainly am not. I *will* break her of this habit.

"You said two weeks on Friday." Hayden speaks each word slowly and without surety.

"I know what I said, but I need to move faster." As I stand from my chair, I shove the now crinkled copy of the *Times* in her face. "See."

She takes a moment to read over the headline: *PRESIDEN-TIAL CANDIDATE DARCY MARSHALL HAS FOUND HIS FUTURE FIRST LADY?*

"Not good," she whispers. I toss the crumpled newspaper onto my desk.

Hayden rubs her temples, tilting her head down to her chest. When she whips her head upwards, the curl comes loose again.

Before my brain processes what is happening, I take a single step toward Hayden and tuck the curl back into her bun. My fingers linger on her hair, feeling the smooth texture. It doesn't feel stringy like I expected it to, but soft and sleek. Like moisturizer on my hands.

The silence enveloping us screams louder than the way Father used to yell at Mother, bringing me to my senses.

Jerking my hand away, I take several steps backward and barrel into the sharp corner of my large, wooden desk. My outer thigh howls in pain, but I grit my teeth to keep the curses in.

I stare at the polished, hardwood floor, noticing the shine of my black shoes, before risking a glance at Hayden. When I do, her doe eyes are wide open, her nude lips parted, and a blush coats her slightly blistered brown cheeks. What have I done?

"Hayden." I say her name with a gruffness that adds another level of embarrassment to this situation. My mouth is a desert, and it feels like I'm swallowing sand when I attempt to clear my throat. "Please maintain a professional appearance while in the work-place." I internally cringe at the hypocrisy of my words because of my recent actions. That was bad. Unbelievably regrettable.

To make matters worse, she laughs. Belly laughs. In between snorts, she says, "Mr. Marshall, that was highly unprofessional of *you.*"

My neck flares with heat. "It meant nothing. I wasn't coming on to you. Please don't take my actions that way." The words rush from my mouth like a criminal denying the very crime he committed. *Keep digging that hole for yourself, Darcy.*

Her laugh becomes a cackle, and my face burns hotter and hotter. Hayden throws her hands up. "Don't worry. I know you hate me. I'll be going now."

I start to tell her I don't hate her, but she turns on her heel to leave before I can utter the words.

Hayden laughs like a hyena all the way out of my office. *Oh, God, please don't let there be a lawsuit for sexual harassment awaiting me at the end of this day.*

I rip a tissue from the box on my desk and dab the sweat beads forming on my forehead line. The best course of action is to approach her, say the words "I'm sorry," and explain my lapse of sound judgment. Instead, I want to choose to avoid her for the rest of the day. Maybe even the week. Confrontation has never been a problem for me, but usually the other person is the one needing to say sorry, not me.

I'm great at confrontation with all of my facts and enigmatic personality, but I'm not the most practiced with apologies.

Avoidance is not probable. I need Hayden to help me with the wife search. It's a team effort; I most definitely can't accomplish the task on my own. Women run from me once they get to know me. They end up loathing me because I'm not the friendly, charismatic man in the portrait that the media ignorantly paints. I'm not mean, just introverted. Maybe that comes off as mean and standoffish and hateful sometimes?

Speaking of...

Why does Hayden think I hate her? Does she aggravate me? Yes. Is she my opposite in every way? Of course. Am I nitpicky about her actions? You bet I am. But pure hate? No, I don't hate her. That emotion is only reserved for my father. I don't even hate Priscilla for walking out on me.

Maybe Hayden thinks I hate her because I can be a little stand-offish and cold in the pursuit of feeling safe in my own skin at times. That's what my therapist said a long time ago when I sought help after Ophelia died and found out I was autistic through our countless sessions. Have I not course-corrected enough?

With a long, drawn-out sigh, I take a seat at my desk and think through possible scenarios.

One. I apologize to Hayden, we move forward, and she finds the perfect wife for me.

Two. I ignore Hayden, pray she doesn't file a workplace sexual harassment claim against me, and she gives up finding a wife for me.

Option one. Definitely. Mostly because I don't want the claim filed against me. And it would be good to apologize to her, show her I'm not the monster she seems to perceive me as at times.

I work through different apologies as I leave my office and head for the conference room where, according to my schedule, Hayden is giving the team a run down of their tasks in preparation for next week's speech in front of Independence Hall in Philadelphia.

I weave through the hallways of my home until I push my way through the tall, red oak doors leading into the rectangular conference room. Twelve sets of surprised eyes turn towards me, but I'm focused on the set of dark brown eyes that slowly narrow as if they were lasers locking onto their target.

A smirk pulls at the corner of her lips, and I swallow the lump rising in my throat.

"Mr. Marshall, is everything okay?" one of the guys asks. I don't bother to decipher who because I'm in the middle of one of the most intense games of "don't blink" that I've ever played. Her brown eyes are several shades lighter than normal, and wrinkles form in the corner of her eyes as her smirk deepens.

"What's wrong, Mr. Marshall?" Hayden echoes. She pouts her bottom lip and tilts her head. She's hiding it well, but a ghost of the smirk still resides on her face.

She knows exactly what happened, exactly what I'm concerned about, and exactly why I shoved my way through the conference room doors panting and with disheveled, fingered hair.

Because apparently I'm in the mood to touch hair today.

That's it. I take a deep breath in, close my eyes, and release a breath that moves slower than Congress trying to pass a bill. Unless I'm misreading this situation, she doesn't seem too concerned that I touched her hair. In fact, I think she might be amused that I did something so out of character for me. Regardless, I still need to apologize and make sure she knows it won't happen again.

"Hayden, may I speak with you alone for one moment?" The rest of the team in the conference room resumes their work, and

Hayden, still wearing the ghost of a smirk, clicks her way toward me.

I hold the door open for her as she steps out of the room, and I let it softly click shut behind us.

"Yes, Mr. Marshall?" Her tone is innocent, childlike. It annoys me.

"I'm sorry for my inappropriate behavior. It won't happen again. The curl kept falling and was distracting me." There. Simple, true, and upfront.

But Hayden's eyes continue to smile like there's a joke I'm missing. "It's okay. I'll invest in better bobby pins."

I nod, unsure of what else to say. It sounds like she won't press charges. I think she finds the entire situation amusing more than anything, based on the sparkle in her brown eyes and the smirk on her face.

"Thank you," I say, running my hand through my hair. Again. I spin on my heel and go on a hunt for a comb to style my waves back where they belong.

For heaven's sake, Darcy. No more hair-touching today.

I crave alone time like a corrupt politician craves money, but when I receive time alone, I feel...alone. A house of this size and prestige was never meant to host one person. Sure, some of the staff lives here, but that's the thing. They live adjacent to me, not *with* me. The pillow beside me remains empty night after night, and sometimes, though I would never admit this out loud, I desire the warmth of a body sleeping next to mine.

This house is too big. Maybe I should sell it and buy a one-bedroom cottage in the mountains? Then again, my history—my story—is contained within these walls. Meandering the hallways and gazing upon the art hanging on the walls leaves me wanting to name and befriend the pictured faces like Anna from *Frozen*. Though I've lived here my entire life, I've never taken to finding rest and solace in painted faces.

Maybe I'm more like Elsa with a deep desire to shut everyone out so I can't unintentionally hurt them when I'm unsure of how to react, confused, overwhelmed, or overstimulated?

It was a long day at the group home, as is every Wednesday, and I sat through two movies—*Frozen* and *Frozen II*, which is why that dang musical is occupying my thoughts. It was worth getting the songs stuck in my head to see the smiles on the kids' faces and to hear their voices laughing and singing along with the movies.

Pausing at one particular picture causes a ripping ache in my soul. *Ophelia*. She's one of the few faces I wouldn't have to name in this processional line of artwork. Her cheeks are rosy, blue eyes sparking with mischief and excitement. This portrait was finished three days before she died, and it serves as a constant reminder of my failures as an older brother.

Yes, maybe I am more like Elsa. Lock me away so I can't make promises to people that I can't keep. So I can no longer hurt those who love and support me the most.

Before I know it, I'm back in my office with little recollection as to how my feet carried me there.

A long-winded sigh escapes as I collapse into my desk chair. When was the last time I took a break? I ask this question every day, and every time, it's the same answer: I don't remember. *Breaks are for the faint of heart,* Father would say.

A knock at the door saves me from taking a trip down memory lane with thoughts of my father. That lane might as well be called Elm Street.

"Come in."

"What's up, my dude?" My short—well, shorter than my six-foot-two self—Japanese friend wearing a snazzy dark green suit saunters through my office doorway.

A grin stretches across my face; my mood instantly lifts.

"Ren, is that any way to greet the future president of the United States?"

"Yep. Better get used to it." He bows. "Ren Sato: Keeping Darcy Marshall humble since the 1990s."

I chuckle as I bow in return, already feeling more relaxed in his presence than I did alone and brooding two seconds ago.

"You look *hansamu,*" Ren says, looking me up and down. "Do you have somewhere to be tonight?"

"Dinner party at the Weatherby Estate. Figured I would wear my favorite suit for a confidence boost."

"*Yabai.* That sucks."

I shrug. "Just another show to put on."

"You're the master of shows." Ren adjusts his low bun, or *chonmage,* as he calls it. "Are you going alone? After hours of making me wait, you texted that the newspaper was lying, but I don't quite buy it. What are you up to?"

With a glare, I only answer the first question. "Unfortunately, no."

"You are naturally brooding, but there is only one person who could put that specific expression on your face." Ren raises his eyebrows. "Is your manager tagging along?"

"Mhmm." My mood sours as I think of Hayden pestering me all night.

"Come on, Darcy-*kun*. She's an awesome woman."

I glare at him, but he stands firm with his arms crossed. "You haven't met her."

"You talk about her enough that I feel like she's our third best friend."

"Hayden Bennett is not my friend," I mumble. *Would it be so bad if she was?* Stella was. But then again, Stella had a moody introverted streak like me. Hayden is extroverted and might be related to the Energizer Bunny. It overwhelms me.

Another knock at my door halts our conversation.

"Must be her." Ren's face lights up. "I finally get to meet the woman who puts your panties in a wad."

I shove Ren's shoulder like I used to do when we were school boys as I walk to open the door. "You can say hi, but after that, take your leave."

"Take your leave," Ren mocks under his breath. Then louder, he sucks his teeth. "Yeah, right."

I slowly open the door, and Hayden stands there with her hair in her signature bun, though she left a few curls to hang in front of her face. *Stay clear of those,* I demand to myself. Her face is practically healed now. Only a remnant of scars from the blisters remains visible under her makeup. I take notice of her yellow pants, black tucked-in blouse, and black strappy heels.

Why doesn't she wear dresses to these dinners like all the other women? I've asked her several times to do just that. *But she does look good in that outfit.*

"I see you didn't take my dress suggestion to heart."

"And I see you still haven't realized that you can't dictate what clothes I choose to wear."

"She's got a valid point," Ren pipes up. I side-eye him as Hayden steps around me and into my office. "And yellow looks good on her."

As soon as I close the door, I turn around and run into a stopped Hayden. She tumbles forward and lands in Ren's arms. Without thinking, I reach out to collect her from him, but Ren has already set her back upright and is mere inches from her face. His arms trail hers while his eyes flick over every part of her body.

"Are you okay?" he asks.

Hayden's chin tilts up, almost as if she is inviting him to—

"She's fine." I force my hands to stay by my side. They want to reach out and pull the woman away from Ren. There's no need for a makeout session in my office involving my best friend and my campaign manager. The thought alone stirs a fire in my stomach.

Ren glances my way, and I watch his top lip twitch like he's trying to suppress a smile. Or a smirk.

He turns his attention back to Hayden. "Are you fine?" Ren asks with honey in his voice.

She swallows and nods her head once.

With a smirk and his eyes still on Hayden, Ren finally creates distance between the two.

I choose to ignore the scenario that transpired. I could blame Hayden for stopping in her tracks, but I still ran into her. "Sorry," I mumble, but I don't think she hears me. Too preoccupied with my best friend.

Ren's smirk has transformed into a smile. "*Konnichiwa*. I'm Ren Sato." He bows. "You must be Hayden Bennett. Darcy-*kun* has told me much about you." I narrow my eyes as he glances my way. That only seems to make his grin grow wider.

"Darcy-*kun*, huh?" Hayden shakes her head. "You two are close?"

"He couldn't get rid of me if he tried."

Hayden chuckles and brings one hand up to cover her mouth. It's an objectively cute action, like she's embarrassed.

Hayden Bennett is never embarrassed. If I know anything about that woman, it's that she's too confident for her own good.

I continue to watch Ren and Hayden. I don't like the way they move around each other. Hayden has fully angled herself away from me and toward Ren. Ren has mimicked the action. They aren't speaking, but their body language seems to be having its own conversation.

Why do I feel like a third wheel in this room?

"We need to get going," I state, clapping my hands together as some unfamiliar feeling heats my veins.

"Will you be joining us tonight, Sato-*san*?"

"Please, call me Ren. Though, I do respect that you understand proper honorifics." Ren continues flashing his million-dollar smile as he bows to Hayden once more.

She bows in return. "Then, please, call me Hayden."

"Okay," I draw. "We've got to go, Miss Bennett."

"I think it'll be fun to tag along," Ren says, boasting a broad smile.

"No," I bark. Hayden gawks at me and Ren shrugs. Then, he whips out his phone and shows me a text invite from Mr. Weatherby.

With a smug expression that could rival the current president, he says, "Let's save gas and ride together."

POP CULTURE NOW!

DARCY MARSHALL'S CYRPTIC COMMENT ABOUT
A NEW LEADING LADY. HERE'S WHAT WE KNOW.

By Krissy Towers

In case you missed our live interview with Independent Presidential candidate Darcy Marshall, here's the latest scoop.

Darcy Marshall has a new woman in his life, only one month since his called-off engagement to Priscilla Weatherby, daughter of Thomas Weatherby, CEO of Weatherby Enterprises. In a recent interview, he stated through a cheeky smile, "I am with someone new, however. We are seeing how things go before becoming public." His nervous energy was palpable, which is unlike our young, political prince. But off the record, just between us, Darcy Marshall didn't smile once before the camera was trained on him. In fact, he was a little cold and aloof. What more can we expect of privileged billionaires, I suppose?

Will this new woman in Darcy's life be the Elizabeth we've all been waiting for him to have? Or will she go down in flames like Priscilla? Finally, does this mystery woman exist, or is she a ruse in order to bury the supposedly mutual break-up between Darcy and Priscilla? Stay tuned because we at *Pop Culture NOW!* are on the prowl for the truth—and the girl.

CHAPTER FIVE

HAYDEN

Sweet goodness. What have I been blessed by the Almighty with?

The answer? My very own Japanese hunk.

I'm sitting in Darcy's fancy black Cadillac. Ren is in the front passenger seat, and Darcy is sitting adjacent to me in the back with only the small middle seat in the space between us. He insisted Ren take the front seat and climbed in the back with me. Of course, I put up a fuss, questioning why I couldn't sit up front and keep Lionel, one of Darcy's personal drivers, company while both the men sat in the back.

Darcy's reasoning: Ren is our guest and should be allotted the front seat.

Honestly, I want that dreamboat sitting next to me in the backseat instead of the stiff-necked, insufferable, too-tall-for-his-own-good Darcy.

"So, Ren." I lean forward, placing my hands on top of the shoulder portion of his seat to steady myself. That *chonmage* of his has my nerves unraveling. "Are you from the States or Japan? Your English is impeccable. There's not even a trace of a Japanese accent."

Ren turns his head in my direction so that he's eyeing me out of one corner. "I am the son of the Japanese ambassador to the United States. I was born and raised here, though I have been on a mission to understand and engage in my roots more."

Suddenly, I feel small in this car of powerful men.

At least there's always Lionel the Driver.

"Oh, Mr. Sato is your father. I believe I met him at last year's Ambassador Ball." I try to sound chill and nuanced, but my heart is racing and my skin is perspiring. This man looks too good for his own good. I can see the resemblance now—bushy (but neat) eyebrows, pointed nose, long neck, and lips that are ridiculously full. I remember thinking the same of Mr. Sato. Regardless of when I meet someone or how many times I meet them, I have a knack for recalling their faces and remembering names. It's quite helpful in my line of work.

Ren chuckles. "He has an affinity for those kinds of things. Me? Not so much."

"Why not?"

"I have more of a..." he hums, "private taste." Ren winks and curls his lips into a smirk.

I'm a loaded spring set loose at his insinuated remark. Mercy, that man could get anything he wanted with that wink and smirk of his.

Releasing my grip on his seat, I fall back with a *thump* against my own seat. Darcy watches me from an angle, but I'm too focused on trying to discreetly fan myself to pay his scowl much attention. Ren turns back to the front, but he lowers his visor and situates the mirror where I can see him, and I'm ninety-nine percent sure he can see me, if the intense smolder is any indication.

This is the kind of sexy stare men give while they do the latest dancing trend on social media.

I never thought one would be directed at me outside of a screen.

Darcy harrumphs, ruining the moment. *Come on, dude. I was in the process of melting into a puddle.*

"When was the last time you had *private time* with another woman?" Darcy asks as he crosses his arms over his chest.

Ren doesn't take his eyes off me as he replies. "A gentleman does not kiss and tell."

"You don't kiss at all. Well, unless we count that one time in tenth grade—"

"I'm appalled you would bring that up." Ren abruptly turns and faces Darcy, who is... smiling?

I didn't know he knew how to do that unless he was in front of a camera or crowd.

The smile is genuine, not forced.

It's kind of breathtaking.

And that's a thought I will banish to the depths of Sheol for the rest of eternity.

"Quit pretending to be the flirt you most certainly are not. You forget how to speak in front of most women you like," Darcy says. His smug expression grows. I turn to look at Ren, whose sexy stare has turned into a sexy grimace.

"It's not pretending if it's working," Ren mumbles. Then louder and with a transfixed smile, "Right, Hayden?" He shifts brown eyes back to me.

Right! However, if he can speak and flirt with me like it's nobody's business, then I'm assuming he isn't interested. What a bummer. We would've had beautiful babies.

"Um, I guess," I dumbly reply while fiddling with a loose curl dangling in front of my face. I focus on deep breaths to cool my heated face and slow down my disappointed heart.

"Stop flirting with my campaign manager." Darcy's voice is dark, making him sound like Batman.

"Why? It's not like she's your woman."

I throw my hand over my mouth as if that would contain the roar of laughter bubbling inside me.

Spoiler alert: it doesn't.

Ren tilts his head to the side in amusement while Darcy narrows his eyes at me, his mouth agape.

"What's so unbelievably funny that you can't control yourself?" Darcy asks, utterly offended.

I shift my finger between us, indicating that the idea of an "us" is terrifyingly hilarious as I continue to boisterously laugh. Me? Darcy's woman? Not in a million years. Not if we were the last two people on this Earth.

Darcy gives his signature scowl, and Ren situates himself correctly in his seat. He flips the visor up.

My manic laughter ceases when Darcy unbuckles his seatbelt and slides closer to me, his tall, built frame fully occupying the center seat plus some.

"There are thousands of women who would jump at the opportunity to be my woman. I've rejected all the women you've brought to me, not the other way around."

With every passing word, I shrink. I don't know if it's the all-black suit he's sporting, the way his eyes match the suit, his husky Batman voice, or his suffocating closeness, but I have the overwhelming desire to apologize for my seemingly offensive laughter.

But enough of that.

I'm not a woman who cowers from speaking the truth.

With every ounce of confidence I can muster, I reply, "You have no idea how hard it has been trying to find a woman willing to even *try* to go on a single date with you. Much less getting the women to the stage of letting them know you want her permanently as a wife."

He leans back against the seat, tilting his head toward the sky with a frustrated grunt. His hands run through his dirty blond waves that have been gelled and styled for the night.

"You're probably scaring them all away," Darcy mutters, though he in no way tried to conceal the statement.

I hear Ren whisper from the front. "Oh, boy."

Then I see red.

Grabbing his tie, I jerk his face down so that he is eye-level with me. "Don't you for one second try to blame me for your lack of social propriety, your unrealistic expectations of women, and your Grinch-like demeanor." I jab him in the chest with a finger from my free hand. "I don't care if you are petitioning to be king of the world. That doesn't give you permission to bully me and blame me for your own faults. I am here to do one job: get you elected to America's highest office. That's it."

As we pass under a street light, the world slows to a halt.

His sapphire eyes, now illuminated by the light shining through the sunroof and windows, widen. His lips, shiny as if he recently applied lip balm, narrow while his jaw clenches and unclenches. What's the cliche references in all the dark romance books? He looks like a vengeful angel...

And I realize I just insulted a billionaire man running to be the president of the United States. More importantly, I insulted my *boss*.

With that awakening, all motion resumes and Darcy's expressions are plunged back into the darkness of the night. My senses slap me in the face.

I let go of his tie and return my hands to my lap.

Ren whistles from the front and then turns to face us. "It's about time someone other than me called him out on his prideful complex." He throws a cheeky grin at Darcy and holds a hand up in the air toward me, which I assume is for a high-five.

Keeping my hands firmly in my lap, I give my head a little shake to let Ren know that a high-five is not going to happen. He slowly lets his hand drop and turns around again.

The moment Ren is no longer visibly peeking over the shoulder of the seat, I cringe. Whatever apology that's going to tumble out of my mouth in about three seconds better be the world's greatest.

"Mr. Marshall, I—"

He holds a finger up, his face turned away from me. I desperately need to fix this.

"Sir, I—"

"Just let me think for a moment." His voice is a growl, and I know I took things too far. The overwhelming desire to win him back over to my good side takes over, and so I do the only thing I can right now. I lean back in my seat and shut up for once.

His fingers fly to his temples and he lightly shakes his head. What's going on up there? I've wondered recently if the way his long fingers find his temples and massage while he practices deep breathing is him trying not get overstimulated and snap. I bite my tongue to resist the temptation to apologize again. Instead, I ask the Lord to fix this situation because I can only screw it up more, it seems. Why did I have to let the anger out? The ugly out?

That's why your Mama left you. You're rotten inside and out. The words of Director Hoggs are seared into my memories, and they like to make appearances every now and then. I take deep breaths and remind myself that I am cherished, loved, and adored by the Creator of this universe. He gave me breath in my lungs. He thought I was worth having on Earth. His opinion is the only one that matters.

Feeling centered again, I effectively get a short apology out to the brooding man next to me without him interrupting, but all he murmurs in response is, "She's it. I should have known all along."

CHAPTER SIX

DARCY

The perfect candidate for Mrs. Darcy Marshall has been under my nose—and under my skin—this entire time. She's the woman I need for the position, but I've been too annoyed by her sunshine-complex to even consider the possibility.

After Priscilla left me, I realized two things. The first realization was that I did not need love. I only needed respect, loyalty, and trust. The second realization was that I needed a woman who would be my sidekick and who understood the world I lived in. Maybe even understand *me*.

Hayden Bennett is capable of taking over the world. I've seen her in action dealing with the press, managing my team, and the million other things she does on a day-to-day basis for this campaign. But the way she confidently stood up to me for admittedly being extremely rude to her opened my eyes to the possibility of so much more. She could be a real confidant. There is no fear of heartache. I don't particularly like her, much less love her.

But I do trust and respect her.

Will making her my wife for my office tenure, if elected, be a thorn in my side? Of course. However, it could also be a strategic move. There's no rule, among countless election rules, saying your fiancée or wife can't manage your campaign. Though we get under each other's skin, and she's one of the loudest women I know, she's also the most qualified candidate for the job of being my wife and possibly becoming First Lady.

We work pretty great together, if the success of this campaign so far is any indication. We are nearing the end of March, and my poll numbers have never been higher than they—

A tap on my shoulder pulls me from my thoughts.

Hayden's doe eyes stir something in my stomach. "We're almost there. Should I stay in the car tonight, or...?"

"Come in with me." I swallow the lump in my throat at the uncomfortable feeling in my stomach. Who cares that she's sad? I've made her sad plenty of times.

No, not sad. I've made her mad. She's cute when she's mad, but seeing her sad makes me... sad.

Wait, no. She's not cute. It just doesn't bother me as much when she's mad because it's usually over something small and insignificant.

The quiet is all encompassing; the only sound is tires on gravel as we enter through the gates of Weatherby Estate. Before long, the car halts in the circular driveway, and Ren jets out before Lionel can open the door for him. Lionel looks back at me, and I wave him out of the car. Now, it's only me and Hayden. The silence and tension is sharp enough to slice through the atmospheric energy around us.

I look Hayden over. She's pretty, in an unconventional way. She's untamed, one could say. But she's smart and would make the perfect Mrs. Darcy Marshall... with a little polishing, of course.

"You mentioned you were only here to get me elected, correct?"

She nods her head slowly. "But Mr. Marshall, I am so—"

"Say no more. You're here for one job? Here's a job for you: Be my wife."

Hayden is a statue, frozen in time with her mouth hanging open from speaking before I interrupted her umpteenth attempt at an apology. A few long moments pass before she even blinks.

"Oh, you're trying to get me back for my outburst." Hayden forces a laugh, interrupting my thoughts. "Good one. I thought you were serious for a moment there."

"I am serious," I state. Hayden opens her mouth to speak again, but I cut her off. "Be my wife."

She is silent again, her mouth opening and closing like a fish. What part of this does she not get? I've already made up my mind. She needs to get on board with my decision. *I've should've known it wouldn't be that easy.*

I continue speaking. "Of course, I will compensate you for your time handsomely. How does two-hundred grand a year sound to you?"

Instead of looking impressed like I imagined in my head, Hayden looks like she might pass out.

Correction. She vomits.

Right into my lap.

The stench is immediately suffocating, and I do what any reasonable person would.

I shove the door open and lean out of the door frame just in time for my stomach to empty itself.

"Mr. Marshall," Hayden exclaims through a sickly groan. From the sound of her door opening, I imagine she's doing what I'm doing, which is getting the heck out of this puke mobile.

Though I can't see her because my back is to her, I hear her heels click on the gravel driveway, drawing closer to me. I wipe my mouth with my jacket sleeve—it's already ruined—and stand up straight.

"I'm so sorry, Mr. Marshall. It must have been the—"

I hold a finger in the air, effectively silencing her. I can feel her eyes boring into my back, but I refuse to turn around. If I did, I would most likely be arrested for murder tonight.

Another crunch of the gravel tells me she is coming closer.

"Mr. Marshall."

I continue staring into the darkness of the night around me. Hayden's stomach contents coat my pants and shoes. My favorite Armani suit. A growl rumbles through my throat.

Did she honestly find me that repulsive? She laughed earlier at the idea of marrying me, but to be quite frank, I thought it was mere shock at the statement. Now, I'm realizing that she might honestly not find me the least bit husband material.

Which is another reason to make sure she says yes to me. How can she think that I am not worthy to be a husband? Much less hers?

I will prove to her that I can be a dang good husband, even if it's just a fake one. I won't be like my father. Ever.

A petite hand rests on my shoulder, and I stiffen.

"I'm so, so sorry. Let me pay for your dry cleaning."

A breath escapes my pressed lips, creating a puff of fog in the cool night air.

"No need. I'll recycle the suit and get a new one." Even if it was my favorite. I turn around, and Hayden drops her hand to her side. Warmth lingers where her fingers had rested.

She bites her lip and looks away from my gaze. An unfamiliar feeling arises in my stomach, a warm feeling that makes my pent-up anger threaten to melt away, though I'm not quite ready for that yet.

"How did you manage to not get a drop on yourself?" There is a dry coarseness to my voice, creating a positively growly and grumpy effect.

Regardless of my tone, she laughs. "I'm a woman of many talents."

With a frustrated snort, I run a hand through my hair. How can she laugh at a moment like this? But then again, I'm standing in front of my ex-fiancée's father's house, proposing to my campaign manager while coated in her vomit. What have I sunk to?

I'm not giving up now. Hayden Bennett as my wife still makes the most sense to me in this pressing, time-restrained situation. "Would one of those talents be marrying your boss and possibly becoming First Lady of the United States?"

"You were serious?"

I sigh. Am I ever not serious? What part of this is she not understanding? "Yes, Hayden. I'm very serious. It would be a real marriage in the eyes of the law, but it won't be real for us. Just think of it as a job promotion with significantly higher pay. And new housing."

With a small gasp, her eyebrows raise and her mouth drops open. At that moment, the wind brushes across my face, carrying unthinkable smells. Hayden then covers her mouth and nose with her hand, and I instinctively scrunch my nose.

"Let's move this conversation to somewhere more...sanitary."

She nods her head, and I pull my phone from the pocket of my black slacks to ask my personal assistant to pick us up in my favorite car—the Mustang. Spotting Lionel facing away from us with his hands laced behind his back, I walk the slight distance away from Hayden and the car to speak with him. He rocks back and forth on his toes, humming an unfamiliar tune.

"Lionel," I say, trying not to startle him with my sudden approach.

"Mr. Marshall." He turns on his heel and faces me with a nod. "Are you ready for me to park the car?"

"There was an incident. Vomit is now soaked into the floor of the backseat."

I expect Lionel to flinch or make a disgusted face, but he doesn't. Instead, he says, "I will make sure it is cleaned by tomorrow."

"I will pay you extra for the service. Thank you, Lionel."

He looks me over, noticing the new additions to my suit. He says, "Should I call someone to pick you and Miss Bennett up?"

"Thanks, but I've already called Bennie. He will be here shortly. You can go ahead and take off."

He nods once and walks determinedly to the car, pausing only to give a slight nod to Hayden, who crosses her arms over her chest and hugs herself. The woman who never gets embarrassed must be dying on the inside right now.

As Lionel drives away, I join a shivering Hayden on the gravel walkway. Not embarrassed, but apparently cold.

I shrug my coat off, but quickly remember it is splashed with unthinkable things.

"It has your...stomach contents on it, but it's warm." I hand the jacket out to her. She stares at it as if it's diseased. Disregarding her look, I step behind her and wrap it around her shoulders. I half expect her to toss it off, but instead, her hands grip the sides and pull it closed around her.

"Thank you," she whispers. In a louder voice, "You need to call Ren and let him know we are leaving."

Ren. Right. I forgot about him.

I send a quick text letting him know that I will be leaving. Two seconds later, he calls me.

"Why are you leaving?" I hear laughter in his voice. "Did Hayden put you in your place again and now you need to nurse your pride alone?"

"No," I bite out. "We just need to go." Hayden would be highly embarrassed if I told him what happened. I'd hate to do that to her, especially if she is my future wife.

"We?"

"Yes. Hayden and I are leaving."

"Oh," he says, his laughing tone shifting to something more incredulous. "Did you two realize you're in love?"

I growl. "No, Ren. We just have to leave. Are you coming or staying?"

"I'll stay here. You two kids have fun." And with that, he clicks off.

"Ren is staying," I state. Hayden only offers a soft smile.

"Thanks for not telling Ren I threw up on you." She tucks her chin to her chest and hugs my jacket closer to her. "I know you were looking out for your image, but you saved mine, too."

I say nothing. There's no point in countering her accusation. I've learned people will always believe what they want to, no matter your intentions.

We stand there outside the entrance to Weatherby's. It's a cloudy night, so only lights pouring through the windows of the mansion offer a slight reprieve from the darkness. Hayden and I look anywhere but at each other, at least, I assume she is trying as hard as I am not to make eye contact.

The smell has faded in the fresh air of the night, and only a trace lingers when the wind begins to blow.

Silence has always been my strong suit, but there is a massive elephant in the area right now, and I'm not talking about an establishment Republican.

I clear my throat. "Hayden, I was serious about my proposal. I think this could work. We aren't romantically inclined, so we can think of this as a business proposal of sorts. Just between us. The rest of the world can say what they will. Of course, we will have to show small amounts of PDA in public, but I don't think that will be a major issue since we know in our minds that this is fake. I will pay you two hundred thousand a year, and it will only last as long as my candidacy, or presidency, lasts. So, eight years maximum."

I offer a smile, thinking of how it sounded like I was offering her eight years in prison.

She stares at me. Her eyes look glassy, but the crease in her brows tells me she is deep in thought.

"That's the longest I've ever heard you speak without pausing."

And for all that deep thought, that is what she concludes. A laugh escapes me.

"Mr. Marshall," Hayden coos. "Did you just laugh?"

I straighten my face out, pasting on my serious look. Well, I guess you could call my serious look simply *my look*.

She continues, "A smile and a laugh tonight. My word. Who knew you had it in you when not in front of a camera?"

I roll my eyes, feeling like a child. "I have a soul, you know."

"I did not, in fact, know that." Hayden chuckles. Her eyes shift away from me as the light banter dies down. "So, how was your meeting today?"

She's changing the subject, but I'll bite this time. She obviously needs time to process. "It was fine. The usual."

"You schedule your further-away meetings on Wednesdays. Why is that?"

With a swallow, I answer. "A mid-week breather from the office." She doesn't need to know where I actually go on Wednesdays. It's my sacred thing.

I hear the roar of the Mustang approaching and my worries fade away.

"Our ride is here," I grin, anticipating driving my baby. Yes, I'm a car guy. They get all my love.

"Another smile," Hayden says. "What am I going to do with you?"

With my heightened mood and the rumble of the Mustang approaching, I respond with words that I know will haunt me for years to come.

"You should marry me, Hayden Bennett."

CHAPTER SEVEN

HAYDEN

He's lost it. Darcy Marshall's mind is gone; it's on an island in the Bahamas sipping a margarita. The most creative, imaginative person could have never dreamt that *Darcy* would propose to *me*. I don't adhere to the belief that he is too good for me or anything. We are all human, none greater than another, but I seem to grate his nerves, and he thinks I'm the bane of his existence. So why would a man propose to a woman he hates even if it's fake?

A knock on the door jolts me from my panicked thoughts.

"One moment," I respond, taking one last swig and gargle of mouthwash before spitting it out and exiting the bathroom. An older woman dressed in a fitted black dress—Mrs. Pellenson, the senator's wife—nods at me before slipping into the bathroom of Mr. Weatherby's estate. There are plenty of bathrooms in this house, but this is the closest to the dining room. At least that's what one of the housekeepers told me.

Darcy's driver brought him a spare change of clothes after hearing about what happened from Lionel because he thought Darcy might want to stay at the Weatherby dinner. I watched Darcy's face deflate at the news, and I knew that we would be staying. Thankfully, my clothes were puke-free.

I round the hallway, embarking on a hunt for either the dining room, a housekeeper to point me in the right direction, or the man who suddenly wants to marry me. Seriously. What is he thinking? I am his campaign manager. I didn't go to college to get an MRS degree, and it's basically selling myself if I were to say yes to him simply for the money. *Pft, ridiculous man.*

Then again, it's a place to live. I wouldn't have to continue my fruitless search for a reasonably priced apartment. I'd be living at my place of work. I could put that fancy espresso machine to good use. No more coffee runs. I can be a normal woman who goes to the coffee shop for the aesthetics and vibe alone.

As I'm walking out of the hallway, two hands grab my shoulders, and instinctively, I wrap my hands to the inside of the perpetrator's wrists and push, knocking the hands off my shoulders as I learned in my self-defense classes ages ago. Looking up to see who put their hands on me without my permission, I come face to face with the man occupying my thoughts. His blue eyes twinkle like stars, and it almost makes me smile.

Almost.

"Will you quit trying to bulldoze over me? You're going the wrong way." His lips twitch as if begging him to smile, but he won't allow it.

I scoff, a flush bleeding red through my cheeks. "Will you quit putting your hands on me without asking first?"

His jaw goes slack and... Is that a blush crawling up his face? "Fine. You can face plant onto hard surfaces from now on."

"Mr. Marshall, what a pleasant surprise to see you here," an obnoxiously-loud voice calls. I break eye contact with Darcy and look over his shoulder.

This night just leveled up in difficulty.

Darcy scowls, staring at me, and then twists his features into the pleasant, friendly presidential candidate. He turns around.

"Mr. Loveless." Darcy nods and shakes the Republican's outreached hand. "It's a pleasure to see you."

As if, I think to myself.

Mr. Loveless addresses me next and grabs my petite hand with his large, pudgy one. I narrow my eyes as we stare at each other in what has to be the world's longest handshake. Giving him a "don't try anything funny tonight" look, I remove my hand.

"I didn't think you'd join tonight due to the *current circumstances,*" Mr. Loveless comments to Darcy.

Darcy maintains his easy-going facade and chuckles lightly. "Priscilla and I may not be getting married, but that does not mean our families are suddenly estranged."

Mr. Loveless smiles in the cunning way that makes me want to revert back to my street days and start throwing hands. "Of course. Well, I see my lovely *wife* down the hall. I better go join her and the rest of the party."

"Right behind you," Darcy says. But he doesn't move as Mr. Loveless steps around us and walks away.

"That no good snake," Darcy mumbles under his breath. "Trying to make me jealous by using his wife."

I glance at Darcy, his mask completely fallen. In its place is a brooding man. Though, the longer I watch him seethe, the more I realize something. The way his eyebrows knit, the shine in his drooping eyes, and the wrinkles appearing vaguely on his forehead... He isn't only brooding, but Darcy is exhausted. It's the expression I sported when I'd noticed myself in department store windows as I trudged back and forth from my minimum wage job, back when I was escaping to the street to get away from the living hell that was Director Hoggs.

A thought punches me in the gut. Darcy is just like me. I have no one in my life to share the chores with, to share the highs and lows of life with, and neither does he. He may have housekeepers and a cook, but he has no one to decompress with, no one to cry to, and no one to hold when he lays his head on his pillow at night.

For the first time, I see a glimpse of the man behind the mask.

"Remember who you are, Mr. Marshall. Mr. Loveless will not get the upper hand tonight," I say. It's not much, but hopefully it encourages him. Presidential candidate Darcy Marshall has to come out to play. He nods in the curt way I'm used to, and then he motions forward. I turn around and begin the short walk down the hall and into the dining room.

Help everyone to remember they are mere human beings vying for various positions to govern a whole country and not petulant children seeking power, I plead with God.

I need to go ahead and enter a calm, cool, and collected headspace. If I don't, I might lose control of myself and run off at the mouth, and that wouldn't be good for Darcy.

Or myself.

CHAPTER EIGHT

DARCY

"And that's the reason we have to maintain Republican control of the House this election cycle. We can't risk left-leaning Independents filtering in. Which means we should only support candidates with the 'R' behind their name," Mr. Loveless drones on.

"People may be more apt to vote for Independents simply due to the corruption rotting through both of the primary parties," I state. "Which means we shouldn't count out conservative-leaning Independents in our endorsements."

Mr. Loveless offers a gentle smile, though I know underneath it he is wishing I would go to the fiery place under my feet. He's part of the corruption, after all. The past hour has gone like this: Richard Loveless has taken shots at Independents claiming that people can never be sure if the party members adhere to more liberal or conservative beliefs, and I have countered that the Republican Party is just as politically corrupt as the Democratic Party.

Senator Pellenson has taken my side, being an Independent himself. Mr. Weatherby has bounced back and forth on varying issues. Ren and Mr. Sato have quietly chatted with Hayden in Japanese, and by the way her wide, excited eyes are animated and her hands flaring as she speaks, I can tell she is loving getting to practice the language. Maybe I should let her in on the fact that I know Japanese as well, thanks to Ren. Then, I could have those lively conversations with her.

No, there's no point. Our conversations get heated enough in English. Though, it's always on the side of pique instead of passion.

The wives of the politicians and donors gathered around the long table have joined in occasionally on the battle between Mr. Loveless and myself, but mostly, they have whispered amongst each other. The food seems to be endless, covering every inch of the table, which one would think would prevent much talking considering how great it all tastes. But no. These are natural-bred politicians. Nothing can make them shut their mouths for two seconds.

Priscilla, thankfully, is nowhere to be seen. Though I was prepared to encounter her tonight, I didn't realize the relief I felt until I settled in for dinner and she was still absent from the gathering.

I take a bite of the steak and chew on the rare meat while I contemplate why Mr. Loveless was invited to this party. Mr. Weatherby is an Independent, the Senator is an Independent, Mr. Sato, though a diplomat, has been nothing short of wonderful for the Independent party and a close friend of many of us. The few other guests are well-known Independent Party political action committee donors.

So why is Mr. Loveless, an establishment Republican and presidential ticket holder for the party, at this dinner?

"When will Marcus arrive?" Mr. Weatherby asks.

"He should be here in," Mr. Loveless checks his watch, "about five minutes."

"Will Priscilla be with him?" Mr. Weatherby glances my way as he asks the question. Why would Priscilla be with—

It takes every ounce of concentration to not let the fake smile slip from my face.

"Yes, they were meeting with a client. It ran a little late," Mr. Loveless says. Right on cue, Mr. Loveless's son walks into the dining room hand-in-hand with my ex-fiancée and childhood friend.

And there's a ring on her finger.

A deadly silence blankets the room. Glances bounce between Marcus, Priscilla, and me. No one dares to move or make a sound, and the uncomfortableness of the situation sits heavily on my chest. I twist my hands together under the table, eventually wiping them down my pant leg as sweat continues to accumulate on my palms.

The mask slips. I can't bear to smile anymore. Anger boils in my blood, and I wish I would have hopped in my Mustang and driven home when I had the chance.

"Mr. Marshall, it's nice to meet you. I'm a huge fan of yours, as I'm in the tech industry." I look up to find Marcus standing beside me with an outstretched hand. It's almost as if I'm looking into a mirror that reveals my younger self—Marcus Loveless and I could be siblings with our similar builds, blond waves, and blue eyes. My face displays a light scruff while he has a clean shave. I search for Priscilla who has already sat down at the other end of the table, for which I am grateful for. Looks like she has a type.

I stand up and take Marcus's hand with a firm shake. "The pleasure is mine, Mr. Loveless."

"Please, call me Marcus. Mr. Loveless is my father's name." He grins. I don't understand this situation, but I can certainly understand not wanting to be completely associated with one's father. I try to find the masked smile to place on my face, but it's buried deep inside. The best I can do is offer a slight nod before I take my seat.

Marcus makes his rounds offering greetings and then sits down next to Priscilla. The look that passes between the two tells me all I needed to know: she was seeing him while she was engaged to me.

By the flush and sweat on Mr. Weatherby's wrinkly face, he knew as well.

Why in the world am I here tonight?

A hand rests on my thigh, and I instinctively scoot my leg away. But when I look to my left, Hayden is smiling at me while she reinforces her hand with a grip that has her fingers digging into the skin beneath my pants.

The only words my brain conjures are that Hayden Bennett's hand is casually gripping my thigh. It's a song played on repeat, clashing with a thousand emotions already plaguing my thoughts.

"Are you okay?" she whispers in my ear. I swallow as the hairs on the back of my neck stand up. Her hand is a hot flame sitting above my knee.

I loosen the tie around my neck and let out a breath. "Of course."

She smiles sweetly, her face lingering in my space. I back away, but her fingernails dig into my leg.

"Don't lean away," she hisses through her smile. The confusion must be plain as day in my eyes because she leans toward my ear again. "Smile like I'm whispering sweet nothings in your ear."

I choke on my saliva at the phrase "sweet nothings" and reach for my glass of water as Hayden backs away with a satisfied smirk. Everyone, once preoccupied with entertaining Marcus and Priscilla, congratulating them on their engagement, now has their eyes trained on me for the second time tonight.

Hayden finally moves her hand, but instead of placing it back in her lap where it belongs, she rests it on my shoulder and smiles at me like I'm her favorite person in the whole world. Like she *sees* me.

I should swat her hand off my shoulder. I should denounce the improper behavior of my campaign manager touching me in this way. Or maybe I should play it cool like she was picking a piece of lint or fuzz from my jacket to save us both a slice of dignity.

But instead, I'm sucked into a strange fantasy where I *am* her favorite person in the world, like she's my person—the one who sees the man behind the mask and still chooses to love him. The me I have to hide to be accepted by society. I believe for a moment that the smile illuminated on her face is one hundred percent real.

And I smile back.

The table erupts in a chaotic cacophony of questions.

"What's going on?"

"Isn't she your campaign manager?"

"Mr. Marshall, what's happening here?"

"You can't date your campaign manager."

"Get it, bro."

And then one voice rings above the rest. One word. A question and a statement.

"Darcy..."

My head snaps, following Priscilla's voice. Our eyes connect from across opposite ends of the long table, and for one split second, I notice the pained sadness in her eyes and the tight pull of her lips—the same expression she would wear when I would stop our chaste kisses from deepening or when she would get upset with me for having too many meetings and not enough time to spend with her. But then, she controls herself and looks down at the food in front of her.

I glance around the table, not hearing the noise as mouths continue to move while pointed in my direction. Cameras continue to flash. The image of my campaign manager and me, looking like a couple, is solidified for eternity and will appear on every news station come morning. My hands grip the wooden table, and I stand up. The chair flies behind me due to the abrupt force, and the porcelain glass dishes in front of me rattle. Mouths no longer move, but I need to escape the stares and implied accusations from Hayden touching my shoulder for everyone to see. *Stupid, stupid girl.* She hasn't said yes to me. If she says no, I have a massive mess to clean up. I wanted to draw up contracts first. My heart beats quickly. Too quickly. My breathing grows shallow and my head spins.

I've got to get out of here...

Without another word or glance at the people gathered around me, I flee the room.

The hallway narrows as I stumble over my feet. The walls cave in, and I find myself leaning against something hard as I struggle to leave. I've been in this house a million times, but I'm so turned around that I'm trapped—held hostage by the ever-shrinking walls. I stumble along for an eternity before I find an open door and hurl myself through it, kicking it closed as I collapse to the ground.

I hug my knees and try to focus my breaths like my old therapist taught me.

Right when I finally feel a smidge of relief from the tightness in my chest, the doorknob rattles and I can't breathe again. I close my eyes.

"Darcy-*kun*."

Ren's hands find my shoulders and begin massaging, working their way across the back of my neck and over the muscles in my upper back. My lungs open, and my breathing becomes deeper and longer, a drastic change from the short and shallow breaths from only moments ago.

"I'll give you two more minutes, but then you *will* tell me what you're feeling. No excuses."

I nod.

By the time I can breathe fully again, I'm ready to talk to Ren. He's the only person I would *ever* talk about my feelings with.

"I feel betrayed. Not because I loved Priscilla, but because she knows what my father did. She knows he cheated on my mother."

I pause to not let the hurt consume me all over again. "There is no way she wasn't seeing Marcus behind my back. Not if they're engaged. And even if what we had wasn't love, I trusted her. I trusted our mutual connection and our years of friendship."

Ren stops massaging my shoulders and back and sits down beside me. We both sag against the wall.

"You weren't prepared to see her with another man. But I have to ask, you didn't fall into this panic attack right when you saw them. So what happened?"

I mull the recent events over. Priscilla walking in with Marcus. Marcus introducing himself to me. The loving exchange between the two. Hayden touching me...

"Hayden. She—"

"Touched your thigh and shoulder," Ren finishes. I look at him, and he smirks. "Yeah, I saw that."

I laugh because it's the only thing that makes sense to do at this moment. "She created a whole new mess that will involve a ton of wordplay and political finesse to clean up if she doesn't agree..." I take a few steadying breaths and try to corral my scattered thoughts. "When everyone looked at me and began shouting questions and accusations, I heard her voice above the rest. Priscilla said my name like it pained her... Something inside of me broke. It was the very expression she wore when I wouldn't do things she liked. It reminded me of those moments, reminded me that we were never in love. But that doesn't mean she should have cheated on me. What gave her the right to..."

"Betray you," Ren answers, using the very emotion I felt. Why did Priscilla deserve the right to be pained after what she did?

"Yes." I shove Priscilla from my mind and recall Hayden and her actions. They were much like the actions of a girlfriend. "I think Hayden was trying to make her jealous, but we all know how that turned out."

"Unless she becomes your wife," Ren says, raising an eyebrow. I had let him in on the idea a little after walking into the party. I had to tell someone who I knew would support the idea and possibly persuade Hayden to say yes.

I laugh at the idiocy of it all. "That was unbelievably stupid of me to suggest. She would never. And now there will be this awkward tension between us, which will serve no one well on my staff."

He clicks his tongue. "The way she played along to try and save your pride back there suggests otherwise, my friend. I think that was her "yes.'"

I turn to face Ren and clasp his shoulder. "Hayden Bennett hates me. That's all there is to it. If I wasn't the one paying her salary, she'd be gone."

Ren doesn't respond, but he looks as if he's fighting a grin.

"Help me get out of this house unseen. And fetch Hayden."

Ren chuckles now. "No wonder you think she hates you. She's not a dog to be fetched, Darcy-*kun*. You've got to learn how to share your feelings with someone other than me. Maybe then you wouldn't scare off women or make them think you're a heartless monster."

"Why do I need a woman to confide in when I have you?" I coo playfully. Ren stares blankly at me. And in that moment, I fully recognize the need for emotional separation between me and Ren.

"Just get me out of here," I growl.

POP CULTURE NOW!

PRISCILLA WEATHERBY ANNOUNCES ENGAGEMENT TO DARCY'S OPPONENT'S SON.

By Krissy Towers

In a staggering turn of events in our Darcy, Priscilla, and Mystery Woman saga, Priscilla Weatherby and Marcus Loveless, son of Republican Presidential candidate Richard Loveless, have announced their engagement. Priscilla and Darcy continue to spew the same narrative that their break up was mutual. But with Priscilla's new engagement coming just after a month of her calling it off with Darcy, we are wondering if the whispering birds were correct in their assumptions regarding Priscilla's fidelity to Darcy. We have reached out to Priscilla, Marcus, and their families for comment.

Did Priscilla unintentionally help out Darcy's campaign while blanketing her future father-in-law's, or is there something more sinister brewing that the public is unaware of? Stay tuned with us at *Pop Culture NOW!* for all of the latest updates.

CHAPTER NINE

HAYDEN

I had shook free of Priscilla's grip once. She'd grabbed at me again, which meant I was in the process of taking the gold hoops out of my ears, but that was as far as I had gotten before Darcy entered the dining room, grabbed my hand, and strode out of the Weatherby Estate with me in tow. I had tried to break free of his hold, but Ren was there to walk closely behind me. After he had placed a firm hand on the small of my back and had shoved me forward, I complied.

Mostly because Ren Sato was touching my back, and I was enjoying every moment of that.

Now, we arrive at the car, and Darcy slides into the driver's side while Ren walks me around. Before he opens my door (what a gentleman!), he looks me dead in the eyes.

"Hayden, consider Darcy's offer of marriage. I know he isn't the most pleasant man to get along with at times, but he has a heart of gold. Once you break through his walls, that man will love you with a ferocity unmatched."

I swallow the lump in my throat at his words. "He told you?"

"Of course. And seriously, consider it. I think the two of you would be a perfect match." Ren winks, then says, "I also think you have the capacity to fall in love, but don't tell him I said that."

Hairs on the back of my neck stand up. "Um, thanks. I–I will think about it."

Ren nods, then he opens the door for me. I scurry inside the vehicle, anxious to get away from Ren's talk about loving Darcy.

Gah! It was stupid of me to let my emotions win. I saw Darcy in a painful-looking predicament that tugged on my heart strings. I had marriage and relationships and love on the brain from his "proposal," if he was even serious about that.

What if he was? Ren seems to think so.

The car jolts into motion, and we are off toward Darcy's mansion, the beginning of the journey quiet and a tad awkward, if I'm being honest. Ren's words replay in my head. Could I work well with Darcy? We work well as a manager and candidate. Could husband and wife work well, too? I choke the words down like swallowing a bitter medicine as Darcy breaks the silence, asking if I'm okay.

I nod and then take a few breaths to ground myself. I recall the events of the night and feel anger rise at the thought of what Priscilla did to Darcy. It was clear that she and Marcus were seeing each other behind Darcy's back. She cheated, and there's no way to hide that now. To be frank, it ticked me off. No one deserves to be cheated on no matter how prickly they are. And what was with Marcus's casualness toward Darcy as if he wasn't a part of the deception?

"I could have taken her, you know," I mumble aloud, gazing out the window of the passenger seat in Darcy's Mustang. He had sent Bennie home with Lionel earlier in the night so that he could drive the car home.

Beside me, Darcy scoffs. "Priscilla has trained in MMA since she was seven years old."

"Yeah? I can fight, too," I whisper under my breath. With a hefty sigh, I lean my head against the cool window.

"If you smudge the window, you clean it," he barks.

I wave him off. "Whatever."

My stomach is queasy, which I don't dare tell Darcy. From the heavy food, stress of the night, Darcy's maniacal driving, and the huge question looming over my head, my stomach can't seem to relax.

"Why did you try to fight her, anyway?" Darcy's voice is softer than usual, and it beckons me to glance at him. His shoulders are slightly slumped, and his typically sharp eyes look heavy and tired under the glow of the passing street lights.

Why *did* I try to fight Priscilla? It's not like Darcy is mine to protect or anything. I barely even like the man. Plus, Priscilla did absolutely nothing to me. But it was that one tiny glimpse into his sadness that so vividly mirrored my own...

Camaraderie. That's why I tried to fight Priscilla. But he doesn't need to know that.

"I had enough of everyone looking at you like you were a wounded puppy. That sympathetic stare they kept giving you rubbed me the wrong way. I figured she was the cause, so she was the one who needed the punishment for hurting you. When you left the room, I started to come after you. Priscilla ran around the table and grabbed my wrists, saying something to the effect of you needing to be alone to process. I told her you were no longer her concern and shook free of her. Then, Ren ran after you and she grabbed at me again, so I thought I would take care of Priscilla while you dealt with... whatever was going on."

I watch him as he sits, soaking in my words. Is that a smile I see tugging at the corner of his lips? No, just a trick of the passing light in the dark. To further confirm that indeed was not a smile, Darcy grunts.

"You don't physically assault people because you don't like what they are doing or saying. Besides, she didn't hurt me."

I press the light above us to get a better look at Darcy. His hands grip the wheel so hard they are bleached white. His hair is disheveled and the tie around his neck is pulled loose. I don't believe him for one second.

"Look at you, Mr. Marshall. She hurt you, all right. What I want to know is why tonight hurt you, but when she called off the engagement, you were okay, just angry."

The lump in Darcy's throat moves up and down as he swallows. He reaches up and turns off the light. "I was fine then, and I'm fine now."

No, you're not, I think to myself, but I don't want to push the issue tonight. There's another issue I need to press him about.

"So, about marrying you," I say.

"Never mind."

"Never mind? After all that? *Never mind?*" My voice inches into a higher pitch the longer I verbally process. "You mean to tell me that I vomited for no reason tonight? That I faked a possible romantic attachment to you during dinner for no reason? *Never mind?*"

Under the passing streetlight, I see Darcy strip his eyes from the road long enough to look at me with a raised brow. A strand of hair falls in front of his face, and it gives him a youthful look. "Unless you want to marry me."

I desperately want to put my face against the window again to cool the burning in my cheeks. "I never said that," I say, my voice lowering to a mere whisper.

"Then never mind."

"What are you going to do?"

He sighs. "I guess take a go at this campaign as a single man. The reporter was right, culture has changed."

"Culture may have changed, but you are still on the Independent ticket. Die-hard Republicans and Democrats alike will be wary of you. We at least need the conservative vote from the people who no longer want to associate with the Republican Party if you are going to stand a chance at winning this thing." I pause to take a breath. "And that means showing you are a man of traditional values while also being open-minded. That is what the people want."

I watch his silhouette—a hand reaching up and running through tousled hair.

"I know." His voice is blank.

"You know I'm twenty-eight, right?"

"Yes."

"And you're thirty-nine."

"And?"

His voice holds no recognition of the age gap between us. I smile. "We are eleven years apart." Darcy still wears a blank expression. Funny. He doesn't seem to care about our age difference. I continue. "You're my boss. We have completely different socioeconomic backgrounds. There would be a lot of talk and speculation."

Darcy mumbles something that sounds like there is already going to be a lot of talk, but I can't quite make out his words. He looks my way again, and my heart constricts at the darkness clouded over his eyes. "I've already said never mind, Hayden. No need to list the reasons my idea was inconceivable."

No matter the darkness, I laugh. "Okay, Vizzini."

Darcy doesn't laugh. Nor does he comment. But the briefest of smiles glimmers across his face, highlighted by the moonlight pouring through the window.

"You know *The Princess Bride?* You must not be as uptight as I took you for. I guess I can marry you then." The words flow freely in the midst of my laugh, but when the last syllable rolls off my tongue, I clasp my hands over my mouth.

Darcy's hands fall to the bottom of the steering wheel as I stare wide-eyed at his darkened frame. As we enter the city lights, I notice he cuts his eyes to me then back to the road before he says, "Good. It'll be easier to spin your little show at dinner if we become an official item in the eyes of everyone. Let's talk about the *job change.*"

"That wasn't a yes!" And I'm back in a sour mood. How does this man have me wanting to throw hands one moment, laughing

without a care in the world the next, and then back to wanting to
throw hands all in the span of a few minutes?

I need time to *think*, for crying out loud!

"No, don't do it!" I yell at the television screen and throw a
handful of popcorn for good measure. I hate this part
in *Fruits Basket*, another one of my favorite anime shows, where
Tohru practically slaves away in the Sohma house in order to live
there. "Just say no to the powerful Sohmas!"

The concept of the show is irritating me a bit more than usual
today. Though I'm sure it has absolutely nothing to do with the
fact that Darcy Marshall, one of the most powerful men in the entire country—probably the world one day, judging by his brilliant
and capable mind—proposed to me last night. And I almost said
yes.

Proposal isn't the right word. More like hired. He wants to hire
me to be his wife. As if I am that type of woman. I may have grown
up running the streets between group homes and foster homes,
but that doesn't mean I will sell out for a dollar.

Right?

He never responded after I reminded him I never said yes. Instead, he drove with an easy smugness as if he didn't hear me. I even
repeated the sentiment that I never said yes to him, but he didn't

seem to comprehend it as his grin grew cockier with every passing mile to his estate.

But I *did* seriously consider marrying him for a moment there. In that one instance, I saw him. I saw the loneliness plaguing his eyes and mirroring my own. We could help each other. We could learn to be friends. We could lean on each other. It's why I placed my hand on his shoulder and tried to let him know that I saw him while we were at dinner.

Darcy wants to pay me to be his wife, and that isn't acceptable, right?

"You have so much student loan debt," I say in an attempt to persuade myself. "And you are being evicted from your apartment. You need the money and a place to live. What's better than living at your workplace? You could save so much time in the morning. You could pay off your loans and finally use your income to go explore. You could go to Japan!"

Japan...

I've wanted to explore the island country for as long as I can remember. Manga and anime were my escape throughout the dark abyss of life, and they stem out of that beloved country. I thought the dream of traveling was a little out of reach, but now...

"No!" I can work my way through the debt even if it takes years. I'm sure there is an apartment somewhere with a dotted line on a contract waiting for my name. Doing life on my own is better than selling my soul to the devil for a lengthy part of my life, depending on the election outcome. Which my career hinges upon.

But didn't he say to view the marriage as a job promotion? Heck, being the wife of Darcy Marshall will be no easy task. So technically, marrying him would be working my way through the debt. Plus, I would have a place to securely lay my head at night.

I throw another handful of popcorn to vent frustration, and then I grab my throw pillow from the other cushion of the couch and hug it close to my body, burying my head into the softness.

What should I do?

Groaning, I yank my head up then pause the show.

I should call Stella. She'll know what to do.

After a few rings, she answers, and I'm met with sleepy eyes, a messy bun, and a yawn.

"Hello, Mrs. Grady," I sing. A soft smile paints her lips.

"It's five a.m.," she complains.

I shrug. "It's six here. Besides, shouldn't you be getting ready for work?"

"I had fifteen more minutes of sleep, you dirty little sleep-stealer. This better be good." Stella yawns again. "Wait, shouldn't *you* be ready for work? You're in pajamas."

"I am taking today off after last night." I tug at my own messy bun with my free hand.

"Well, what happened? Go on. You woke me up."

"And me," Lucas grumbles from the background.

"Hold on. Let me get out of the room." Stella grunts as she gets out of bed. A few moments later, she's in Lucas's kitchen—her kitchen.

I'm silent as she begins to make coffee.

"Hayden, what is it?"

"Well, um... Darcy thinks he found a wife."

"Hmm, that's good," she mumbles as she dumps coffee grinds into the filter, then picks up the pot. "Who is it?"

After a beat, I answer. "Me."

The sound of glass shattering echoes from the other end of the phone.

"Stella! Are you okay?" Lucas shouts. Moments later, his face enters the screen. He stares at Stella as she stares at me with wild, gray eyes.

"You said yes?" she finally asks.

"What? Of course not. I haven't said anything."

"Somebody tell me what happened," Lucas demands. "My favorite household appliance is shattered on the floor."

"Darcy proposed to Hayden," Stella responds, still seemingly in shock.

Now, Lucas looks like a deer in the headlights. "Hayden. He's a billionaire. And running for president of the United States. *The United States!*"

"I know," I groan.

"You could be First Lady. I could say I know the First Lady of the United States," he continues in his southern drawl. "Do it. Marry him."

Stella and I both glare at him.

"What?" he asks in an innocent tone. Stella shoves him out of the frame.

"Will you clean this up, Luca? I really need to talk to Hayden." There's a pause, and then she adds, "Alone."

"Fine," he sulks. "Though you broke it."

"I owe you one." Stella smiles broadly off camera, then leaves the kitchen.

"Well, I guess I don't need coffee. That news alone is like an IV line of caffeine straight to the heart."

"Stella. I need help," I snap a finger in front of my face to capture her attention. "I'm actually considering his offer. Talk me out of it. Tell me I'm being utterly ridiculous and anti-woman. Tell me that I'm not being a good Christian and am making the biggest mistake of my existence."

Stella hums to herself for a moment, her eyes looking everywhere but at me. "What's in it for you?" she finally asks.

"No more student loans. A place to live. A nearly tripled salary," I huff. "A big enticer, right?"

"But if he wins—"

"When he wins," I correct her. She raises an eyebrow.

"When he wins, then you will become First Lady of the United States. Hayden Bennett, First Lady. It has a nice ring to it," Stella muses.

Heat creeps up my face. "Um, well. I think my name would legally be Hayden Marshall."

"I'll be." She shakes her head, while I bite my tongue not to comment on how southern she sounds right now. "That sounds better than your real name. Hayden Marshall, First Lady of the United States."

My stomach twists, and I have the urge to vomit. I swallow it down. "No more vomiting just because something makes you uncomfortable," I chastise myself. Hayden Bennett. Hayden Marshall. Hayden Bennett Marshall. Hayden has-no-middle-name Bennett Marshall.

How can a woman without a middle name be the First Lady? Or marry a man of Darcy's caliber? I don't like this feeling of inferiority; I work hard to remind myself that the Lord says no human is above another human. But right now...

"What's that?" Stella asks, pulling me from my thoughts.

"Nothing. I just..." I close my eyes, "can't do this." My phone drops to my lap.

"Hey, Hayden." Stella's voice is soft and gentle. "You're pretty. Even at this angle."

I snort, and Stella laughs alongside me. I pick the phone up from my thighs.

"Look, hon. I understand if you don't want to do this. But, you *can* do this. I know Darcy is a thorn in your side, but he's a good man. He genuinely cares about people, which is why he's running for president even though the political arena isn't his favorite place to be. He wants to make a change, and he's willing to go through the fire to see it happen."

"In the public's eyes," I scoff. "He's a scrooge to me. Why would a man propose to someone he doesn't tolerate well?"

Stella is silent. It's a type of silence that makes me squirm.

"What is it?" I finally ask.

"I can't say, but you should ask him about his Wednesday meetings. It may change your mind about his character."

I roll my eyes. "He takes breaks by going to faraway meetings on Wednesdays? Yeah, I know that. And I don't think he has a bad character. I wouldn't support him for president if I thought that. I respect him, and I—"

Whoa.

"I trust him," I finish in disbelief at the realization. He is capable and well-off. He takes care of his team. He never misses a deadline or an event. He's committed and trustworthy. "I may not like him, but I *trust* him." Does marriage really have to be about love? Or is trusting the person more important?

"You always said you never wanted to fall in love." Stella sounds skeptical, but she's only repeating my words back to me. Yeah, I've said that. But I never really meant it. I think she knows that. I only wanted to portray my independence and confidence within myself instead of a man. I've always depended on myself alone. Well, and God. Though I could benefit from not making Him an afterthought these days.

"Do you think it would be morally wrong for me to marry him and then dissolve the marriage after everything is said and done?"

Stella contemplates this on the other end of the screen as she begins to dress for work. "Biblically, they married for reasons other than love all the time. Marriages were often transactional in nature. I don't think that it's wrong. But if you were to consummate the marriage and then—"

"Take your horses and hold them tight, Stella. Nobody said anything about consummating." My stomach rumbles with nausea at the sheer thought.

"I'm just saying..."

"No!" I bark. "Go get ready for work. We can talk later when your brain lets this whole consummation thing go."

Stella laughs heartily. "No matter what you decide, I'm in your corner."

"Bye, Stella." But before we click off, I hear her laugh and say to Lucas, "Oh, they're *so* going to fall in love."

The phone drops to my lap again, and I stare at the paused image of my anime show.

Tohru falls in love with the grump at the end of the show. Turns out, Kyo, the love interest, was misunderstood. Is Darcy simply misunderstood? Can I dig underneath the surface to try and understand him? Could we work together as a marital team, guiding this country? Could I learn to like him? Possibly even love... No. Let's not go there.

A place to live, student loans paid, a heftier income, and not to mention the chance to become First Lady...

If I became First Lady, I could use that to land my dream job of becoming Secretary of State one day. Hillary Clinton did it, and I'd be ten times—a million times—better than her. Bonus, I look better in pantsuits than she does.

Can I do this? Am I going to marry a man for reasons other than love? It's a completely counter-cultural thought.

This is the life I've been given. My parents abandoned me. I grew up bouncing between group and foster homes, and I've spent a lot of time running away to the streets. And now, I'm going to marry for money and stability over love.

We won't technically be married because consummation will *not* happen. So when it comes time to divorce him, I can have a clean conscience.

Am I really doing this?

God, is this what You want me to do? Please give me direction.

CHAPTER TEN

DARCY

I tap my pen against my wooden desk.

Hayden didn't come in to work today.

I found out about her absence by formal email instead of the text she usually sends when she'll be out of the office for the day.

It has to be because she still thinks I want to marry her. I heard her loud and clear when she kept repeating that she didn't say yes to me, but I didn't say anything because of how unsure her voice sounded. It was almost as if she wanted to say yes but something was stopping her. So, I let it ride.

That's what I get for not communicating my thoughts properly as my mother always tried to teach me.

The door opens, and Ren walks in.

"Two days in a row. I feel pretty special right now," I jest, lightening my own mood. Who else will do it for me?

"You're always my special person, Darcy-*kun*." Ren sits on the edge of my desk, ruffling a stack of papers. A warning snarl ripples from my throat. He laughs and relocates to the perfectly comfortable seat in front of the desk. My desk is...my space. I don't like people behind it, on it, or even touching it. It's organized down to the grouping of pen color and tip styles. There are some things in life a person can control, and I choose to control everything I possibly can. It lessens the sting when uncontrollable things arise.

"I wanted to check on you in person, and I was on my way to a meeting."

"You have a meeting in my neighborhood?"

Ren smiles, all teeth. "Nope. This was completely out of my way."

A warmth stirs in my chest, and I am grateful for this one person in my life who cares. *Sheesh, Darcy. Get out of your heart and back into your head.*

"That was unnecessary."

He shrugs and slumps into the chair, legs splayed.

"How are you after last night? Did anything happen with Hayden on the ride home?" He lowers his voice when he mentions her name. He had stayed back and caught a ride with his father.

I, however, go red with embarrassment at the mention of her name. I can't believe I actually asked my campaign manager to *marry* me. And then I reiterated over and over that I was serious. That I don't joke.

Which I don't, and she knows that, hence the embarrassing situation.

"No. I let her off the hook." Not the best choice of words, but my pride is in jeopardy after the way she so adamantly turned me down last night. I've never thought of myself much as a ladies' man, but I also know I have my name, wealth, and much more to offer a woman.

"So that's how it went down, huh?" Ren snorts. "Whatever you say, my friend."

Ren Sato, the man who reads me like an open book with a sixteen-point font.

"Gosh, this reminds me of when Anna May turned you down as her date to the school dance. You were brooding for weeks."

Is it bad that the memory still stings a bit? Like a week-old burn. I don't like rejection.

"You're too prideful for your own good, but it's okay. I still love you, Darcy-*kun*."

"Just leave if all you're going to do is rehash old memories and taunt me." I run my hands through my hair, then check my watch. "I've actually got a meeting to attend in about ten minutes."

"Okay, my wounded puppy. Go lick your wounds before your meeting. Let's have a drink tomorrow night."

"My Fridays don't look like your Fridays, Ren," I say, picking up my agenda for the day. I can tell Hayden was not the one to type it out by the way the bullet points are regular, round points instead of a different design. Every day, she uses something new. A sun, a star, an arrow. But never the classic dot. I miss her schedules.

"I just happen to know you have tomorrow evening free." Ren bows his head. "Hayden told me yesterday." Then he is out the door.

Do I have tomorrow evening free?

Checking my calendar, I realize I do.

What did Hayden Bennett do to make this magic happen?

Another knock at the door.

"Come in," I say.

"Are you ready for the meeting?" my personal assistant, Bennie, asks.

I nod, grab my coat, and follow him out the door.

We wind through the hallways until we enter the conference room where my team waits for me. It's our weekly Thursday Debrief meeting before the weekend comes where we share updates, review polls, and talk strategy. We do this on Mondays too, but I much prefer the Thursday meetings because we get to review our successes and failures of the week. It's productive, informative, and...

"Sorry I'm late!"

Hayden's voice turns me into a block of ice.

Or a blazing fire?

Can a person feel cold and sweaty at the same time? Maybe I have a fever.

"Oh, Hayden. Thank goodness you're back." Paul, the one redhead on my team, breathes a heavy sigh of relief. "Trying to be you and me is a difficult task."

Hayden laughs. "I know the feeling. Trying to be me and Stella for a month nearly did me in."

"Now I feel bad. I only had to be you for half a day."

"Being me is going to get exponentially more difficult," she says, her eyes finding mine.

I swallow and command everyone to take their seats. "Let's begin with polling. What is the current data?" It's not that I don't know the trends, but polls can update at any given moment depending on where you pull numbers from. And the last time I checked was last night when I got home after dinner. Mainly, I was obsessively googling my name to make sure nothing leaked from last night's dinner fiasco.

Translation: I wanted to make sure the media never caught wind that I was having a fling with my campaign manager. It's still odd to me that Mr. Loveless didn't leak pictures. He must have something up his sleeve.

After Hanson, my polling executive, debriefs us, letting me know I am beating Richard Loveless within the conservative sphere in more liberal states while losing to him in traditionally more conservative states, we move into discussing campaign stops. Most everything is planned in that department as we had to strategize our route ages ago, but now we are simply checking in on the little details.

Hayden is detail-oriented. She may look and act like a hurricane bottled in a jar, but she pays attention to what's important and knows how to finesse any situation. Alongside Stella, they planned the route we would take. Our "Route to Victory" as they called it. And so far, it's been more successful than anything I could have dreamt up.

I watch her eyes light up as she talks about lineups and merchandise at the upcoming rallies. Her smile inches wider and wider with every passing moment she rambles on about the inner workings of the stage placement and timing to music. Technically, those things are not in her job description, but she enjoys them nonetheless, so she works with event planners quite a bit to create successful and engaging rallies to promote my candidacy for president. The vibrancy in her voice draws a small smile out of me, and for a moment, I'm filled with immense pride to have her as my campaign manager.

And there it is. That's why I proposed to Hayden. She's an unstoppable force when it comes to this world I live in, and she'd make a great companion. If I can trust her to help me win the presidency, I can trust her to walk beside me through it. Marriage doesn't have to be about love, but it must always be about trust and respect.

"Mr. Marshall?" My name in her sing-song voice captures my attention.

"Mm?" I snap my eyes to hers. That smile that's not really a smile because she's trying to hide it appears, and her eyes practically dance. Why does she love taunting me after catching me having thoughts about her? Does it give her a serotonin boost to embarrass me?

Her heels click with every step she takes toward me. She stands beside me now, and the heat radiating from her nearness makes my palms clammy.

"What do you think of the idea?" She cocks her head to the side as I meet her gaze. She hovers over me as I typically do her, and the corner of her lip twitches. I swivel my chair so that my body is facing hers, trying to rack my brain for any hint of the conversation happening before I lost my thoughts to what a successful pairing me and Hayden could be in the political world. Especially when she wears this black and white plaid skirt with a slit on the side and black stockings...

Eyes up, Darcy! What is wrong with you?

Before I realize what's happening, Hayden leans down, placing her mouth at my ear. Sucking in a breath, I'm filled with her soft, floral scent and decide it's best not to breathe right now. Not after staring too long at her legs. She exhales a puff of air, and it tickles my neck. But it doesn't stop there. The weird sensation travels down my spine, filling me with angst and... pleasure? Her breathing is shaky as she whispers one word, "Yes."

My legs move of their own accord, catapulting me out of my seat. Hayden stumbles backward on her heels, but I reach out with one hand and grab her waist and pull before she tumbles to the ground. Her chest connects with my own, and I tighten my hold to keep her steady.

The last thing I need is a broken campaign manager.

"You are no longer allowed to wear heels," I attempt to tease her, though my voice sounds harsh.

"Must wear dresses, but can't wear heels." She clicks her tongue as she narrows her eyes. "Got it."

I smile, trying to let her know I was joking, but then I remember what she said and holy smokes!

"You said yes?" I search her deep brown eyes for any trace of humor or amusement. Instead, I realize gold flecks circle her irises, and it's mesmerizing.

She nods her head once, and my heart takes off.

Not because I love her and it's the happiest moment of my life, but because a weight that's been sitting on my shoulders, compressing down continuously, has finally been lifted.

"Yes," I repeat the word. For a moment, I squeeze my eyes shut and then open them. She's still here, in my arms, and...

In my arms.

A throat clears, and I suddenly have the need to build a tiny house halfway underground and live my life as a very tall hobbit. My whole team is watching me embrace her.

I shove Hayden away from me, and she stumbles over her heels before catching herself against the table.

She smooths down the front of her tantalizing skirt. *Maybe I should ban that instead of her heels.*

"I'm sorry," I hurriedly state. Those words are getting easier to say with practice, though I don't know if that's a good thing. That I have to say it so often.

"It's fine," she mumbles.

"Hayden, can I see you outside for a moment?" I don't dare look around at my team, though the silence seems to broadcast their every thought.

The boss has a thing for Hayden?

Is this appropriate?

A secret political affair?

Should we say anything?

"Of course, Mr. Marshall." Her smile is biting and tone sarcastic.

I turn on my heel and walk out of the conference room, already heading for my private nook. Her heels echo behind me.

We arrive at the door, and I hold it open for her to pass through.

"Don't shove me to the floor from behind," she says with squinted eyes, passing me by and entering the room.

Why did it have to be the most obnoxious, stubborn woman that I fell in trust with?

"This will be a long eight years if you keep up that attitude." I close the door and turn around to Hayden seated in my chair like she owns it. She smirks, crossing one leg over the other and tapping her fingers in unison against the forearms of *my* chair.

"Oh, Mr. Marshall. The fun is just beginning."

I bend at the waist to look her dead in the face. The close contact and prolonged eye contact have me a bit squirmy, but I press on hoping she's feeling the same uneasiness. "In that case, call me Darcy."

She's not getting out now.

CHAPTER ELEVEN

HAYDEN

A stack of papers hits my distressed white desk with a soft thud. Annoyed, I inhale through my nose and then cut my eyes upward, not bothering to tilt my head in the direction of the hovering man. I know who it is, and I know he knows throwing papers on my desk without explanation is a pet peeve of mine.

"What's this?" I ask, biting my tongue to try and keep the snark under wraps.

"The marriage contract."

Papers threaten to cut my fingers as I quickly flip through the pages, counting them.

"This has to be at least fifty pages." Panic settles in my chest as I continue to count. "Okay, more than fifty. How did you draft this already? We've been engaged for two hours."

Unamused, he says in a gruff voice, "The wedding will happen next Saturday. Read through the document and add any changes in the margins."

"But I—" I look up just as the door shuts, and I realize Darcy has left the room.

"Nine days." I choke on the words as I process aloud. "Nine days. In nine days, I will be legally married to Darcy Marshall. In the eyes of the law, I will be his wife." My heart struggles to maintain proper beats as reality sets in.

Being his wife is better than not having a place to live. Or drowning in student debt.

I think.

I've tried to find places to live within my budget, but nothing is available. The apartments that are open are in sketchy locations I no longer care to live. I've begged my landlady not to sell, but it's no use. What's happening is happening.

How does one put together a wedding in nine days? Not to mention, a wedding that will capture the attention of every news outlet and tabloid? My breathing becomes rapid and sweat prickles at the edges of my hairline.

It's rare I wish for a mom since I've been on my own for so long, but... *God, I could really use a mom right now.*

My door opens without a knock and Darcy saunters back in.

"Mr. Marshall." His name is a rasp on my lips. I meet his eyes.

"About the wedding..." He trails off, looking away before continuing. "Mother will take care of everything. My networking company, COFFEE, will pay for it."

I stare at the man in front of me, watching his Adam's apple bob up and down. He finally looks my way again, and I simply nod, not trusting words.

He tilts his head to the side, almost as if he is expressing sympathy, and then he walks out of the door.

His mother.

The thought of in-laws never crossed my mind when I agreed to marry Darcy. Student loans, a place to live, a possible trip to Japan, Secretary of State, and a higher income were occupying my thoughts. Not a mother-in-law or a dead father-in-law with an unpleasant reputation. Goodness, is it hot in here?

I close my eyes and flap my hands wildly around my face.

Two hands wrap around my wrist mid flap, then my hands are engulfed by a much larger set.

"Darcy," I say, recognizing his spicy scent. I don't open my eyes.

"If you want to back out, now is your chance. I will not force you to marry me. But I think this can work." The sincerity in his voice takes me by surprise, and I finally open my eyes. If his voice was sincere, his eyes are sparkling blue pools of truth.

I trust him.

Though he is cold and standoffish, I think it's because he doesn't process the world like the rest of us. I've been getting glimmers of that lately. He apologizes when he needs to, and he's never done anything to intentionally hurt me. Stella is right—he cares for his people even if he doesn't always do the greatest job at showing it.

I can do this.

We can do this.

My breathing finally begins to slow.

"I'm okay. Let's do this."

He releases my hands, and they suddenly feel cold and lonely, as if his hands were a comfy blanket ripped away without warning. Ignoring the feeling, I pick up the contract.

"Read through it. Contact me if you have any questions." And with that, he's gone again. Hopefully, for good.

Because the flush burning my face now has nothing to do with anxious thoughts and everything to do with Darcy's hands on mine.

He has *never* been that kind and considerate to me. He gave me an honest chance to back out. I should have taken it. I should have said never mind and started apartment hunting again.

But the thing is... I didn't want to back out. The look in his eyes and the loneliness in my heart says we need each other. Even if it's not for love.

Alone with my thoughts and a hefty contract to sift through, I crank up J-Pop music and get to reading. If majoring in political science and studying public relations and policy has taught me one thing, it is to always read contracts.

Fujii Kaze fills my ears and my eyes stare at the bolded words: **Marriage Contract.**

Here goes nothing.

Two hours, three cups of coffee, and an entire J-Pop playlist later, I stand up to stretch my stiff muscles. A headache has set in during the last forty-five minutes of the endeavor, and my eyes pulse and ache from dryness and strain.

So far, I've read about possession security, grounds for divorce, and the terms of dissolving the marriage at the end of the candidacy or the presidency. And I'm only twenty-eight pages in. Nothing has been inherently disagreeable at the moment, so I'm hopeful it will remain that way. A yawn rips through me; it's time to go home. I pack up my things and navigate the hallways of Darcy's estate—the very place I'll soon be living at—to find the exit and my car waiting for me.

As I'm driving home, the world seems to sing a different tune. Everything is going to change, and I can't help but wonder if it will be a change for the better or for the worse. If I was a person who suffered from anxiety, I would be falling to pieces right now. But thankfully, I've thought through this decision, and I've come to terms with it.

Mostly.

Whatever is going to happen will happen.

I am marrying Darcy Marshall next Saturday. I will be Hayden Bennett Marshall. My student loans will be paid, I will have a place to live, my dreams of becoming Secretary of State one day will be closer than ever, and I might even get a trip to Japan.

In nine days, I will change my last name on the basis of trust, not love.

And the world is going to erupt at the news.

Has anyone told the PR and Social Media departments about this? They need to be prepared for the media storm.

Wait. That's my job. I have to tell my team.

"Ugh!" I'm groaning when my phone rings. "Hey, Stells."

"So, how did it go? I've been on pins and needles over here waiting to hear from you." The excited tone tells me everything I need to know regarding her feelings toward this fake marriage. She's delusional and thinks it'll become real.

"I'm currently driving home after drowning myself in pages upon pages of marriage contract details. How do you think it went?"

Stella yawns before responding. "He must have already had that prepared."

"Makes sense. He was searching for a wife after all."

"You're really doing this." We sit in silence as I mull over my thoughts. If you would have asked me only six months ago if I would have said yes to something like this, I would have laughed in your face. Furthermore, if you would have told me that I would real fake-marry Darcy Marshall, I might have passed out from shock. What changed? Because he hasn't changed. I haven't changed.

Yet, I said yes.

"I have my reasons," I say to myself more than to her. I contemplate inviting her to the wedding. But it's not real, and I don't need her by my side to witness me marrying for reasons other than love. She got the love of her life, and though I know she would be here in a heartbeat if I asked, I don't want her to watch me practically sell myself out. She can watch online anyway.

I pull into the parking garage and click off the phone with Stella. For once in my life, I want to be alone with my thoughts tonight.

And there's still so much contract to read.

Once I am snugly inside my blue sherpa blanket with a hot cup of cinnamon tea, I flip to the page of the contract I left off on. This section is titled "Arrangements."

A quick scan reveals this is about how I will live at his house, travel with him, have personal security with me at all times when I'm out, and give up my apartment. I laugh bitterly to myself. If I wasn't already being evicted, that would have been scratched out with a red pen. As a matter of fact, I think I'll scratch it out anyway. He doesn't get to tell me what I can and can't keep that belongs to me. A girl can fight for her own living space against an all-controlling tyrant such as Darcy Marshall, right? Even if it's all a facade because I'm losing the apartment.

But he doesn't need to know that.

As I continue to read, I put my red pen to good use. Apparently, he should have consulted me first when it came to writing this arrangement section because there are countless things I firmly do not agree with. For example, he wants me to wear dresses to dinner parties and other formalized events. Darcy Marshall must have some kind of dress fetish; I'm convinced. And what's with the "Party Two will sleep in the same hotel room as Party One when traveling" nonsense? Because heck no. Party Two will not sleep in the same room as Party One.

Ever.

I check the time and debate calling Darcy to settle these "arrangements" right now, but I'd rather see his face when he meets the mighty force of my red pen, so I will wait until tomorrow.

With that, I zoom through the remaining few pages of the contract, all of which I agree to, or at the very least, don't feel like fighting him on, and then hit the hay.

CHAPTER TWELVE

DARCY

S he sips her coffee slowly, her brown eyes, so different from mine, never looking away from me. The sounds of espresso machines whirling and light chatter from the people in and out of Five Four Coffee provide background noise while I focus on trying to decipher her expression. I once thought Hayden's stare was the most intense thing I could experience, but I was clearly wrong.

I don't remember Mother ever looking at me this way before.

"Son, you don't have to do this," she finally says after several long seconds, setting her cup of coffee down. I fidget with my hands in my lap, shrinking under her constant gaze.

"It's my best shot at winning the presidency."

"Forgive me for speaking this way, but she is a nobody. How will marrying this woman create a better opportunity for you? If anything, you are raising her status."

"Because marriage isn't about status," I retort, internally flinching at the way she sounds like Father. "You know that better than anyone." A flash of hurt crosses her eyes, and I immediately regret my words. "I'm sorry, Mother. You know I didn't mean it like that."

"No, you're right. Marriage isn't about status. But it also isn't about one person taking from the other. What can she offer you?"

I let out an exasperated laugh. "She's giving me anywhere from one to eight years of her life. And a solid chance at the rural conservative vote. What more could I ask for?"

"But do you love her?"

"Marriage isn't about love, either," I bite.

"Regardless of what happened, I loved your father, Darcy." Mother's gaze finally shifts from me to the chromatic, abstract paintings on the wall of the coffee shop. "He messed up. And he died before we could make it right. But I believe we could have made it right."

Gracious, I wish she would quit deluding herself. Father was scum to cheat on her after everything they went through together. He found solace in the arms of other women while Mother strove to be strong for me as I struggled to pull myself from the brink of despair after losing Ophelia.

"Trust and respect are more important than love." I reiterate my earlier sentiments when I told her about the marriage happening. "A man in my shoes, of my position, needs to know he can trust the woman by his side. Love is subjective. It's fleeting. Trust is solid and real. It's not easily obtained."

Mother sighs then places her hand palm-up on the table. I place mine in hers and let the warmth of her frail, wrinkled hands take over my senses. "I trust you, Son. If you say this woman is the one you need by your side, I support you."

"Thank you." I squeeze her hand, then bring my coffee to my lips. The flavor is sweet and smooth, warming my throat as it goes down.

"But I would love to meet her today. Could you arrange that?"

The hot liquid trickles down my chin as I choke. The sounds of conversation around suddenly seem too loud and the small shop too crowded, though there are only a handful of other people in the building. She wants to meet Hayden? *Today?* I was hoping to briefly introduce them at the rehearsal and be done with it. This marriage is only in the eyes of the law, so there is no need for family bonding and such things.

"I don't know, Mother. We both had today off, and I'd hate to bug—"

My phone rings, and I take it from my pocket.

Hayden.

"Her." I finish my sentence in an irritated whisper before answering the phone. "Hello?"

"Let's meet. We need to talk about the contract."

"I'll send you a location to meet me at. I'm already here," I respond, though my chest is tightening. I hang up and text her the address to the coffee shop.

"Looks like you'll get your wish." I smile grimly at Mother. "But once you exchange pleasantries, you will need to go."

Mother's eyes light up and a grin inches across her face.

She spends the next twelve minutes asking me a million questions about Hayden—questions I don't know the answer to. What's her favorite color? What's her favorite type of music? Is she a cat or dog person? The only question I knew the answer to was about her home life, thanks to the background check completed on her when she joined my campaign team. She's orphaned and has constructed her life on her own from the ground up, which is one of the reasons I respect Hayden immensely. Not many people can overcome a situation like hers, go to college, earn a living, and secure the position of campaign manager of a presidential candidate.

"Mr. Marshall." Hayden's voice brings me back to the present, and I stand up to greet her. Mother follows suit.

"Hayden, this is my mother, Ruthanne Marshall." I gesture my hand toward Mother. "Mother, this is my campaign manager, Hayden Bennett."

Hayden holds out a trembling hand, but Mother wraps her in an embrace. Hayden's hands fall to her side while Mother bear hugs her, and I wish I could see Hayden's expression. Her body language says she's not a hugger, which is surprising to me because of her loud and outgoing nature. No, I've seen her hug several people. People she had just met. Hayden Bennett is definitely a hugger, the opposite of me.

"It's so nice to meet you, Hayden. I'm excited to have you as my daughter. You can address me as Ruth. Ruthanne takes me back to my upbringing in Tennessee." She winks.

I cough, and Hayden shimmies out of Mother's grasp. *Daughter.*

"You have a daughter." Did she forget about Ophelia so easily?

"*Another* daughter." Mother smiles sadly. Hayden stands frozen.

"It's nice to meet you, too, Ms. Marshall," Hayden says with a smile that flickers on and off her face as if she's glitching.

"Please, call me Ruth." Mother takes my arm. "He says I was only allowed to introduce myself right now, but I will see you tomorrow bright and early. I will get your number from my son and text you so that you can reach me if you need me."

Hayden only nods, the obviously fake smile seeming to decide to stay on her face rather than vanish.

"Goodbye, Mother," I say.

"Text me Hayden's number." She kisses my cheek before walking away from us and out of the little coffee shop.

I stand behind the chair Mother was sitting in and pull it out for Hayden. She side-eyes me but sits down. I take my seat across from her at the small, round table.

"Sorry about that. She was here when you called." I sip my sweetened coffee. "Would you like to order a cup?"

"Yes, please," she says, standing back up.

"No, sit down. I will get it for you. What do you want?"

Hayden stares at me like I sprouted a tail. "Um, an Americano. No cream or sugar."

I turn away and head for the counter where the blue-haired barista who looks like he hates his life jots down the order of the person in front of me.

What was that? Hayden, the most outgoing, bubbly person I know, completely shut down meeting my mother. Maybe it was the awkwardness of the situation? Then again, Hayden isn't one to embarrass easily. No, that woman will talk to herself if there is no one around to talk to. I've walked past her office many times and have heard her mumbling to herself.

"Next," the barista calls in a monotone voice.

I tell him I want a large Americano for the name Hayden. When he asks if he should leave room for cream and sugar, I say no. A little thrill runs through me. For all the things I don't know about Hayden, at least I know her coffee order now.

"Does this guy do it for you?" Hayden's sassy voice is at my ear.

I flinch, accidentally knocking into the person behind me. Quickly, I apologize to the older gentleman I about bulldozed and then glare at Hayden, who had approached me from the side without my noticing.

"What do you mean?"

"You were smiling. Does the monotone, blue-haired, anime look excite you?"

The quirk of her brow and the upward pull of her lip tells me she's joking, and I should retort, but I'm stuck on the fact that I was smiling and didn't realize it. And I was thinking about Hayden when it happened...

"You know, if you shrunk, lost a little of your bulk, and dyed your hair blue, you'd be just like my friend Kale here."

How'd she know his name? Oh right, the name tag. I hardly look at those.

Looking Kale over, I realize she's right. We sport the same blank, slightly irritated facial expression. Our voices share that disinterested tone.

"Friend?"

"This is where I come to get *your* coffee in the mornings since it's your favorite shop. I know his name, but he doesn't know mine. I use a different fake name every time I come in."

"Hayden," Kale calls out, and I refuse to look her in the eyes. Oops.

"I guess he knows my name now." Snark oozes from her words, and the side of my face burns with the lasers Hayden is shooting at me.

If I looked at her now, I'd probably drop dead from the beams.

From my side gaze, I watch her grab her coffee. As she attempts to chat with Kale, I make a beeline for our table.

The marriage contract is sitting face up, stirring anxiety within my chest. I flip it over with a harsh thud and my hand lingers pressed on the contract. She should know better than to leave a document like this out in the open for the world to see. I glance to the two men in suits standing in opposing corners of the room. I guess they could easily catch anyone attempting to take my stuff, but still. That's not my agents' responsibility. Hayden sits down at the table, and now it's my turn to shoot eye lasers at her.

"Why did you leave this document unattended?"

She makes a show of looking around at the shop, and I follow her gaze—only the baristas, the old man I bumped into, a couple of teens, a young woman, and my agents occupy the building with us.

"Who's going to care?"

"You never know." I'm feeling more at ease remembering Five Four Coffee isn't crowded like usual. The Marshall name has been dragged through the mud because of my father's cheating scandals, and I've put my blood, sweat, and tears into my image to burst from his dark shadow. People rarely associate me with him now, and it's of utmost importance that this marriage contract with Hayden never leaves the hands of the few parties involved. All anyone needs to know is that we fell madly in love while she comforted me post break-up with Priscilla. A quick, whirlwind romance.

The media would have a field day if they found out I was paying my campaign manager to marry me. Hayden has garnished enough respect from fellow politicians and has a positive image in public opinion. I'm banking on her small, but growing popularity within the public sphere to nail my father's reputation into the grave forever. Hopefully people will love our "love" story: two people who grew to love one another while working side by side as I grieved the ending of my previous engagement.

"Um, Mr. Marshall? Are you going to sit down?"

Coffee shops are too public for this conversation. "How do you feel about going back to the office?"

A quizzical expression streaks across her face, but she stands up and grabs her coffee. I tuck the contract back into the manila envelope, wondering why she even took it out just to leave the table in the first place.

Hayden reaches for the contract after I've closed the envelope, but I hold it out and away from her. "This stays in my hands from now on." I begin to walk toward the exit.

"Starting soon, what's yours is mine, my *darling Darcy*."

My feet freeze on their own accord hearing my first name on her tongue. She's only used it a few times now, but I'm not sure it will ever cease to stop me in my tracks.

"Goodness. I almost ran into you. Stop stopping on a dime. That would have been twice in two weeks that I've spilled coffee because of you."

Abruptly, I turn to face her. She's way too close for comfort, so I step back from her burning chocolate eyes. I swallow. "No pet names. Just Darcy will do."

Hayden's eyes lose their playful spark, and she nods her head. I did it again. I said something in a harsh tone that hurt her feelings.

Is hurting her feelings worth not hearing my name on her lips? Is making her eyes dull with sadness worth avoiding the thrill that ricocheted through my body because of the velvety way she said my name? Like promises of things to come.

Yes, it has to be worth it.

When it comes to Hayden Bennett, thrill is not an emotion I can let myself experience. I can't let the woman who embodies sunlight continue to thaw my icy, controlled exterior. The moment I let someone in is the moment they will use my story against me.

"You don't need an apartment anymore, Hayden. What would people think if it was leaked that you had a place of your own?" I'm doing some serious rethinking about marrying this stubborn woman. How can she not see the obvious conundrum she is putting us in by demanding to keep a lousy apartment?

She leans forward, placing a forearm on her crossed legs. Her chocolate eyes glare daggers at me. "Because I need a space away from *you*."

"Ha," I scoff. "As if I would be in your way often enough for you to need privacy. I will be the one needing to get away from *you*." She sneers, but I continue. "Come to think of it, maybe *I* should have my own apartment."

"Get your own apartment then, but I am keeping mine, Darcy."

A slight shudder runs down my spine at my name on her tongue. That will take a while to get used to, I fear. Maybe it would be good for her to be able to get out of my space.

"Fine," I bite. I make a mental note to contact her landlord later and find out more details about this apartment she's so desperately wanting.

"Fine." She sits up and crosses her arms, a smug expression filling her face. She only won because I decided to let her, but I keep that information to myself.

"Why did you cross out the dress requirement, Hayden?"

The smug expression falls, and Hayden looks like a woman about to give me a piece of her mind, as if she doesn't do that enough.

Instead, she laughs. "We live in the twenty-first century, not in your namesake's era, Darcy."

I make a mental note to call Mother and let her know one more time just how much I hate my name. "Class is timeless, Hayden Bennett. Besides, you sport the last name of the heroine in that story, if I remember correctly."

She shrugs, a momentary dark look crossing her face. "Can't help your last name, Darcy."

Marshall. Is that a better last name to flaunt? Darcy Marshall, son of the late Gerald Marshall. Father ran our last name through the mud. He soiled it completely, even if the media is unaware of all his failures. I can't call them mistakes because he knew what he was doing.

No, Gerald Marshall failed his wife, his daughter, and his son. He failed the Marshall name.

"Wait a second." Hayden's voice brings my focus back to the task at hand: finalizing the marriage contract. "Are you saying I lack class, Mr. Marshall?" Her voice teeters on the edge of teasing and playfulness, but her expression is sharp.

"I wouldn't fake marry you if I thought you were incapable of class, Hayden." Why in Heaven's great design are we using each other's names after everything we say?

She uncrosses her arms and tilts her head. A loose curl falls, and I swallow, folding my hands in my lap.

"Good answer, fiancé."

I choke on my next breath at her words. Maybe we should stick to using each other's names instead.

"I need to know you will wear dresses to formal events. I need my wife to look the part of First Lady."

"I can do that in a pantsuit, Darcy." Here we go with the names again.

"The conservatives are all about trad-wife culture, Hayden. You are the one who brought that research to my attention a couple of months ago. Which means you need to wear dresses most of the time."

She grins. "Ah, so there is the compromise. Most of the time, I can do it. Just let me be myself every now and then, okay?"

"Just be the refined version of yourself."

Her grin falls, and she stands up, hands on her hips. "I am so sick of your backhanded compliments." And with that, she storms out of the room.

I flinch as the door slams shut.

She is refined; I meant that. But sometimes, she can be... a bit much. Too eccentric. She knows this, right? People are generally self-aware of their personalities. She's a grown woman who's obsessed with anime and video games, for heaven's sake.

Regardless, I said the wrong thing again. And if I keep this up, it's going to be a long fake real marriage.

CHAPTER THIRTEEN

HAYDEN

"**S**tella! What should I do? I don't know how to be a daughter, much less an in-law." I'm pacing my apartment floor, trying to burn the anxiety from my veins. T-minus 90 minutes until I am supposed to meet Ruthanne Marshall, or Ruth, as she asked me to call her when she told me that I would be another daughter to her.

"Honey, you just be your bubbly, sunshine self and that woman will adore you just like I do," Stella's mom, Marian Harper, hollers, appearing beside Stella in the face chat video.

My heart warms at her words. "You've been a great stand-in mom to me, Marian." She told me at Stella's wedding that I could be another daughter to her, and she has intentionally reached out to me since then, making sure I was fed, socializing appropriately, and emotionally full.

"I've talked with Ruth before, and you will love her. Better yet, she will love you. You have nothing to worry about." Stella offers a broad smile before looping an arm around Marian's waist. I notice Marian lean in, and I feel a momentary stab of pain in my heart. The brave woman has been living with crippling rheumatoid arthritis for years.

I stop pacing and swipe at the sheen of sweat on my forehead. I'll need to blot my face with a tea tree wipe before I leave.

"You both are right. I've got this," I say unconvincingly. Maybe the more I say it, the more I will believe it? "But what if she doesn't think I am good enough for her son?"

Stella raises an eyebrow, and Marian's expression closely matches with her daughter's. I wonder if any of my expression matches my mother's. "I don't think that will be the case, but even if it is, your worth is not attached to what she thinks of you."

"You're right," I relent. "But I'm still a nervous wreck."

"That's okay," Stella says. Marian nods. "Drink some decaffeinated tea to soothe your nerves, do some deep breathing, pray about it, and then tilt your head and put your shoulders back and go meet your mother-in-law."

I shudder at those last words.

"And remember it's only temporary," Marian adds. I release my breath, letting that word wash over me. Temporary.

"Thanks, ladies. I should get started on that list." I paste a smile on my face and wave goodbye. The call ends. My smile drops.

I slump into my chair, still thinking of the word "temporary." Marian is right. Ruth will not be my permanent mother-in-law. Once Darcy and I divorce at the end of this thing, I'll divorce Ruth, too. Done. Simple as that.

With that settled, I make chamomile tea, blot my face, whisper a prayer, and head out the door to meet my *temporary* mother-in-law.

The walk to Five Four Coffee is short and cool. The March weather is pleasant, and the light breeze is enough to keep me from perspiring. Once inside, I order an Americano under the name of Tohru, since *Fruits Basket* has been my choice of anime lately, and sit in the back corner so that I have a full view of the door as I wait for Ruth Marshall.

Two minutes later, she walks through the door and quickly locates me in the back. I stand up and wave enthusiastically, which translates to an awkward not-sure-if-she's-a-human look for me. Ruth doesn't seem to mind because she grins widely and waves back with a wildly flapping hand that matches my energy. Her walk—a bouncing cadence—is cause to believe the lively woman isn't actually in her sixties.

Her blonde hair is the same color as her son's, though there are many streaks of gray. Somehow, she works the look. The closer she gets, I'm startled for the second time by her eyes. They are a deep brown that warms the soul of the one looking into them—the complete opposite of Darcy's icy blues.

"Hello, Hayden. It's good to see you again. Thanks for meeting me." Ruth wraps me in a hug, and unlike last time, I let my arms circle around her slim frame. I don't pull her close, but I don't have to—she smashes herself against me with enough force to push my boobs to my chin.

Is that what motherly love is supposed to feel like? Hugs that smash boobs? Because that's how Marian hugged me, too.

"It's no problem," I reply, still smushed against the smaller woman. I drop my arms and begin to step away. She releases me. "So, what's on the agenda for today?"

"Sit down, sit down. Let's chat for a little while first. I'll go order coffee."

"No, let me! What do you want?"

Ruth smiles. "You're precious. Thank you. I'll take a skinny vanilla latte."

"One skinny vanilla latte coming right up." I grab my purse and walk back to the counter where blue-haired, boring Kale stands with a slight frown. I order and give him the name Ruth. There is no way I'm giving a fake name for my mother-in-law's drink. The coffee is made quickly, and I return to the table with the coffee in hand.

"Thank you again, Hayden."

"My pleasure." *What?* Do I work at Chick-fil-A all of a sudden? I mentally facepalm myself.

"So, tell me about yourself. Darcy has told me very little."

I sit down in my chair and try to hide the fact that I feel slighted that Darcy hasn't spoken about me to his mother. But then I remember this is all a ruse.

"Oh dear. Don't feel bad. Darcy hardly talks to anyone about anything personal," Ruth continues before I can respond to her question.

I snort. "No, ma'am, it's not that. I know better than most people that your son is a tough shell to crack."

Immediately, I regret the words, but Ruth simply laughs. "Right you are. Having to work side by side with him all day is a tedious task, I'm sure."

My head wants to nod along with her, and it wouldn't be amiss to do so, but Darcy isn't all bad. "You raised a good man, Ruth. Yes, he can be complicated, picky, stubborn, cold, quiet, and demanding, but he is also considerate of his subordinates. He takes care of us and respects us. He values our time and energy. I think he even wants to be more socially involved, but maybe he doesn't quite know how..." I trail off, contemplating that last tidbit. Darcy is a difficult man, but what if it's because he has so many walls up? What if he is afraid of something? What if he is more like me than I realize?

"My son couldn't have chosen a better woman," Ruth says, dabbing a tissue at the corner of her eye.

"But you don't even know me yet." If she knew I was orphaned, grew up bouncing between homes, running away, and the things I have seen and done in my past, she would take back that statement quicker than Kakashi mirroring his opponent's moves in *Naruto*.

She reaches out her hand and takes mine, squeezing gently. "Hayden, you listen closely. The fact that you see the person behind my son's carefully crafted exterior tells me you are what he needs. Just be patient with him, Hayden." She looks off in the distance before turning back to me. "I also trust his judgment in choosing you. Regardless of when—or if," she winks, "this marriage ends, you will always have a mother in me. I know you don't have parents of your own, but I will gladly be a stand-in mom for you."

Now it's my turn to cry. "Thank you," I choke out. "But how did you know about my past?"

"What kind of mother would I be if I didn't run a background check on the woman marrying my very important son?" The gleam in her eyes says she may be joking, but I don't think she is.

"Right," I say, drawing the word out. I lean back in the chair, and Ruth lets go of my hand. "Anything I can share that you don't already know?" I smirk, and she matches my expression with humor in her eyes. I think we will get along just fine, even if it's temporary.

"Let's start with your favorite color. It should be the color of your wedding."

I grin, thinking of the one color that Darcy would loathe having as his wedding color. "Yellow. Bright, sunshiny yellow."

How am I going to pack this place up by myself in two days? I shouldn't have procrastinated this inevitable task over the past week. It's Wednesday, the one day a week I actually get out of the office on time due to Darcy's out-of-town travels, and I have to have my things ready to go by Friday evening before the rehearsal.

Dirty dishes still sit in the sink, the trash overflows, and nothing is in its assigned spot. In lieu of actually cleaning the apartment, I hunt for boxes to pack my things in. Luckily, I don't throw out boxes from my online shopping and have plenty of cardboard to stuff kitchen appliances, clothes, and bathroom necessities in. Though, come to think of it, will I need kitchen appliances? Darcy's place is massive. He is bound to have everything I could possibly need. Also, he has a kitchen staff who does the cooking for him.

Heck. Yeah.

That reason alone is enough to move in with him. I hardly cooked for myself anyway, but now I will have access to full yummy meals I don't have to prepare. Part of me cringes at the excitement I experience knowing I will have a kitchen staff prepare meals for me, but then again, it's natural to be happy over such a thing when you have been on your own for so long. I'm definitely not one of those women who will hold onto her pride when it comes to food. Other things, sure. Food? No way.

My phone rings with the special ringtone set just for Darcy: "Love Yourself" by Justin Bieber.

"Yes, Mr. Marshall?"

He takes a breath. "I just spoke with Deborah, your landlady. She says you are being evicted."

The phone slips from my hand and my heart rate picks up. My first thought is that I could sue Deborah for giving out my personal information to him, but then again, what good will that do?

My second thought is more of an encompassing feeling—embarrassment. I fought so hard to make Darcy believe that I would be keeping this apartment the other day, and now he knows the truth.

I bend down and pick up the phone, and then I do what I do best: ramble.

"Sorry, I dropped the phone. Yeah, someone bought the complex out and I have to leave. But it's kind of perfect, you know? Because I am moving in with you and stuff. I definitely had options of places to stay, and I'm still considering renting a new space so that I can—"

"Hayden." His voice is stern, but also... concerned?

"Hmm?"

"You will have plenty of space for yourself here. Don't look into other spaces. Do you need assistance packing up your apartment?"

"I, um..."

Knock. Knock. Knock.

"Hold on, please. Someone's at the door."

With my mind a muddled haze from embarrassment at Darcy learning the truth of my apartment situation, I fan my face and then open the door.

"Stella!"

"Hayden!"

We jump into each other's arms with delighted squeals. That's when I notice Lucas behind her.

"And you brought your sweet, southern hunk."

"Good to see you, ma'am." Lucas tips an invisible hat.

"Bring it in," I say, breaking free of Stella and embracing Lucas with a big hug. He awkwardly taps my back a few times, then he steps away.

"I'm all here for the surprise, but what in the world are you two doing here?" I ask, glancing between them.

"I heard there's a wedding Saturday, and you're the star of the show." Stella steps around me, letting herself into my place. "And apparently we've got some cleaning and packing to do."

That's when I remember I'm holding the phone and Darcy is on the other end of it. I drag it to my ear. "Oh, well, Stella and Lucas just showed up. I think I have enough help."

Darcy clears his throat. "Okay, then. I'll let you go." He hangs up, and I'm left wondering why he sounded off. Maybe he heard the mention of the wedding? Hearing it from Stella made it seem too real to me. Maybe it did for him, too?

"Who was that?" Stella asks.

"Oh, it was Darcy. Just checking to make sure I had everything ready to go."

Stella and Lucas exchange a grin, and I don't like the look of it. Stella speaks first. "How sweet of him."

Then Lucas, "This is going to be the realest 'fake' wedding ever."

Stella and I give him a confused look, but he shrugs and pulls out a beat-up iPhone that has to be a single digit model.

My heart sinks. "I know it's a televised wedding, but it's not going to be huge. Only the people who need to be there for political face are coming. You didn't need to come all this way for that. Especially for a fake marriage."

"You're signing papers. It's real, Hayden," Lucas says, following Stella inside. Now I'm standing in my own doorway while they scrutinize the condition of my apartment, talking back and forth about the best methods for cleaning and packing my place up.

I watch them, my chest tightening and sweat rolling down my spine. Did the room start spinning? I'm not one prone to anxiety attacks, but I can't help but feel a little on edge knowing my best friend and the love of her life are going to witness me make a decision that is the equivalent of selling myself out. Realistically, I know they don't see my decision in that light, but my internal monologue hurls insults at me saying that I'm going against my morals, desires, and standards.

Nobody knew I wanted to marry for love. Not even Stella. Since I was a girl, when someone would bring up the idea of marriage, I would cringe and tell them, "No way." Around twenty-three, I changed my mind, but for some reason, I couldn't admit it out loud.

I still can't.

The world tells me wanting marriage and love is for the birds. I should chase my career and excel. So that's what I've been doing, all while secretly pining for some handsome prince to come sweep me off my feet.

My stubbornness is once again biting me in the rear end. If Stella knew my heart, she'd persuade me not to marry Darcy.

But it's my secret, and I'm still not bold enough to admit it aloud. Darcy will take care of me, regardless of his snippy comments and frosty exterior. I've seen the man behind the mask, and he isn't that bad. He just needs some love, like a hurt puppy.

And he wants this, too.

He chose me.

Me.

The girl who has always been disposable.

He trusts me enough to take on the responsibility of becoming his wife, and *he wants it to be me. He dismissed so many other women.*

The thought thaws something in my chest I didn't know was iced over.

"Earth to Hayden. Where are your spare boxes? I know you keep the packages from your online ordering." Stella places a hand on her hip and cocks her head at me with a smirk. "Are you already lost in the idea of sharing a bed with Darcy?"

"You can leave now," I deadpan, motioning outside the door. She laughs, a carefree, joyful sound, and another bullet rips through my heart. I want that. I want to be as happy as she is now that she has Lucas. I want my forever person.

"Just kidding. But for real, what are the sleeping arrangements like?" Stella asks. Enough. I have to stop wallowing in my circumstance. It is what it is.

"I'll have my own room across the mansion from Darcy's room." At least I hope it's far away from his room. With the amount of rooms that estate contains, I'm sure it will be no problem for me to tuck myself away unnoticed unless it's working hours. "Okay, Avengers. It's time to assemble." I place my hands on my hips and tilt my chin to the air. "This apartment isn't going to clean itself."

Stella and Lucas chuckle, but then they follow me to my hoard of boxes and—being the blessed souls that they are—help me pack up my home.

F ive hours later, panting and collapsing on the floor, I wheeze out one word: "Finished!"

Stella groans as she crumples beside me. "How did you accumulate that much stuff over four years in this apartment?"

I shrug. "Just happens. I'm a sucker for a sale, after all."

Joining us on the floor, Lucas harrumphs. "You both are."

"Soul sisters," Stella and I say at the same time, then we give each other a high five before falling to our backs on the bare, wooden floor.

Without warning—or my permission—tears prick the corners of my eyes. This little apartment holds so many memories. Stella and I lived in this complex together, right next door to each other. We've spent Christmases, Thanksgivings, and birthdays here, just the two of us. I discovered my love of coffee here—prior to Stella, I never drank the stuff. I've laughed, cried, celebrated, and sulked in these very walls and on this very floor. Apartment 11H is the first place that truly felt like home to me.

"It's a new page, Hayden. And it's okay to mourn the closing of this chapter." Stella's hand finds mine and our fingers intertwine. I hear Lucas walk out of the room, giving us some much-needed alone time and privacy.

I squeeze her hand as tears roll down my cheeks and off to the floor. "We had so much fun here, didn't we?"

"The most fun." She sighs, her nails drumming against the floor. "I miss New York, not going to lie."

I prop myself up onto my elbow, taking my hand back. "Already? I thought marital bliss would prevent that from ever happening."

"Don't get me wrong, I love Lucas more than anything and would always choose him, but I do miss the hustle and bustle and convenience of the big city. And how everyone ignored me for the most part. I can't go anywhere back home in Dasher Valley without being stopped for an hour-long chat."

"That must exhaust your introverted self," I say.

"Yes and no. I do love people, but I also need some time to walk alone on the street without someone stopping me to ask how my mama is doing." Stella sighs again. "But enough about me. I'm very lucky to be back with my family and friends, and of course, the love of my life. Let's talk about you and how you're coping. Because it's not great, apparently."

Family. Friends. Love of my life. The words ricochet from my heart to my brain, leaving bruises with each bounce. It's not Stella's fault. She doesn't know everything about me, despite being my best friend. Some things are too embarrassing, too difficult to say aloud even to the person you trust and love the most.

"I'm just sad about leaving," I say, attempting to hide the shakiness in my voice. "Like you said, it's the end of an amazing chapter of my life."

"No matter what," Stella pats my thigh, "I'm always with you. A plane ride or phone call away."

"I know," I whisper. I bring myself to my feet, and she follows suit. "Let's find out what I'm doing with all my things."

We look around the bare room littered with packed boxes and other miscellaneous items strewn across the wooden floor.

"Do we bring this to Darcy's, or..."

I swallow. "I don't know. Which means I need to call him."

"Oh, I'm excited to see y'all interacting as an engaged couple. Well, I guess you were technically on the phone with him when I got here, but still. I didn't see or hear the entirety of it." Stella waggles her eyebrows.

"Don't get too excited. It'll be more bickering as usual." With a big breath of confidence, I whip out my phone, scroll to his contact—accurately labeled Killjoy—and press the call button.

As it rings, Stella hits my arm repeatedly and tells me in a hushed tone to put the phone on speaker.

Per usual Darcy etiquette, he answers at the last possible second. "This is Darcy Marshall."

I know, my brain mocks him while using his stern, no-nonsense tone of voice.

"I have my things packed up, and I was wondering when I could bring them over?"

A pause.

"Oh, so you do need my help after all?" His voice is... teasing. That's a teasing lilt, right?

I swallow, feeling embarrassed that Stella is hearing this. "Yeah, I guess I do."

"I'll send a vehicle over to help you move. It should be there in an hour."

My heart thumps at the earnest tenderness in his voice, and I chastise it internally. "Thank you, Darcy."

His voice lowers to a whisper. "You're welcome, Hayden." Then he clicks off.

My heart seethes. Why wasn't he cold like usual? What's wrong with him? How dare he treat me like this in front of my best friend? Like he actually cares or something. "See, nothing eventful. Same old Darcy."

Stella laughs. "Yeah, right. That man was definitely teasing you and was kind to you. You're already breaking through his walls. Oh, this is going to be so much fun to witness."

"Why do you get so much pleasure from my misery?" I mumble.

"Because I truly don't think you'll be miserable for long. That's how these marriages of convenience go in romance books, at least."

"Stella, my life is not a romance book, and I am certainly not cut out to be a heroine."

She rolls her eyes. "That's what they all say."

POP CULTURE NOW!

WEDDING BELLS ARE RINGING!
PRESIDENTIAL CANDIDATE DARCY MARSHALL TO WED
CAMPAIGN MANAGER HAYDEN BENNETT.
WE SMELL AN ARRANGEMENT.

By Krissy Towers

It's no secret we at *Pop Culture NOW!* are obsessed with bringing you the latest gossip on the nation's young, hot, and (formerly) eligible presidential candidate, Darcy Marshall. He sent shockwaves through the nation when he announced his engagement to Hayden Bennett, the woman who took over his campaign from sought-out political princess, Stella Harper, when she made the move back to her roots to marry that hunky hometown hero of hers. Now, we are all asking the same question: Was this a ploy to get back at Priscilla Weatherby and Marcus Loveless? Or, like Priscilla, was Darcy having an affair?

Here's what we know about Hayden Bennett:
- Twenty-nine
- Holds a dual masters from Harvard in Political Science and Public Policy & Communications
- Grew up an orphan in New York City in a now shutdown group home
- Has assisted Stella Harper for seven years
- Holds a conservative-leaning voting record
- Speaks English, Spanish, and Japanese

On paper, she's an excellent example of a woman who has pulled herself up by her bootstraps and has overcome the odds stacked against her. But we must not forget where she came from. Is Darcy forcing her into this marriage, did she agree in exchange for money, and/or did she truly fall in love with her boss?

Stay tuned to your favorite pop culture platform as we bring you all the delicious tea in the coming months. We are digging for the answers you want.

CHAPTER FOURTEEN

DARCY

E minem's lyrics about sweaty palms and weak knees echo through my brain. I don't make a habit of listening to the rapper, but his early stuff hit me in the soul more times than I care to admit. Even privileged rich kids go through hard things.

It's not real, chill out, Darcy.

However, the rows of chairs with sunshine yellow bows tied around them, the same yellow color aisle runner, yellow and white roses along the aisle, and the swarm of rabid press outside of this old, echoey cathedral creates a concrete feeling to this wedding. I try to imagine every chair with a human sitting on it as I stand at the altar and suddenly want to vomit.

You stand in front of crowds all the time. This is no different. Imagine it's a rally.

But the pep talk isn't working. And this is not a rally. It's a wedding.

My wedding.

Hayden Bennett will be my wife in three hours. We will say sacred words standing in this very spot with the sunlight shining in through the stained-glass windows that boast images of saints.

With all the yellow, it's as if Ophelia was in the room today. It was her favorite color, and the thought of her spirit in this room makes me want to shout at the sky, demanding a reason as to why nine-year-olds have to die.

A clearing throat shakes me from my momentary raging stupor.

"Sir, I know it's your wedding day, but can you take a quick look over these papers and sign?"

I side-eye my assistant but relent. It's all a ruse, so what's the point in celebrating the occasion? "Hand them over." I take the papers and skim while returning to my dressing room. As soon as I close the door to the room, the papers are snatched from my hand.

"It is your wedding day, Darcy-*kun*. What are you doing reading papers about," Ren looks over the front paper he grabbed, "campaign finances?"

I snatch the papers back. "Because it's not a real wedding."

"You are exchanging rings and saying 'I do' in front of people and God. This is as real as it gets, my man." Ren claps me on the shoulder, and I finally glance his way. My first thought is how nice he looks in his all-black Italian suit, and my second thought is that though he looks good, yellow is not his color; he should burn the tie after this occasion. My third thought is that he is right.

Regardless of my feeble attempts to downplay this wedding, it is a real wedding. My heart may not be in it, and Hayden may not love me (nor I her), but the papers are real. Our signatures on the marriage license are real. God overseeing us standing at the altar is real.

And now the thought of lying to everyone makes me sick.

The press has been hard on me and Hayden. Public opinion of this impromptu engagement is low. Sure, some people are rallying behind our "romance," but the majority are calling bull. Hayden and I have to do one heck of a job selling our love today. All eyes are on us.

"God, what am I doing?" I bury my face in my hands, guilt clawing at my throat. My yellow necktie feels a little too tight, so I pull the knot loose a fraction.

"What you need to do to win this election." Ren pauses. "You never know... You may end up falling head over Italian-leather Oxford boots for the woman."

I glare at Ren. "You're not God. I was asking Him."

He smirks, then gives my face a harder-than-usual smack. "No, but I am your best friend. And as your best friend, I bet you'll fall for her."

Fire consumes the previous guilt. "I don't know how anyone could fall in love with Hayden Bennett. She's boisterous and clumsy, is always swarming around like an annoying gnat, smiles way too much, and has a hidden Machiavellian complex to her, which is why I hired her, but that doesn't make her lovable."

Ren laughs. "As if you aren't the quiet schemer and plotter yourself, Darcy-*kun*. You two are a match made in heaven. You'll see it one day. You will wake up and realize you married the woman of your dreams without ever realizing it."

"No, I won't," I say through clenched teeth, though something inside me is fighting that resistance. Hard. Because I do want to smile when Hayden smiles these days. And her boisterousness hasn't gotten under my skin like it used to. I release my breath. "Can you stop now and help me get ready for this stupid wedding?"

"I will stop. But remember my words and don't take too long to realize you love her, or she will move on." Ren tosses a comb in my direction. "Now do something with that hair."

Three hours later, I'm standing at the altar with a yellow boutonniere pinned to my black tux wondering where the hours had gone. It's all a massive blur; the only feelings associated with the past hours are sickness, guilt, and confusion.

That's not the way one should enter a marriage, right?

Finding Mother in the crowd only heightens the guilt. *Wave of nausea.* When I find Ren standing in the back waiting to escort Stella—who like Ren should burn all the yellow that she owns—down the aisle, I'm met with a smirk and two thumbs up. *Stomach twisting.* The other smiling faces in the crowd blend together, and my head begins to spin.

No. I cannot have a panic attack standing here in front of the world.

Smile.

Yes, I can do that.

I smile.

What's next?

Put your shoulders back and tilt your chin up.

Done.

Breathe. In. Out. Subtle. Slowly.

I focus on my breaths and realize Ren and Stella are now at the altar and the wedding march has begun.

Everyone stands.

The wide double doors open.

Hayden stands with her chin tucked down, wearing a beautiful, pristine white gown that radiates brighter than her sunshine personality. It cinches at her waist, and the rest of the dress poofs out around her like she is actually a princess. Her hair is up in a bun, as usual, but this bun seems to have all her curls at the right places with yellow flowers dispersed throughout. It's the first time I've enjoyed yellow as a color since my sister died. She isn't wearing a veil, which, according to Mother, Hayden fought hard to win that decision.

No one escorts her down the aisle.

And when she is halfway to me, she looks up.

Her eyes scream, "Help me," and I'm moved by a greater power to protect this woman who looks helpless in this situation.

The storm of anxiety raging inside me calms in the name of being needed by Hayden. My breath hitches, and my feet make their way to her. I loop my arm with hers and bend down to whisper in her ear.

"I've got you."

She smiles, and her eyes widen with happiness; she is genuinely grateful. The expression warms me.

I can't look away from her smile as I walk her down the aisle. Everything else seemingly fades away. Her smile declares she trusts me, and that is all I need to guide us forward to stand before God, our friends and family, and the world to say, "I do."

Like the preparations, the ceremony passes in a fuzzy haze. Hayden's gentle, warm smile, the sincerity in her eyes, and the soft squeeze of her hands keeps me rooted.

Trust. This is why I am marrying her. I trust her to carry me through, and I will carry her through.

And that thought eases the guilt of this marriage of convenience. Love might not exist between us, but mutual trust and respect do.

That's enough.

We repeat the traditional vows and say those two words.

"You may now kiss your bride, Mr. Marshall," the priest says, and I swallow a lump.

How could I forget that I would have to kiss her? Why didn't we discuss how we would kiss beforehand? Why didn't we at least practice?

As the thoughts keep me frozen in place, Hayden's face draws close as her arms wrap around my neck.

She pulls me down to meet her without hesitation.

I let her lead and close my eyes.

Our lips brush carefully, and just like that... Hayden releases me and steps away, slipping her hand into mine.

Did I even bother to put my arms around her waist?

My world trips and stumbles as I grasp her dainty hand; I'm a thread in a sweater—nicked and quickly unraveling. I desperately need to get out of the public eye so I can think. So I can fall apart.

I drag Hayden down the aisle to loud cheers and claps, and once we are through the doors, I release her hand and make a beeline for the nearest dressing room.

My breathing becomes erratic, and I slam the door shut behind me and collapse to a seated position against it, pulling my tie loose from my neck. The tiled floor is cool and comforting. Steady. Unmoving. Unchanging.

Too much change has happened at once, and it's overwhelming. Yes, I asked for it. It's a needed change, but that doesn't negate the fact that it's unnerving and terrifying.

A soft knock at the door, then, "Darcy?"

Instead of answering, sobs rack my body.

"Darcy, let me in." Hayden's voice is gentle and understanding.

I scoot away from the door. "Come in," I manage to say between sobs. She opens the door.

"Hmm. If I ever got married, I definitely wanted to bring my groom to tears, but this isn't what I had in mind." She places a hand on top of my shoulder and lowers herself to the ground. "These are tears of regret."

I sniffle. "Not regret, just... overwhelmed by change."

"Thanks for being honest with me. It scares me too, you know?"

Sobs continue to pour out of me. I should care; I should be humiliated that Hayden is seeing me in this condition, but when one can't breathe appropriately, it's hard to care about the opinions of others.

"Here," she says, placing both hands on my shoulders and shoving me forward. "Let me get behind you."

She moves my body with guided nudges as if I am a machine and she is the pilot. I have no clue what she's doing, but her bare legs end up sprawled on either side of me and I lean back against her chest. Her arms wrap around me in a tight hug, and the scent of sunshine and sweet spice is all-encompassing.

My head rolls back against her shoulder, and she whispers, "I learned this technique from Stella. She had panic attacks, too." Then, "Breathe. Hold. Release."

Hayden repeats the commands, and I eventually sync with her. Our chests rise and fall together. Our breaths rush in, we pause, and we release.

We become one.

"Better?"

I nod, feeling much more relaxed. The fog lifts and my thoughts begin to clear.

"Better enough to go out and face the masses ready to congratulate or scrutinize us at our reception?"

My heart quickens again, but I take deep breaths and ground myself back to this moment.

"Do you think we can feign being so in love that we wanted to ditch the party and head back to my—er, our place?"

Hayden laughs and releases me from her arms. "Give me at least thirty minutes to enjoy the food. Then we can sneak away."

I stand and offer my hand to Hayden. I lift her to her feet and she smooths the satin gown that makes her look like Princess Tiana from *The Princess and the Frog*. "What if I could make you a more delectable dish at home?"

"Hmm. What are you offering?"

I grin. "I make a mean ramen dish. The master himself taught me. I know how you like all things Japanese."

Hayden's eyes light up. "You mean Ren?"

"Indeed."

She thinks for a moment before answering. "Let's blow this popsicle stand."

As we navigate escaping through the dressing room window, which is a sight to behold with Hayden in her sparkly, poofy dress, one thought grips my mind: Hayden calmed me down from a panic attack, a feat only my best friend has ever accomplished.

We slide into the car, most of the backseat taken up by Hayden's gown, and I tell Lionel to head for home. The atmosphere is near silent, with only the light pants of our breaths to be heard. I side-eye Hayden to see if she's still breathing as hard as me (making a mental note to add more cardio into my workout routines), but she is side-eyeing me too, and we simultaneously burst into laughter.

"That was..." Hayden begins through laughter.

"Something." I finish. We laugh a little longer, then both take a few grounding breaths to mellow out. I place my elbow on the siding of the door and rest my head into my open palm. The sights of the city creep by as we drive through the crowded city, and with each moment closer to home, my stomach tightens.

I am married. To Hayden Bennett. My campaign manager. And I'm paying her to be my wife.

Sneaking another glance her way, I notice she's in the same position as me—her elbow resting on the doorframe with her head in her hands. Is she having the same daunting realization as I am? That we are married and heading to live together?

My throat tightens, and I reach to loosen my tie, forgetting it was already undone from earlier. There's no relief for the panic setting in, and I refuse to let Hayden see me like that again. Yes, she was comforting and helped me, but I don't want her to see me as weak. I take deep breaths in and then let them out, focusing on the passing buildings and people.

Hayden has already broken something down within me—I enjoy her smile and her laugh, and she brought me comfort in the midst of my panic attack. She seems to understand me in a way no one else does, and it causes me to wonder if she knew my secret about my sister's death, would she understand my pain instead of blaming me? I know I'm at fault, but what if someone other than my therapist, best friend, and mother told me that I wasn't? That I had permission to let Ophelia go?

Would I listen?

The questions stirring within me become too overwhelming. I shut my eyes and rub my temples.

"Are you okay?" Hayden asks in a gentle, concerned voice.

I simply nod my head.

She sighs then says, "I'm here, Darcy."

I want to believe her. Some small part of me does believe her. But Hayden has already seeped into my life in ways that I never would have imagined, and I have to throw walls back up to protect myself. I can't let her in anymore. Everyone that gets too close leaves.

And frankly, I don't want Hayden Bennett to do the same.

CHAPTER FIFTEEN

HAYDEN

"So," I draw the word out as I rock back and forth on my heels, standing at the front door of Ophelia Estate with Darcy—my husband—by my side. My eyes are firmly planted on the golden door knobs and not on the groom dressed in a killer black tux. During the duration of the ceremony, my brain kept short-circuiting over how handsome Darcy looked—still looks. I see him in a suit everyday, but there was something about him saying covenantal marriage vows, holding my hand, sliding his grandmother's 10-carat marquise diamond (I choked on my coffee when Ruth told me that would be the ring I was receiving) on my finger, and our lips briefly touching that sent my hormones into a tailspin. I sneak a look at him from the corner of my eye before joking, "Aren't you supposed to carry me over the threshold or something?"

He gives me an incredulous look, rolls his eyes, then shoves the door open. Not being a complete caveman, he holds the door open for me to walk through first. I stare at him and wonder where the soft, vulnerable, raw man that I sat on the floor in my wedding dress with went. The man who suggested ramen instead of the spread that the reception party offered. Where did he go? Why is Killjoy back?

Be patient with him, I remind myself, Ruth's words floating through my head.

As I walk through the door, Darcy makes sure to stand as far away from me as humanly possible. I step across the threshold into my new home.

I've walked through this house a million times, but this time...

It doesn't feel different like I expected. This is a job, and I am only here to fulfill my newfound duties as his campaign manager.

But still, it feels like I'm supposed to be here.

Surely time will bring about the feeling of change, like I don't belong here. Ophelia Estate isn't truly my home.

Home is a concept that doesn't exist for me. Until Heaven. Yes, that's the only place I'll completely belong.

But can I be honest? When Darcy met me halfway down the aisle and looped his arm with mine, it felt like home. It was a moment of undoubted safety and belonging.

It's all a ruse, I remind myself. *He did it for the cameras.*

My intuition, however, gnaws at me, arguing that it wasn't an act at all.

"Do you plan to stand there all night?"

Shaken from my thoughts, I turn to face Darcy, who is standing a few feet behind me. "Where is my room?" Looking around the entryway, I take small steps forward.

A small-framed woman wearing a black dress approaches me. "I'll show you to your room, Mrs. Marshall."

I stop in my tracks. *Mrs. Marshall.* I heard the new name when the priest pronounced us husband and wife. But that was just the priest saying those words, and I was too wrapped up in my thoughts for it to fully process.

But hearing it roll passively off the tongue of the maid of the house I'm now living in...

That makes everything real.

Darcy sighs and runs a hand through his styled hair. "I'll call for you when the ramen is ready. Go get settled and comfortable."

I swallow, not sparing another glance at Darcy in favor of hiding my face from him. I don't know what I need to process, but there's something I need to think over, and I can't do it in his presence.

"Thank you," I squeak, and I quickly follow the lady wearing rolled long sleeves, slacks, and an apron.

She leads me through the halls until we finally arrive at a plain-looking door. Plain for the mansion, I should say. When she opens it, I realize it is the colorful room Darcy brought me to when I had the unfortunate coffee incident. Was that only a few weeks ago?

What was that Tolstoy quote I learned in one of my college classes? Something about true life only being lived when small changes happen.

Change has hallmarked my life recently. Moving here isn't a small change, but maybe it's a sign that I can really start living? I don't have to let the suffocating pressure of this new role or Darcy's continuously sour attitude hold me back. I can choose to continue to live. Truly live. Regardless of Darcy's reactions to me. He chose this just as much as I did.

Might as well embrace the change and have some fun. He signed a marriage and business contract, after all.

"Thank you," I say to the maid again. "What's your name?"

"Janice." She shifts her eyes away from me as if she shouldn't be interacting with me on such an informal level.

"Janice, you're my new best friend here." I pat her shoulders and her mouth forms an "o" shape. "Seriously," I continue. "You know how Mr. Marshall is. I need a lady confidant in this place."

She snickers and covers her mouth.

"Thank you again, Janice." I give her a hug, while she awkwardly stands shocked and frozen. Then she leaves me with a click of the door closing, and I take in the wonderful, chaotic hues of yellow, orange, and pink swirling around my new room.

Exhausted from the day, I vow to unpack the boxes that are stacked against the walls tomorrow. I also make a mental note to tell the staff thank you for getting my things in here so quickly after I left all the boxes that I decided to keep in the lobby yesterday.

Stripping off my clothes and makeup, and wrapping my hair into my durag, I slither into the cozy bed and try not to fall asleep. Ultimately, I fail, drifting off to the memory of Darcy's genuinely concerned eyes when he ran to meet me in the middle of the aisle.

"Mrs. Marshall."

I stir, aware someone is calling for Darcy's mom.

"Mrs. Marshall. Wake up. Your food is ready."

My eyes snap open as I remember that *I* am Mrs. Marshall.

Janice stands at the foot of my bed with a tray. The intoxicating smell of ramen reaches my nose and I inhale, immediately transported back to my childhood.

Ramen and anime were staples of surviving within the foster care system.

"I thought Darcy and I would be eating together?"

Janice turns her head away from me and says, "He asked me if I would deliver your food to your room. He took his bowl to his office."

What is with him? We connected at the wedding. It was as if we were actually friends. And now he has the food that he said he would make me delivered to my room like this is a hotel?

No. That isn't how things are going to operate around here. I can be patient all day, but that doesn't mean I'm not going to insert myself into his life. It can be a loveless marriage, but it will not be a companionless marriage.

"Janice, could you return the tray and food to the kitchen? I'll take my meal there."

Janice nods, but I don't miss the upward pull of the corner of her lip.

I march out of the room on Janice's heels and stalk forward toward Darcy's office—a place in this house I've been many times—instead of the kitchen. After winding hallways come to a halt, I stand outside his office door. I twist the knob before I talk myself out of standing my ground with the man who gives me whiplash.

He's mid-chopsticks to mouth when I barge through the door.

The noodles plunk back into the bowl, splashing the soup broth onto him and the desk. Darcy hisses a curse before rolling his chair away from his desk.

"To what do I owe this pleasure?" His tone and false smile indicate this encounter is nothing close to pleasurable for him. He yanks a tissue from the wooden box on his organized desk and dabs at the splashes covering his face and white button up.

"I was under the presumption that we would eat ramen together." I cross my arms, only feeling a wee bit bad about the soup on his shirt. He has plenty of other button-ups to choose from.

"You were incorrect."

He begins wiping soup splashes from his desk, and I notice the way his sleeves are rolled and cuffed on his forearms. My eyes are drawn to his flexing muscles as he wipes the desk, but then I deflect my eyes because I don't need those muscles burned into my brain when this marriage is a sham.

My fists clench, and I drop my arms and anchor my fists into my hips. "Look. We need to set ground rules for living together. Rules that are not outlined in the contract. Basic human decency rules."

Darcy mutters under his breath and tosses the tissue in the nearby trash can. He turns to me, and we engage in a battle of the silent game. The darts we fire through our gazes speak volumes.

Finally, he breaks the intense silence, scrunching his brows together as if the words on his tongue taste sour. "You live here. During non-working hours, you stay on your side of the house and I will stay on mine. We will eat at separate times or at least in separate locations. For no reason should we enter each other's bedroom or use the other's bathroom." He pauses, then adds, "We will be like two ghosts in the night who never meet."

Somewhere through his statement, my hands fall to my side. Sadness grips my heart at his words, and I can't decide if it's because of the twinge of loneliness in his voice or if it's because I don't want to live like a ghost in my dwelling place. Nor do I want to live with a ghost.

"You met me in the aisle," I blurt. Realizing too late I can't take the words back, I drop my eyes to my feet and chew on the inside of my cheek. The new silence in the room settles in awkwardly, and I want to bolt. I was so vulnerable walking down the aisle alone. He heard the rescue call in my heart and saw the pleading in my eyes. No man has ever read me like that before, and I thought... I just thought... "Never mind."

I turn to rush out of the room, vaguely hearing the scrape of a chair behind me, but before I make it through the door, he grabs my wrist, and I freeze.

Different anime scenes float through my mind of the man grabbing the woman's wrist as she tries to walk away from him. My heart always fluttered, but I never thought it was something men did in real life.

No, in real life, they let you walk away.

But Darcy isn't letting me go. And I can't bring myself to turn around.

"Trust," he says in a low tone. He clears his throat. "I trust you to be by my side in the capacity that I need you to be. And you," he clears his throat again, "you can trust me to be by your side."

"Then eat ramen with me tonight. And have dinner with me every night moving forward." Should I tell him the meaning of that statement in Asian countries? It is our wedding night. I fight the urge to laugh hysterically at the absurdity of this entire situation. *How did I end up here, God? Is this what you want?* I once again question His will, though admittedly, there is a peace within my soul.

Another heavy silence hovers over us. But then he releases my wrist and nods. "Okay."

POP CULTURE NOW!

DARCY MARSHALL'S AWKWARD FUMBLE:
DOES HIS WIFE HATE KISSING HIM?

By Krissy Towers

Hi, *Pop Culture NOW!* babes. We have a short and sweet (sour?) report for you today. Is it just me, or is Hayden Bennett Marshall disgusted by kissing her husband? Let me set the scene for you in case you missed the live stream of the latest campaign rally in Ohio: The governor of Ohio calls Presidential candidate Darcy Marshall to the stage, but before Darcy steps out of the wings, his campaign manager-turned-wife pulls him in for a hug. Darcy looks to make a move to kiss her (watch it in slow motion, friends, trust me). Hayden, however, turns her head at the last second, causing Darcy's perfectly-shaped lips to smush against her ear. Talk about a weird wet willy! We want to know your thoughts. Does Darcy Marshall kiss like an animal? Or does he kiss like an *animal?* Let us know in the comments. All I know is that I wouldn't turn away if those lips were headed my way. Stay tuned for more *juicy* gossip.

Click <u>here</u> for a recap of the wedding.

CHAPTER SIXTEEN

DARCY

"On Wednesdays, we wear pink. I've told you this a thousand times, Mr. Marshall."

I pull the edges of my pants up to reveal pink socks. "I didn't forget, Keisha."

The fourteen-year-old rolls her eyes and crosses her arms, and I think my wife, when she was young, might have resembled this girl.

My wife. How does that phrase sail across my thoughts so smoothly now?

"It needs to be visible at all times. Here, I have a pink scrunchie you can wear around your wrist today." Keisha yanks my hand and drags me up the steps of the group home and into the common area. She's a force for a short, scrawny teen. "Wait here."

I do as I'm told because if I've learned one thing during my time volunteering here, it's that these young adults are always right and you better listen to every word they say and complete every task they ask of you.

Maybe teens should manage campaigns. Or at the very least, be the ones knocking on doors.

Hmm. That wouldn't be a terrible idea... But would I get slandered for forced child labor?

Probably. If Mr. Loveless had anything to say about it.

He's slandered my marriage, calling it a political sham and a hoax among the people over the past month. Some people are listening, but surprisingly, we've gained support and he's been touted as a racist. I don't condone using that word lightly, but I'd be lying if I said it doesn't help my campaign. It's when I catch Hayden meandering around our kitchen with puffy eyes, reddened skin, and mumbling over articles she's read about our interracial marriage that makes me want to go kill the idiot politician with my bare hands.

"Mr. Marshall! You came!" Keegan, Keisha's twin brother, is like a bear running toward me because of his thick frame. He pummels me to the black and white tiled floor of the group home and puts me in a headlock before I can get a word in.

"You've been practicing, huh?"

He grins down at me, his gap tooth showing proudly. "You betcha. I've been waiting all week to show you this."

"Okay, big guy. You've shown me, now why don't you assist this old man off the ground?" I tap the floor three times, and he releases his grip before helping me to my feet. This is why I changed into jeans and a t-shirt before coming here.

Landon, an eleven-year-old boy whose growth spurt seems to keep getting the best of him, bumps Keegan with his shoulder.

"Keegan! Move. He's mine today. He hung out with you last week."

"Like Mr. Marshall wants to spend time with a kid like you. He wants to hang out with men like me." Keegan puffs his chest while Landon's shoulders droop, bringing his height down closer to Keegan's.

My heart goes out to both kids. Though I've always been more of a Landon-type, passive and quiet, I can also understand Keegan, the angry and protective type. "Why don't we all hang out together today, huh? I may have brought something you'll both like."

The boys look at each other and then back at me with wide eyes and a hint of a smile. Keegan nods his head at me. "Whatcha got?"

"Follow me."

We head through the lobby and out the midnight blue double doors to my Mustang where I have all the supplies tucked away. Maybe I should have gotten permission, but sometimes, the most fun happens when you ask for forgiveness later.

"Mr. Marshall! I told you to wait." Keisha runs out of the three story building, taking long strides until she's by our side. She holds out a pink scrunchie. "Wear this on your wrist."

"Don't make him wear that," Keegan swats Keisha's wrist. "He's a man."

I grab his wrist. "And men don't hit ladies, Keegan." I receive the scrunchie from her and tell her thank you. "Men can wear pink, too."

"She's not a lady," Keegan mumbles, but goes on about his business opening my trunk. "Whoa..."

"What is it?" Landon rushes to Keegan's side and peers into the trunk. I watch his face light up. "Are we going shooting?"

Chuckling, I correct him. "There is no way I can take pre-teens and teens shooting, Landon. But I can suit you all up for a thrilling game of paintball."

The boys whoop and holler, and even Keisha checks out the gear. They call the rest of their friends—their family, basically—over.

While they haul the gear out of the trunk, I try to speak over their excited chatter. "I hope you all don't mind, but I have a friend coming to join us today. He's been my buddy since I was around your age. He should be getting here shortly."

As if right on cue, the decked-out black Toyota Tundra that belongs to Ren powers down the gravel road. The man spends his money on three things: clothes, travel, and his truck. His home? It's basically a shack that he frequents every now and then.

The kids don't notice the vehicle approaching because they're too busy bickering over who gets which paintball gun. Ren pulls up beside me and rolls the window down. I'm about to tell him where to park when I notice a person in the passenger seat.

"You brought a frie—" The question cuts short when the person pulls down her sunglasses.

"Hey, husband!" Hayden's cheerful voice and bright smile send coursing waves of annoyance through me. I attempt a smile in her direction, then glare at the menace in the driver's seat.

Ren grins ear to ear. "Hayden wanted to know what you *really* do on Wednesdays, so she tagged along." Oh, Ren. If looks could kill...

Hayden is already sliding out of the passenger door before I have a chance to tell him to take her home. Instead, I give him directions on where to park and mentally condemn him to solitary confinement for the rest of his life. He's clearly lost his mind.

Closing my eyes, I begin to count to ten. *This guy*. If he is going to continue dragging Hayden to places she doesn't belong, I will—

An arm loops through mine. I smell her—sunshine and lemon—before I see her. "Happy to see me?" Her voice sounds like all things yellow—dandelions, honey, and fire. I open my eyes and examine the woman who has attached herself to my side. If I actually believed in auras, hers would be canary gold.

I hate it.

Because the woman covered head to toe in skin-tight black athletic gear is still golden.

"Of course." A lie straight through my teeth.

Ren is the only person I've brought out here. I never even brought Stella though she knew about it. It's my special place to shed my walls, give back in a small capacity. Being here, around these lively kids, reminds me of my sister. I guess I show up every week for these kids because I can't show up for Ophelia. I failed her.

I don't exactly understand why I'm having an adverse reaction to Hayden stepping into this sphere of my life. I trust her. We are married. But I don't want her to start asking questions about Ophelia. I would rather take that secret to my grave than confess what I did all those years ago, putting my sister in harm's way, just to get away from my father.

"Who are *you?*" Keisha asks, her arms once again crossed as she eyes Hayden up and down. I put the harrowing phantoms in my mind to bed, tucking them in and commanding them to go to sleep. Forever, preferably.

With one hand lazily resting on my forearm, Hayden extends her other out to Keisha. "I'm Hayden Bennett Marshall, Darcy's campaign manager and—" she pauses, side-eying me, "his wife."

Keisha's jaw drops before she shakes her head and adjusts her expression back to one of suspicion and disdain. She cuts her brown eyes to me. "Since when are you married? And why didn't you tell us?"

"In a few days, we'll have been married for one month," Hayden says with a smile that looks genuine. She's a great actress. She's proven that for sure over the past weeks with her loving, doting, enamored wife bit for the media hounds.

"I wasn't asking *you,*" Keisha bites. She glares at Hayden one last time before walking away. The kids stop fighting over the paintball guns and train their eyes on me and Hayden.

Hayden's smile doesn't falter. Instead, she stands on her tiptoes and whispers, "What's her name?"

I tell her, then Hayden nods and hurries after her.

Doesn't she understand that Keisha will rip her head off? But then again... I have no doubt that Hayden can match wits with the teen. While Hayden disappears into the group home, I join the kids in picking out gear while they taunt me about the "beautiful woman" I'm with.

Hayden is beautiful.

Once upon a time, I was a man who never had physical-touch desires. Fast-forward nearly one month into marriage, and any contact she initiates feels like giving a drop of water to a man stranded in a desert.

I don't know who I've become, but I don't like him much.

But it's still not enough to want to consum—

How in the world did my thoughts end up here? I place the back of my hand onto my cheek, angry at the evidence of my thoughts painting my face.

Thankfully, at that moment, Ren jumps into the group, loudly proclaiming he will win because he is a real-life Japanese ninja, making him an instant hit with the kids. Most are suspicious, demanding he prove it, while a few of the younger kids stare up at him with rounded eyes and jaws agape.

Clapping my hands together, I shout, "All right! Time to pick teams."

"But I want to do a free-for-all," complains Martin, the oldest of the kids. "One last moment to shake these kids up before I age out."

"Then I expect you to lead your team well, captain," I respond. "You'll always work better with a team. Remember that when you leave this place."

Beside me, Ren snorts. "Take your own advice every now and then."

Martin high-fives Ren and says, "Ninja's my first pick." Ren claps him on the back with a grin.

"That's fine with me." I point to Ren. "I'm coming for you."

I assign the next oldest, Cynthia, as captain of the other team, and she immediately picks me. We finish picking teams, then I finally tell the director what I plan to do with the kids today. Needless to say, she isn't thrilled, but when she sees the excitement and feels the energy radiating from the group, she relents and tosses me the van keys so that I can haul everyone to the arena together.

I crank the van as soon as everyone finishes fussing over who gets the back seat and loads up. Hayden and Keisha come running out of the building waving their hands wildly at us.

I open the door, and they get in. Ren offers her the passenger seat, but she declines.

"Whew. We made it." Hayden sits next to Keisha, and they start whispering and giggling, verifying my earlier thoughts that Keisha was a teenage version of Hayden.

"Looks like Hayden won her over," Ren says.

"I had no doubt she would."

The thought of Hayden getting to know Keisha stirs something inside me. Keisha and Keegan's story isn't pretty. I've been able to crack Keegan open, but Keisha is a girl, and there are boundaries I can't cross with her. Hayden must have gotten her to open up quickly. She was an orphan herself, so maybe she relied on her past experiences to relate to Keisha in a way most people couldn't.

For the first time I wonder what Hayden went through as an orphan. Was it anything like some of these kids' stories? If so, Hayden must carry burdens I can't imagine. And she carries it all with a smile while illuminating every room she walks into.

Whereas I carry my trauma like an ostrich with its head stuck in the sand.

Respect for Hayden swells, and I find myself thankful she's the woman by my side. That she's here with me today.

It's nice to share this, even if I was originally upset by Ren's blindside attack of bringing her here without telling me.

We arrive at the paintball arena I'd previously booked for the afternoon, and the kids immediately gather into their teams to start planning tactics. Ren is already showing his team the best hiding spots.

"Can I be on your team?" Keisha asks. I glance at Hayden who is standing behind her, and she nods her head. The soft smile she wears says everything I need to know: Keisha really did confide in her.

"Of course." I smile at Keisha, and she punches my arm.

"Great. I want to nail Keegan with a paintball."

"I'm off to keep Ren in check," Hayden shouts with a wave as she turns to join the other team. Another wave of respect hits me, and then guilt. I've been so cold and standoffish to her. Forcing her to take inititive with me in the public eye out of fear I'll make the wrong move when it comes to physical contact. When I do attempt something, it usually goes awry and makes pop culture headlines. And really, it's not on purpose. I just don't know how I'm supposed to act with human beings on a personal level. I prefer the business-level.

Hayden is always cheerful to those around her, attracting everyone into her orbit, and I'm always so... awkward. Tense. Unsure.
Maybe I'm a little jealous of her joy and her ability to befriend a
fly? Of the confident way she carries herself?

How can I be charismatic and confident when it comes to my
business or running for office, but when it comes to personal
relationships outside of Ren and my mother, I'm a bag of nerves
and what-if questions?

"Mr. Marshall! Ren is making battle plans with them. Help
us!" One of the younger kids tugs on my shirt. Putting a pin in
my thoughts, I gather my—Cynthia's—team and help coordinate
strategy.

After the tactics have been drawn and we have all sat through the
safety lesson and rules, we find our previously scouted spots within
the arena and wait for the start signal.

I'm tucked in an alcove with my rifle at the ready through a small
opening when someone taps me on the shoulder from behind. I
turn my head to find Hayden smirking with her rifle pointed at me.
She's in all-black gear with her hair tied in a bun, and I'd be lying
if I said she didn't look like she belonged as the leading woman in
a superhero film.

"You ready to be taken down the moment the start signal
blares?"

Slowly drawing my rifle from the window opening, I say, "You'd
really take the fun away from the kids? I'm sure they want to be the
ones to bring me down."

"Oh, but that's where you're wrong, Darcy. Part of our strategy is for me to take you down in the beginning." Hayden winks. I point my rifle at her.

"Game point."

"Only if your finger is faster than mine." She cocks her head. "I can't believe I'm playing paintball with you right now. Who is this version of you? Where have you kept him hidden? Also, you should wear jeans more often. You look good in casual clothes. And in all-black tactical gear. Swooooon."

Did she just compliment my appearance? She compliments my work all the time, but my physical appearance? Heat creeps up my neck. *Who am I, indeed?*

She doesn't let up. "I mean, really, Darcy. You look dangerous right now. You could be the morally gray hero in a romance novel. The type of man who is grumpy and cold and ruthless." She crouches, the tip of her rifle at my chest. "The kind of man who would bring a city to ruins to save the woman he loves. Who would—" she pauses, leaning in closer from her crouched position so that our noses are inches from touching, "get on his knees in front of his woman."

I'm fully aware of the dirt beneath my knees as I kneel in front her. Hayden's words spin around in my head, and the look she's giving me? It's as if she wants to be the woman I'd destroy a city for. Her gaze unabashedly falls from my eyes to my chest, where the barrel of the paintball gun rests, down to my knees, and back to my eyes, a smirk playing on her lips.

My body is aflame, and...

I don't want it put out.

Be bold, Darcy. Take a risk. She's your wife.

I lean in.

A blaring horn goes off, and Hayden grins before pulling the trigger.

Click.

I realize two things at once: One, she played me. Hard. Two, she didn't load the CO_2 container correctly.

Her face falls.

I raise my gun to her chest with a wicked grin, confidence still surging in my veins. "I guarantee mine would go off if I pulled the trigger, but since I'm obviously the kind of man who destroys cities for his woman, I won't take the shot. Instead, you'll stay by my side as I bring this arena to ruins, keeping you safe until it's down to me and you."

Hayden swallows, something akin to fear and desire pooling in her brown eyes. Electricity hums around us like the barricade wall enclosing our location is a hot live wire.

It's invigorating. I want to guzzle it down like a man deprived of water. I want to make Hayden's breath hitch and heart race faster with my words. I need her to feel like she made me feel.

"And then," I continue, leaning in to whisper in her ear, "I'll destroy *you*."

She turns her head, her lips parted, and our faces are only breaths apart. If I just inched forward, I could press my lips to hers. *Taste her...*

She doesn't move, and neither do I. We sit, staring into each other's eyes. The stand-off of the century. Who will fire first? Who will fold?

Screams begin ringing out.

Hayden knocks my rifle from my hands, then sprints away.

Grabbing my rifle, I slump against the alcove wall and take a few steadying breaths.

What the—*curse*—was that?

CHAPTER SEVENTEEN

HAYDEN

"Divine Princess!" His voice booms and carries across the house. A couple of days ago, I discovered this nickname he had for me because he couldn't find his phone and asked me to call it for him. Turns out, it was near me, and I got to it first, discovering my supposedly unflattering nickname.

Little did he know I liked it.

I cover my mouth to hide my laughter as the curtain around me ruffles with each little shake of my body. He's too close to finding me in the sitting room for me to respond now. *Be still,* I silently scold myself. It's almost midnight, and on nights like this when Darcy's up late, stressing out, and on a horrendous rampage, I try to lighten the mood by being childish and silly. I admit it's not the most becoming method for me to use, but it works.

I think he secretly likes it.

The curtains open with a swoosh, and I stare into the deadly blue eyes of my husband. *Wow, the term comes so easily to me now. Has it been a little over a month already?*

"Yes. A month of literal hell," he barks, answering my apparently spoken thought and grabbing my arms, yanking me from the curtains. Since the paintball game last week, he's started touching me in little ways—and if I'm being honest, it's almost as if he finds reasons to touch me. I still initiate in front of cameras, but Darcy? He's taking initiative *off-screen.*

The thought causes a wave of heat to crash over me.

One month of suffocating in Darcy's presence every day and every night has done something weird to my brain. Sure, he's always been attractive. But living with him? It's like a switch buried deep within me labeled "wife mode" has been flicked on while my hormones harass me—not just for physical encounters such as the little touches, but also for emotional connection, which I get on occasion from him. It's making me spiral into a pit of longing.

Not for Darcy, necessarily, but for something genuine and *real.*

"Admit it," I tease as I look him over. He's still sporting his suit from work today. "You like being married to me. I bring a bit of fun into your life, Killjoy." It was only appropriate that I shared my nickname I had for him. At least he hasn't realized my ringtone for him is "Love Yourself" by Justin Bieber.

"Chaos. That's what you bring. Maybe I should change your nickname to that?" He drops his hands from my arms. This has been another change for the better. Darcy says more than simple sentences to me on the daily. Even when it's not work-related. Sure, most of the time it's grumpy with a sprinkling of condescension, but I'll take what I can get.

Secretly, I desire more of the man from the paintball arena, but I could never bring myself to admit that aloud. That would be equivalent to admitting that I *like* like Darcy.

And I'm 85 percent sure I do not like him like *that*. I just like the flirty and playful banter and the light touches letting me know someone chose me and cares.

I would almost call us friendly now. At the very least, we are no longer awkward people learning the ropes of a marriage of convenience who ignore each other as we pass in the hallway or end up in the kitchen together. He nods his head, sometimes says hello or hey, and then I respond with a peppy smile and something out of the ordinary. A perplexed expression will cross his face, and then he will continue with whatever he was doing. I enjoy those moments the most. He can't figure me out, and I love that.

"I much prefer Divine Princess." I bat my eyelashes.

"All the more reason to change it." He smirks, then fixes his expression back to his regularly scheduled scowl. It's the flashes of expression that key me into his true emotions regarding situations. His media mask is perfected, but with me, the mask has holes. Darcy sighs and runs a hand through his tousled blond hair. "I'm sorry it's late, but I need your help finalizing the schedule for the rally. I didn't know I would have to play a game of Marco-Polo to find you and make my request."

"Eh, it was more like a game of Divine Princess-Killjoy, but anywho. You found me!" The background music to Link finding a Korok in the video game *Zelda: Breath of the Wild* plays in my head. I have the sudden urge to do Hetsu's dance. It's funny how little phrases such as "you found me" bring the silliest memories to the surface.

Speaking of *Zelda*, I need to call Stella soon. I miss playing her favorite game with her.

"Yes, I found you." Darcy rolls his eyes and shifts his weight. "Now, would you mind assisting me with this schedule?"

"That's what I'm here for, boss." I salute him, and he rolls his eyes again. "I mean, who needs sleep? Not me. Certainly not you. I'm technically off campaign managing duty right now..."

He crosses his arms, and I try (but disastrously fail) not to notice the pull of his suit around his biceps. "I'll make you ramen."

Yes! But no. I need to drive a harder bargain. "And it's midnight. No matter what the schedule says, we do have to leave at 5:30 a.m."

"I'll add a cinnamon roll for dessert," he says without a smile. He then looks me over, his stoic expression holding his thoughts on my pajamas captive. "And you may remain in your night clothes."

I give him a friendly pat on the shoulder. "Ha, like I would have changed. You still don't get to dictate my clothes, Killjoy. But I'll take you up on the cinnamon roll." And then I prance out of the sitting room and toward his office while wearing my *My Hero Academia* Deku onesie proudly.

The click of his dress shoes follows close behind. I wish for once he would let himself be free. I have never seen Darcy around the estate dressed in anything less than a suit. Sometimes, he gets a little wild and takes his jacket off, but that's the extent of his "dressing down." It would do the man some good to let loose.

Or maybe just to bring back those bootylicious jeans he saves for Wednesdays.

"Actually." I stop in front of his office door and turn around, only for my face to come unreasonably close to his chest. I shift my gaze upward and immediately drag it back down. I'd much rather be unreasonably close to his chest than to his face. "Could you, um..." I motion my hand for him to back up.

He does no such thing. "You suddenly stopped."

I place my hands on his chest to shove him away, but he leans closer and my back presses against the door to his office. Swallowing the growing lump in my throat, I risk tilting my face to meet him.

His eyes are fierce, locked into mine. His face seems to grow bigger.

No, he's moving closer.

My breath hitches.

Closer.

I should push him away. My hands are on his decidedly muscular chest. I admit, I've wanted to know what he's got going on underneath these stuffy shirts he wears every day.

His face pauses inches away from meeting mine, and I rise on my tiptoes without a second thought.

Darcy Marshall is going to kiss me.

And I'm going to let him.

I close my eyes.

His breath tickles my ear and his arm brushes my waist.

"Hayden, I—" he whispers in a gravelly, broken voice. The way he said my name has my bones crumbling to dust.

A moment of nothing passes before something clicks and Darcy's body heat no longer seeps through my pajamas and into my skin.

I stumble backward, dropping onto my backside through a now-opened door.

"What the—" It takes a second to comprehend what just happened, but once I do, I snap my head up to glare at the heinous man. "You let me fall!"

Can a voice achieve a higher pitch than mine did?

The marble floor is cold against my palms, which thankfully, do not hurt. My butt, however, is a different story.

Darcy ignores my accusation and walks around me with clenched fists. I hear his desk chair scrape against the floor. How does he have a right to be angry right now? His mood swings are giving me more whiplash than the car accident I was in when I was eighteen, driving a beat-up Kia, and speeding away from the demon of my past: the group home.

I push myself off the floor, wincing at the slight pain in my lower back. It's nothing a bag of ice and ibuprofen won't fix, but still. Turning to face him, I repeat my statement with a tone of disbelief.

Darcy takes his dear sweet time shuffling papers on his desk before clasping his hands together until his knuckles go white. "Sorry, but I'm not a seer. How was I supposed to know you would fall when I opened the door?"

Agitation spreads through my veins. "How were you—what? It's common sense! It's gravity. What do you mean—" Anger fills my vision, and I can't string coherent thoughts together, much less words. How dare he? One minute he is offering ramen noodles and cinnamon rolls and is making fiery eyes at me like he wants to devour my lips. The next minute he lets me fall to the floor while I am close enough that he could have caught me or at the very least grabbed my arm or clothes.

The teenage girl who didn't know how to control her emotions begs to be set free, but one thought keeps me grounded: Darcy Marshall, regardless of his abhorrent behavior, is running for president and is my boss...and my husband.

I finally speak through gritted teeth. "Let's just get this schedule fixed so that we can go to bed."

Darcy's face remains emotionless, but his thumbs circle each other over and over. I've learned to recognize this as a sign of uncertainty and confusion. Does he truly not understand what just happened?

No. I shake my head. *It doesn't matter. Whether he understands or not, it doesn't mean you have to take this treatment.*

He nods. I sit down in the chair in front of his desk while trying to mask the pain I feel. The anger. My own confusion.

I don't bother to ask if his uncertainty is over not catching me, almost kissing me, or the crazy mood swings he makes me endure.

Because it doesn't matter. I can't keep letting him mess with my emotions, regardless of if he understands what he is doing or not. He doesn't want to have a friendship with me? Fine. That was all I was asking for, but not anymore.

I will be the epitome of professionalism.

About an hour of brief statements and formal speech passes between us before Darcy, taking me by surprise, actually has cinnamon rolls delivered to his office. Janice brings them in and tells us to have a wonderful night and to enjoy her secret family recipe before scurrying out.

"I'm sorry I let you fall, Hayden," he says, offering me a plate with three cinnamon rolls. There's a trace of uncertainty in his eyes, and I have to hold in my laugh. He's such a paradox.

"Thank you," I reply, taking the plate. It's warm on the bottom, and the smell of the cinnamon rolls leave my mouth watering. Taking a bite, I relish in the gooeyness. "Okay, you're forgiven." The words come out mumbled because my mouth is full of deliciousness.

Darcy smiles softly, watching me eat. I gesture for him to get one, but he declines with a shake of his head. Once I've devoured the first cinnamon roll while he's fidgeted awkwardly with his shirt sleeves and straightened the pens on his desk three times, he says, "I'm autistic."

Again, I find myself holding in a laugh. Not because I find the situation funny, but because it's so obvious. I should have known. So many people go undiagnosed, and I had an inkling he may fall into that category, but it wasn't my place to pry. I set the plate down, blot my face with a tissue from his desk, and look into his eyes. Blue irises search me, waiting for a reaction. He's scared.

"Thank you for telling me, Darcy." I reach for his hand, and surprisingly, he allows me to take it from across the desk. "It helps me understand you better. But it doesn't change who you are in my eyes, okay?"

He laughs lightly. "Is that a good thing? That I'm still the same in your eyes?"

"Yes." I grin. "You are the same stoic, sometimes robotic, man that I married. Now I understand why you're that way."

"Do you think it's bad that I'm that way?"

The uncertainty in his voice pinches my core. I squeeze his hand. "No. Not at all." I lean across the desk, and when he warily eyes the papers I'm accidently shuffling around, I can't help but laugh, which brings his attention back to me. I smirk. "I like your sourness. Balances my sweet nicely. For example," I wiggle against the papers on his desk, "I can mess up your desk and watch your frustrations grow. It's fun to crawl underneath your skin."

He sighs, closing his eyes, and I laugh again as he removes his hand from mine and stands, opening his eyes once more.

But they've darkened. He steps round the desk, and I stand to meet him, a mild fear he's going to reprimand me for leaning over the top of his desk. That signature spicy and sweet scent he carries mingles with the cinnamon rolls, creating something enchanting. We're toe-to-toe, him towering over me as his mussed hair falls against the side of his face, when he whispers like a spoken lullaby, "What am I going to do with all of your sunshine? You're chasing away my cloudy skies."

The alarm on my phone goes off too early. Why did he schedule our flight so early? It's ungodly to be awake at 4:15 in the morning, especially when I didn't collapse into bed until a little after one in the morning.

Three hours of sleep to run on. *Dream-filled sleep. Dreams where Darcy cleared off his desk with the sweep of his hand, lifted me by the hips, and set me on top.* We won't talk about what happened next.

I drag my heated self out of bed, throw on my robe, and begin the lengthy process of transforming from regular Hayden Bennett to Hayden Bennett Marshall while not thinking of the all-too-vivid dream. Since we are flying to Texas today, I opt for flowy yellow linen pants and a white sleeveless blouse, a light layer of makeup, and an updo. A stylist will be waiting for me to change my entire outfit, face, and hairstyle before the event, but I still have to look dressy and presentable for travel. I never know when the media will snap a picture of me and Darcy together, and I cannot make him look bad.

Being his wife is only an extension of my campaign manager position, after all.

About an hour later, I'm standing by the front door with a travel bag waiting on Darcy. I check my watch, realizing he is three minutes late. Darcy Marshall is never late. Never.

"Mrs. Marshall!" One of the housekeepers scurries down the corridor calling my name over and over.

"Janice," I state as she comes into full view. "What's wrong?"

A little out of breath, she responds, "It's Mr. Marshall. He's in a lot of pain, complaining about his side and back. He can barely move. I think it might be kidney stones again. He used to get them even though he hasn't had them in a while."

Coldness sweeps through me. "Has anyone contacted the doctor?"

She nods her head emphatically. "But he won't be here for another twenty minutes, and Mr. Marshall is adamant about making it to his flight."

"We're flying on his private plane," I state. "We have the power to easily reschedule. We can bump departure time back a couple of hours. We can dress on the plane for the event tonight if we need to."

"Will you come explain that to him? He simply isn't listening to us." The frail look on her face persuades me.

Plus, I get the opportunity to go into Darcy's room. It's one of the few rooms I haven't stepped foot in since working here and moving in as his wife.

"Let's go."

A little over a minute later, we stand at his doorway. The urge to knock and make my presence known is overwhelming, but I also don't want to be screamed at to go away. If normal Darcy is grumpy, there's no telling what in-pain Darcy is going to be like. Putting on my mental armor, I shove open the double doors to his bedroom.

He sits on his bed slumped over with one pant leg on and the other dangling off to the side, revealing boxer briefs that... have prickly cacti on them? How fitting. I bite my tongue to hold in my laugh. His hair is disheveled, sticking up like a classic anime character, and his white dress shirt is only buttoned halfway. *Like that dream...*

The laughter I was holding back over his boxers fades, replaced with something more akin to a bomb igniting in my chest. My heart stutters, then begins pumping triple time when I get a good look at the man I'm married to. When his gaze cuts to me, I throw my hands over my eyes as if I wasn't ogling my sick husband.

However, his perfectly proportioned pectorals are branded into my brain now. I'll die dreaming of that chest.

Not the time, Hayden, I reprimand myself.

"Darcy, you need to take care of yourself and wait for the doctor. We can push back our flight if we need to."

"Hayden, what in the world are you doing in my room?" His voice is tired and scratchy. "Turn around."

I do as he says because I can see the pain in his eyes and hear the suffering in his voice. Darcy Marshall is not a man who will tolerate being seen as weak. "Janice informed me of your possible predicament. If you push yourself too hard, you'll take that much longer to heal and could end up in the hospital. Then we will have to delay and reschedule a lot more than a flight."

"We have a schedule to stick to," he says, though by the end of the slow statement, he's groaning in pain.

"No. You are going to the hospital," I state, making my decision. "Janice, we can't wait on the doctor."

Darcy groans again, clutching his side. I've never seen his face contorted in pure agony. The flight *will* wait.

"Fine," he breathes out with yet another groan.

Immediately, Janice and Bennie, whom I didn't realize had entered the room, are on the phone and making arrangements for Darcy to be secretly admitted to the hospital. A whirlwind of preparations begins, and I remain a wallflower, watching the whole scene play out.

Helplessness plagues my thoughts, and I wish I knew what I should do at this moment. But all I can do is watch.

Bennie dresses Darcy in joggers and a t-shirt. Janice packs a bag with Darcy's things in case he has to stay overnight.

And I watch.

What kind of wife am I that I can't help my husband in such a time as this?

Forty-five minutes later, Darcy and I are in the largest hospital room that I have ever seen—so large there is a small tree occupying the room. Seriously, they must reserve these for future presidents and billionaires. The walls are the typical white color, but the space is aesthetically pleasing with green accents and earthy decor.

Darcy is dressed in a hospital gown, but a white sheet covers him. He's not sleeping, but his eyes are squeezed shut, creating creases in his forehead and a scrunch to his nose. My heart aches at the sight, and I send a silent prayer to God for quick healing and pain relief.

I need my future president functioning properly.

I need my husband to not to be in pain.

Bennie talks on his cellphone right outside the door, rearranging our plans, presumably. Janice did not come with us, so now I must step up and be the actual wife in this situation, not his campaign manager. When the doctor waltzes into the room, I whip out my phone to take notes. That's what a wife would do, right?

"Mr. and Mrs. Marshall," he begins with a friendly smile. His gray hair puts me at ease—a doctor with practice. Not to knock the young and upcoming doctors in the world, but for some reason, I trust this man a little more than someone looking fresh out of medical school.

I reach out to shake his hand. One sideways glance at Darcy tells me he is listening due to the new tilt of his head, though his eyes remain sealed shut.

"My name is Dr. Karl, and I will be your husband's doctor for the duration of his stay. We will need to run scans to check for kidney stones due to his history and the symptoms he is currently experiencing. My team is right outside the door ready to take excellent care of Mr. Marshall. This team has all signed nondisclosures, as have I. Do you have any questions?"

I shake my head, fully at ease. Doctor Karl has a certain energy that gives me peace.

"Thank you for your expertise," I say dumbly. He only smiles and motions his team inside. Two young women and a man wheel Darcy out of the room.

He never opens his eyes.

CHAPTER EIGHTEEN

DARCY

F ifteen years.

It's been fifteen years since I last had kidney stones.

I groan, clutching at the invisible pain in my side. In an instant, Hayden is at my bedside offering to give me water and to page a nurse. I swat her away, but she only moves a few inches, gripping her phone in her hands, which are positioned in front of her chest. Like she's hugging the device.

"Do you need to, um, use the restroom? I have the strainer right here."

An ulcerated laugh escapes me at her stilted awkwardness.

"No," I say through another groan, a wave of nausea washing over me. What caused this? My diet hasn't changed. I've kept dairy and acidic food intake to a minimum. Another swell of throbbing, unbearable pain pulsates within my side and back. Nausea builds and—"Give me the bucket!"

Something shatters on the floor, but I don't have time to be concerned. I heave over my bedside, praying to God that Hayden made it in time with the bucket.

Through the torment, vomiting, and tears, my thoughts center around one thing: Hayden will never see me the same way, and all authority I thought I once held with her has run away screaming.

With the amount of blackmail material she has on me now, she's the boss.

"Here, drink this." Hayden's soft voice caresses my chilled, sweaty skin like a gentle kiss. She holds a cup of water with a straw in front of my face. Closing my eyes, I part my lips and take the plastic straw between my teeth and relish in the cool taste of water.

"Ah, that's good." I sigh, letting my head fall back into the pillow.

"Maybe you should try to go to the restroom," Hayden says, concern lacing her voice. "If you pass it, you'll feel much better."

"Page a nurse then." The last thing I need is for Hayden to escort me to the bathroom. Walking is beyond complicated right now.

"It would look," she swallows, "bad if someone other than me helped you get to the restroom."

"They've signed nondisclosure agreements."

Hayden huffs. "Just let me help you, *husband*. It's our two-month wedding anniversary, after all."

My stomach stirs again, and I'm reach for the bucket Hayden set beside the bed. Nothing comes out, though.

"Fine. But just help me get to the handrail inside the restroom."

Hayden places one of her hands on my back while I clasp the other with my own hand. I take notice of her outfit at that moment—a thin number, but professional. Yellow, of course, but cute and fitting for her. Perfect for the sweltering, Texas weather we should be sweating in right now.

Not cold hospital room temperatures. She must be freezing.

With sheer willpower on my end and strength I didn't realize Hayden had, I'm heaved out of the bed and onto my feet. The moment they touch the cool floor, my knees wobble and buckle. Hayden's arms scoop and catch me under my armpits, and I'm horrifically aware she is carrying my full weight. Even though she is slightly taller than the average woman, I still tower over her slim frame.

With a tug, she lifts me back to my feet, and I manage to find some semblance of steadiness. "There you go," she whispers, adjusting us so I have one arm around her shoulders while she holds me by my waist. Her thin clothes cling to her body, not in a revealing way, but in a cute way.

And that's the second time I've thought of her as cute in the span of minutes. I really am sick. Hayden is beautiful; I will always acknowledge that. But cute? That's a special term of endearment.

We wobble our way to the restroom, I take hold of the handrail, and she vacates the premises. Very carefully, I untie the hospital robe in the back and situate myself into a more comfortable position when the door flies open.

Our eyes lock for a moment, wide with a certain horror that would rival my childhood expression when forced to watch something like *Freddy Kruger* with Ren. Hayden's eyes flick downward before two high-pitched screams ring out. I scramble to close the hospital gown around me as she slams the door. I'm mildly concerned at how my voice managed to match hers. The greater concern is that Hayden saw me practically buck naked preparing to urinate to pass a kidney stone.

Mortification doesn't begin to describe the feelings I'm experiencing. I'd rather live with this stupid kidney stone than walk out of this restroom. I'd rather lose the presidency than see Hayden ever again. I'd rather...

"I'm sorry! I'm sorry! I'm sorry! You forgot the cup you need before using the strainer and I didn't think to knock and—"

"Just," I begin, fighting the urge to die right here and now, "stick it through a crack in the door."

The door creaks open just enough for her hand to slide through, holding the clear cup. Careful not to touch her skin in any manner, I take the cup and shove the door closed.

"Gosh, dangit!" she screeches, and the cup falls from my startled hands.

"What is it?" I holler. As I bend to pick the cup up off the floor, excruciating pain floods my side and back, causing ripples of nausea. Falling to my knees, I dry heave into the toilet knowing nothing is coming out, while Hayden curses under her breath on the other side of the door. When my stomach settles, I collapse against the toilet and glance in the direction of Hayden's mumbled words. The door is wide open, and Hayden is clutching her right wrist with tears in her eyes.

A curse slips from my lips as I realize what happened. "Hayden, jeez." I take a panicked breath. "I'm so sorry."

"It's fine," she hisses. No. It's not fine. Not even remotely.

I hurt her.

Grabbing the railing, I lift myself to my knees. "Come here. Let me see your wrist."

Her eyes meet mine, and something inside me fractures at the pain twisted into her features. Her normally perky eyebrows are knitted, and her eyes, which usually contain the power of the sun, are dim. Her full lips are frowning, not emitting their typical glossy glow.

"Cover yourself first," she chokes out, closing her eyes.

I look down and see way too much hip and thigh on display, courtesy of loose ties. Thankfully, she's not getting a full-on picture of my backside again. I quickly adjust the gown and re-tie it. Triple knots.

"All good." I say, attempting to mask any ounce of embarrassment from my voice. She faces me again and takes a few cautious steps into the bathroom. I hold out my hand for her wrist, but she stares at my hand as if it's covered in leprosy. "Let me see your wrist, Hayden."

Maintaining dignity and control is vital in situations like these where your legally-real but emotionally-fake wife has seen your bare-naked butt, held your vomit bucket, and now looms over you as you are on your knees in front of a hospital toilet.

She places her wrist in my open hand. I wince at the sight of the open cut, the blood, and the bruise that's already forming around said cut, traveling from the bottom of her thumb across the bottom of her wrist. Gently flipping her hand over, I find a perfect mirror of the wound already forming on top of her wrist.

"I'm so sorry, Hayden. I should have waited for you to be completely clear of the door before attempting to push it closed. Let's call a nurse to attend to this."

She snorts. "So that they can accuse you of abuse and run a smear campaign? Yeah, right. I'll take care of this myself." Hayden removes her hand from mine. The space in my open palm suddenly feels cold.

"Again, nondisclosure agreement. We could sue the pants off them if something from this hospital visit leaks to the press."

"Maybe you should sue their pants off anyways. You seem to be in desperate need of them." Hayden looks me over, and I swallow the heat crawling up my neck and face. "Still," she continues, "if it leaks, the damage is done. You know how they will twist every narrative."

Ignoring her bad joke, I sigh. "You're right. At least let me help you bandage it."

Hayden laughs dryly as she holds her wrist. "After you pee in the cup and pass this kidney stone. I need my candidate back in action. I don't want to play wife anymore. It's kind of exhausting."

Is it really that exhausting to be my wife? My partner?

After this fiasco of a day, she's probably right.

"Don't worry. I'll be good as new in no time."

"Good." I don't miss the way her eyes softened alongside her voice. I glance at her, remembering I'm on my knees. Judging by the catch in her breath and the smile playing on her lips, she's noticed it, too.

Remembering the encounter from a month ago in the paintball arena...

Hayden crosses her arms—careful of her injured wrist—and leans to one side. "I like this view, come to think of it. This is the second time you've been on your knees in front of me, Darcy."

I scowl, and she grins. "Get out so I can," I look anywhere but at her, "do my business."

"Yes, sir, Mr. Marshall."

"Don't call me sir."

"Okay, Killjoy." She laughs, genuinely this time, and the ache in my chest loosens. But not the one in my back and side. I groan as a new tsunami of pain crashes into me. Hayden's laughter comes to a screeching halt, and she's quick to assist. "Here. Let me help you up."

There is no point in denying her help. I can't get up on my own. I need her. "Okay."

With her uninjured hand, she aids me in standing. Most of my weight leans onto the handrail in the bathroom, and I am back on my feet in a matter of seconds. "Thank you." I drop my gaze, unable to meet her eyes. Amidst the exhaustion, embarrassment, and excruciating pain, Hayden has stood tall by my side. Even as I thanked her by (accidentally) slamming her hand into the thick door.

She's the bravest soldier fighting on the frontlines in my army of one.

Hayden is walking out when I snap my head up and call out her name. She spins around, eyes wide with concern.

"Hayden, I—" What am I trying to say? What words are hiding in the depths of my consciousness? What is this that I'm feeling?

"Yes?"

Unable to formulate a coherent thought to tell her just how grateful I am for her, I speak skin-level words. "I'm glad you're here."

My bones ache, but not because of illness. At least, not the physical kind.

She tugs her phone out of her back pocket, and I notice the screen is cracked. Is that what she dropped earlier? "Say it one more time. I'm going to record it and replay it every time you go all surly cave man on me, okay?"

I narrow my eyes and scowl. She laughs, and then Hayden and her sass finally exit the bathroom.

Careful to make sure the door is firmly shut this go round, I untie my gown and begin the excruciating process of passing this dang kidney stone. I think I'll put the stone in a jar of acid and watch it crumble after what this thing has put me through today.

Maybe that's a bit harsh, but that's me. I'm harsh. And apparently the cause of my *wife's* exhaustion.

The words sting more than I think they should, and I know now, as clear as day, what I have to do.

I have to consider the possibility that I have real feelings for my real wife.

Because if I'm being one-hundred percent honest with myself, I don't think I would have made it through this without her.

And there's no universe where I would choose to go through it without her if given the opportunity.

CHAPTER NINETEEN

HAYDEN

Chronic stress and dehydration. According to the doctor, that was the cause of Darcy's kidney stone. Thankfully, he passed it due to the apple cider vinegar and ample amounts of water the nurses (and I) kept forcing down his throat.

Eight hours and countless awkward bathroom situations later, we sit on opposite sides of a private jet and refuse to acknowledge each other's existence. After the first show in the hospital bathroom, I can never look at Darcy Marshall the same. I would say it was highly unpleasant, seeing him so sickly. But the reality? The man is fine wine. An eleven-year difference between the two of us doesn't amount to much when he has a body that looks like it stepped out of a fitness magazine. He's lean but has muscles in all the right places. And he can rock a hospital gown like it's nobody's business.

And that backside of his. Mm. Good heavens. Lord, have mercy!

"Gah, Hayden. Shut up. Quit lusting after your husband," I chastise myself under my breath. I would lust away if he was truly mine, but this whole marriage is a sham, regardless of what the law says.

I sneak a peek at him across the aisle. When I see he is safely gazing out the window, I allow myself to fully turn my head in his direction. He's back in a suit—a lighter navy blue that complements his complexion well—with his blond hair gelled back in a way that screams, "Run your hands through me." I mean, we *are* married. I could simply flip a switch in my brain and act on my intrusive wifely impulses. I could make us real. Two months is long enough, right?

No. "He's annoying. He's rude. He's dirty words you shouldn't say. He's prickly. He's incorrigible. He's your opposite. He's sour and vexing," I whisper, listing all the reasons I can't continue to entertain the thought of Darcy as *mine*. We would never work on an emotional level together, and that's why this marriage has to stay *strictly platonic* even if I think we'd make beautiful children together.

Whoa. Never thought I'd string those two words together in a sentence.

I guess it's okay to think of my strictly platonic husband as hot, right?

But I'd be lying to myself if I said I hadn't fully noticed lovely, hidden qualities that almost outweigh his broodiness. Qualities I once took for granted, but as his housemate, I finally see the full picture. Like how he genuinely cares about his constituents. He isn't another politician out to manipulate the masses. Or how he works into the wee hours to make sure he is pulling his weight for the team. He never leaves us hanging or stuck with an unmanageable amount of work. And who could forget to mention the fact that he spends his free time with orphans?

I was an orphan. I understand the significance of that weekly Wednesday hangout and just how much those kids love him for it.

"Mr. Marshall, can I get you a drink?" a flight attendant asks. Darcy turns to face her but instead catches me gawking at him. Raising my chin and pasting a smile on my face, I refuse to look away. My face may be burning hot right now, but thankfully, the plane is on the darker side.

Like my hormonal settings at the moment. *Dark mode.*

"Will you bring two glasses of red?" he asks her, still not taking his eyes off me. My intuition beckons me to turn away, to duck under the plane seat and disappear. The look in his eyes is no-good.

He's up to no good.

I'm thinking no-good thoughts.

Abort mission.

I look away.

"You shouldn't drink wine after a kidney stone and grueling hospital visit," I say, gazing out of the plane window into the dark abyss of the night sky. Seconds pass before he responds.

"Or maybe I should reward myself for making it through."

Shudders ripple through my body, originating at the nape of my neck where his breath touches my skin. My soul screams at me to lean back and into him. No, that's probably just the flesh talking.

"Uh... Darcy?" I take a deep breath to settle my flesh and resist turning my head to face the phantom in the dark who suddenly appeared next to me. "Why did you move?"

He reaches around my body and clasps my hand with his. The heat of his breath tickles my neck again. "Wouldn't a newlywed couple sit together on a plane?"

I try to yank my hand away, but his grip is firm, a cage around my fingers. "Maybe a real one," I whisper through a shaky breath. He still doesn't budge.

"The flight attendants are unaware it's not real."

"Sitting next to me doesn't indicate anything other than you're a clingy husband." I try—it's a grand endeavor—to maintain a steady, sure voice. But somehow the word "husband" rolls off my tongue with a sigh that sounds loaded with longing. Maybe I should take talking off the schedule for the duration of this flight.

Darcy's hand tightens around mine. "I also would like to further know your thoughts about me. So far, I've learned I am incorrigible, rude, sour, vexing, and dirty words that that mouth of yours is too good to speak."

I'm stone cold, but his breath is still hot against my neck. Too hot. If only he knew I repeated the negative trait mantra to restrain my mind from dwelling too long on all his wonderful qualities. Ones that I've grown to admire.

"Your wine, sir," the flight attendant graciously interrupts. Darcy releases my hand and leans away from me. I want to move, but I'm still frozen solid. How did he hear me? I don't talk that loud, do I?

"Turn around, Hayden."

I feel like the Tin Man, like I need to oil every joint to make them cooperate and move.

Darcy releases a long and dramatic sigh and holds a glass of wine over my shoulder. "We are going to talk. I'll wait in this plane all night if I have to."

What is with him? He's being his usual direct and demanding self, but it's giving... sexy demanding. Hot directness. Flirting with fire and preparing to go up in flames.

I take the glass and sip it, hoping it will give me an ounce of courage to face him. The wine burns going down my throat, and I realize I'm halfway finished with the glass by the time I'm ready.

Inch by inch, I turn until I am face to face with him. Darcy's eyes smolder; his lips twitch as if on the precipice of an amused grin.

"Finally." He clinks his full glass to mine. "You know, you really shouldn't be speaking about your husband that way in public. Someone could overhear."

I cast my gaze away, feeling ashamed of what I said. "I really am sorry."

"I'm not that easily offended." He snorts, and it signifies to my body that it can officially loosen up. "You may be right with one or two of your observations."

"That still doesn't warrant a vocalization of them."

He nods, contemplative. "Maybe put your frustrations in a journal next time?"

My hand flies to my mouth to cover a hiccup. "Already have one." I wonder what he would think of it? It's currently a hodge-podge of hating him and respecting him all at the same time.

Hiccup.

"You don't drink much wine, do you?"

"No," I confess. "My choice of beverage on the occasion I do drink is an Old Fashioned."

"Hmm." He taps his fingers on his thigh. I shift my eyes back to his face. "I never would have pegged you as an Old Fashioned woman."

"There are many things you don't know about me."

Hiccup.

I slap my hand over my mouth again for two reasons. The obvious reason is because of the hiccupping. Not attractive. Reason number two is so that I don't speak more unintentionally flirty words.

"You're right. There are many things I still need to learn about you." With that, he hands his still full glass of wine back to the flight attendant.

"Was there a problem with your drink, sir?"

He stares at me as he speaks to her. "No, I realized my *wife* was right. It's probably best not to drink right now."

I choke on my last sip of wine and hand the empty glass to the attendant.

"Would you like another glass?"

I wave my hand. "No, I'm good. Thank you. Maybe some water."

She nods and disappears.

Silence stretches between us as the distance closes between us. I'm not sure who's leaning in more, but I know it's a team effort.

Just like everything between me and Darcy.

Because we are a team.

He's inches from my face, and I let my eyelids wrap me in darkness, preparing to experience his kiss for the first time with every sense but sight. We are wrapped in the dim glow of the plane light while the night sky zips by us through the windows. Cozy. Soft. Inviting.

"Hayden." My name is rumbly on his lips as his mint breath caresses my face.

"Darcy." His name is a plea on my lips. I don't know if it's me or the wine taking charge, but...

No. I do know.

It's me.

Just with the confidence of wine.

Because if I'm being honest with myself, I've wanted this to happen for a while.

With every demand rolling off his tongue, every snarky remark on my end, and every unmasked moment between the two of us, I've fallen for Darcy Marshall.

"What are we doing?" His fingers find the small of my back, and I arch into his shaky touch.

"Nothing right now," I whisper against his ear, intentionally blowing softly before taking his lobe between my teeth. He gasps and his body stiffens. "But we are about to be kissing."

His fingers splay across my back, pulling my body into his as if he is gluing us together. The kind of glue that requires high amounts of pressing to stay combined.

I let out a noise I'm not proud of when his lips press against my neck, blazing a trail up the side, across my collarbone, and landing at the corner of my lips.

"I've wondered what you taste like since the paintball game," he murmurs, hovering over my mouth.

Probably like wine right now, I think, but my thoughts are too scattered to form words. Not from the alcohol but from *my husband.*

I make another whimpered noise, begging him to put me out of my misery. I want to taste him, too.

A throat clears. "Your water, Mrs. Marshall."

I expect Darcy to jump like a skittish cat.

He doesn't. While we both open our eyes, molten lava pours from his gaze as I look over his shoulder at the flight attendant, preparing to take the water from her to be polite.

But Darcy moves his hand from my back to the back of my neck, gently tugging my hair down and angling my face to the perfect kissing position. I snap my eyes back to his as he says, "Come back later, please." His voice is husky and hungry and hot. The sound of the women's heels fade.

And then Darcy drags my lips to his in a kiss that should be banned in all one-hundred and ninety-five recognized countries. His soft lips are explorative as he controls the kiss, coaxing my mouth to fall into tune with his. He tugs at my hair again, eliciting a moan from the depths of my soul.

He growls in return, and I didn't realize men actually did that sort of thing. The passion pouring out of Darcy as our lips dance opens a well of feelings within me, and I match him stride for stride.

I admire this man. Respect him. Trust him. Cherish him. I—

The L-word is on the brink of my thoughts, but I'm not ready to jump off that edge just yet. Not even as he slows the kiss and wraps both arms around me as if I'm his lifeline of safety out in the ocean of wild waters.

I really, *really* like him.

The taste of salt registers in my senses, and we both part for air.

Is he crying?

Lifting my good hand, I cup his cheek and wipe at the water running down his cheek. His hand mimics mine just as he asks, "Why are you crying, Hayden?"

I touch my face, realizing it's damp with liquid. "You're crying, too."

This should be funny, a hitched-for-convenience husband and wife crying as they share their first real kiss, not the quick pecks in front of a camera. But nothing is funny about this moment.

It's real and raw.

It's two souls connecting.

"I like you, Divine Princess." Darcy uses the nickname with utmost reverence, taking me by surprise. "I don't know what these feelings mean, but, I know I like you. And I'd like to date you."

POP CULTURE NOW!

BUSTED! EVIDENCE TO PROVE DARCY COERCED CAMPAIGN MANAGER HAYDEN BENNETT COMES TO LIGHT!

By Krissy Towers

Our favorite presidential candidate to keep tabs on has been a naughty man.

Richard Loveless's team has brought a scandal to light. Leaked photos from a bomb-drop dinner where Loveless, Marshall, and Weatherby were all in the same room (the very one where Marshall learned his ex-fiancée, Priscilla Weatherby, was now engaged to Marcus Loveless) reveal Darcy and Hayden seemingly coming to an agreement before they entered Weatherby Estate. Once inside, reports state the two announced they were seeing each other.

The timing is fishy, don't you think?

Which leads us back to our original question: Is Darcy and Hayden's marriage a hoax? Did the two tie the knot to get back at Priscilla and Marcus, or was it arranged for Darcy to appear as a more appealing candidate? Social media is aflame with rumors and conspiracies. But we can't forget to ask one more question: Are they truly in love?

Check out these incriminating leaked photos below, and then examine these photos we took three days ago when the two were spotted exiting their private plane to attend a rally in Arizona. Judge for yourself if this marriage is a facade or a genuine union of love. As always, stay tuned to *Pop Culture NOW!* as the story unfolds.

CHAPTER TWENTY

HAYDEN

F ive months.

    We are five months away from the election, and let me tell you, Ophelia Estate has been in manic mode. And I've been wearing my manager hat and wife hat simultaneously lately, so much so that I'm not sure where the campaign manager ends and the wife begins.

And to add to the chaos that is my life right now?

Dating my husband of convenience!

Because Darcy Marshall knows *nothing* of true dating.

"Are you ready for our date tonight?" Darcy slides his arm around my waist and kisses my cheek, sending annoyed butterflies swarming and rioting in my stomach. I'm simultaneously peeved and turned on. Not a fun combination.

"For our dinner date?" I toss a sweet and sour smile up at him. "With your COFFEE business partners?" See, this is Darcy's idea of a date: blending business with pleasure. He hasn't learned to separate the two. Don't get me wrong, I enjoy spending time with him wherever or with whomever, but when I'm having to act as his wife and campaign manager while on a "date," it's not exactly ideal.

He hasn't planned a single date for us. Just the two of us. Out of the public eye where we can just be together without the pressures of this real-but-fake marriage.

"Don't worry, Hayden," he says, completely misreading me. "I'll still kiss you on the doorstep when we get home tonight as if we are parting ways instead of walking inside these four walls together."

I snort at the idea of this mansion having a mere four walls, but Darcy seems to take that as proof I'm feeling better. I'm not, but as he smiles softly at me and places a chaste kiss on my lips, I let my frustrations melt away into understanding.

He's in the middle of a presidential campaign and a marriage ruse, and I'm at the heart of both. This has to be our version of dating right now. We don't get the luxury of down time just for the two of us. Darcy has made it clear and reiterated over and over again that he likes me and wants me and is in this with me. Because that's the type of man he is—determined. Once he sets his mind to something, there's no stopping him.

"Will you kiss me inside, too?" I ask, batting my eyelashes in a dramatic way that makes him roll his eyes.

But then the icy blue color darkens. "I'll kiss you wherever and whenever, Divine Princess."

He makes good on this promise for a solid minute before his personal assistant takes him away from me so he can join in on a virtual meeting with some diplomats.

I stand dumbfounded that this is real life, wondering when Darcy Marshall became so much more than a man I simply tolerated for my career. Edith Hamilton was right; "Love cannot live where there is no trust."

Trust.

It all comes back to those five letters.

Trust is not built from love; love is built out of trust.

The two crossed-shaped letters stand sturdy on either side of the word like a protective barrier. That's what trust is. It's knowing you are safe. Protected.

With Darcy, I am those things.

He, alongside God, make the two t's on either side of my life.

I don't know when I came to need Darcy, but I do.

And the idea of ever dissolving this marriage sends spiders straight to my stomach.

"Hayden, we need you in the conference room!"

I startle, following the voice to find Paul at the edge of the hallway, breathing heavy, eyes set with panic.

"What's wrong?"

"Loveless is running his mouth again. He's saying Mr. Marshall is paying you to be his wife, and unfortunately, he says he has proof."

The earth tilts on its axis, and everything that once felt safe, secure, and steady crumbles beneath my feet. The earth rocks, the ground opens, and down the rabbit hole I tumble.

"Wh-what?"

Paul's frantic expression hardens. "Listen, Hayden. I don't know what the two of you are doing. It's not my position to call it love or not. I trust both of you and know that neither of you would do something to intentionally sabotage this campaign. But the team needs the truth, and then we have to figure out how to manage this."

I nod once, not trusting my voice.

And for once in my life, I wish Darcy was by my side.

I need my shield to take some of these bullets for me.

Following on my assistant manager's heels, my mind whirs. How did Loveless find out? We were so careful. Only told people we trusted. Had our bank sign NDAs. What receipt is he bringing to the table? Should we lie to the public or come clean?

I step through the double doors and into our meeting room. All eyes turn to me, waiting. Examining. Wondering.

"It's true."

A collective roar rises around the room.

"Why didn't you tell us?"

"You lied to us!"

"We could have helped!"

"Is he forcing you?"

The last one snaps me out of my nervous haze. "No!" I shout, silencing the room. "Darcy is not forcing me. I chose this. And we are dating."

Perplexed and doubtful faces fixate on me, waiting for me to elaborate. I swallow the lump in my throat. "Yes, our marriage is for convenience to help him win the rural vote. But, as we've spent more time together and have gotten to know each other on a more...personal level, we decided to start dating within our marriage. I like him a lot, and, well—" I close my eyes to cool the heat kissing my face.

"Well, what?" Brittney, our campaign merchandise coordinator prompts.

"Our marriage will be real. One day," a deep voice that I've come to recognize by sound alone says. I turn around, and all of the anxiety building within my bones vaporizes. Darcy takes two long strides into the room, wraps his arms around me in a tight embrace, and then kisses me. "I'm so sorry."

The sound vibrates against my lips. "I thought you were in a meeting."

He kisses me again. "Bennie saw the alert. I had to check on you. The diplomats can wait."

Happiness swells within me. He chose *me*. I plant one more kiss and say, "We'll get through this."

Applause rings out around the room, along with new shouts.

"I called it!"

"Let's burn the receipts!"

"Get a room!"

Darcy's forehead drops to mine, and we laugh. I take a mental snapshot of this moment, one that if you would have asked me if it would happen even a month ago, I would have laughed in your face. But now? This is a memory I'll cherish to my grave.

For once in my life, I have a teammate.

But I also have a job to do. I let go of Darcy, but only to take his hand and lead him to the front of the room. "Micah, I need your help," I say to our social media manager. "This is what we need to do..."

After a grueling three-hour long meeting, we dismiss the team. Turns out Loveless's proof was out of context photos from the night of the dinner party where he made it seem like me and Darcy struck the deal that night. One is a picture of me and Darcy standing outside the door before we entered into Weatherby Estate. The photo is altered to look like we are shaking hands and securing a deal, but in reality, I remember Darcy avoiding eye contact with me while I tried to get him to smile before walking in.

We released a statement denying all charges, since no real receipts were brought to the table. A small part of me feels guilty for lying, but this is politics. And despite how we started, what Darcy and I have now is real.

However, people are easily manipulated, and it's going to take some time for the accusations to pass. But honestly, I'm fine with it because it means Darcy and I can PDA-away the allegations. And that will be *fun*.

Grinning, I head back to my room to get ready for the business dinner that Darcy's masquerading as a date. As I wind down the halls to the other side of the mansion, I shove away thoughts of confessing the truth to the public because something Darcy said before the meeting rings through my ears: *"Our marriage will be real. One day."*

A real marriage entails not sleeping on opposite ends of an estate.

A real marriage means drifting off to dreamland with arms wrapped around you.

A real marriage consists of long nights and twisted sheets.

And I should be nervous, but honestly?

I'm waiting for that man to invite me into his bed.

Because regardless of how this started, I think I know exactly how it ends. With forever.

Nearly tripping as I walk into my room because I'm so lost in midnight fantasies, I notice a long, white box sitting right inside the room where I accidentally kicked it. Off to the side and tumbled to its side sits a smaller white box. I pick them up and bring them to the bed, opening them. Inside the larger box lays a note written in perfect cursive atop lemon-yellow fabric.

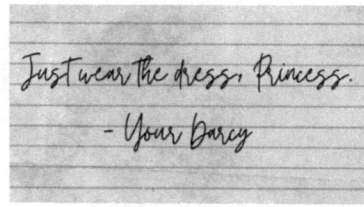

Just wear the dress, Princess.
— Your Darcy

The smile overtaking my face is nothing compared to the way my heart is swooping and soaring while I set the note on the bed and pull out the dress. The texture is stretchy and soft to the touch. The fabric unfolds, revealing a chic capped-sleeve cocktail dress. It's a solid piece with a v-cut neckline and a cinched waist, and I already know it will fit me like a glove. Quickly digging into the smaller box, I pull out a pair of black stiletto heels begging me to try them on.

Tears fill my eyes.

No man has ever bought me a whole outfit before.

Most of my clothes growing up were hand-me-downs or thrift-ed.

Though I don't want to be paraded around in this dress for Darcy's business associates, I change into the dress.

Tonight, I will wear the dress.

For him.

For the teenage version of me who would have kicked adult-me in the teeth for not wearing such a nice article of clothing.

For me. For the successful, hardworking woman I've become.

As I stand in front of the mirror, I let down my hair. It falls into a heaping mess of coiling curls, and I set to work styling it to wear it down.

But sometimes, no matter how much I've changed and grown, I still see the scared eight-year-old girl screaming and crying in the shadows on the street while rain poured and soaked her to the bones. I sometimes still see the other girl, her chest rising and falling for the very last time.

And for the first time since things became real between me and my husband, I wonder if I'm worthy to call a man like him by that title.

Chapter Twenty-One

Darcy

"Yellow is your color." I trail my eyes up my wife, from her strappy black heels to the classy dress that's draped so perfectly around her body that I'm jealous of a piece of fabric. The killer? She's wearing her hair down, and it's a little untamed. Just like her.

She smirks. "Some guy calling himself mine left it on the floor in front of my door for me to trip over. The least I could do was show him what he's missing by taking me out to dine with his business partners once again. He could," she sweeps her hands down her body and spins, "have all this to himself tonight."

I bite my lip to keep from laughing. Her clues have not been subtle, and she doesn't know I've been planning this date for a week after she sat me down and blatantly said she wanted some time for just the two of us. I did have a business dinner on my schedule tonight, but I emailed the team and rescheduled for tomorrow.

Tonight, I wine and dine my wife.

Or, uh, sako and hibachi my wife. Because Japanese food is the way to her heart, and that's where I'd like to set up permanent residence.

Placing my hands on her waist, I tug her close and whisper, "And what will we do when I get you all to myself, *wife?*"

Hayden, to my surprise, pats my rear. "Don't tempt me, Killjoy. I wouldn't allow you to murder the mood like you usually do if you were taking me out alone."

I swallow, the realization that she is legally my wife and I am legally her husband sinking into my system like a rock in water. Of course, I've had these moments before, but it doesn't change the intensity when it hits me again. I could take her back to my room, shut the door, peel this fabric right off her skin, and—

No. Not until we agree to make things real. Not until I'm ready to open up to her about my ghosts. I don't want her to run away screaming; it might break me.

I kiss her cheek. "We should get going. Don't want to be late."

Twenty minutes later, we're parked in front of Ginger & Sesame, one of the most sought-out hibachi restaurants in the Upper East side. Tonight, it's bought-out.

Just for me and my date.

I can't fight the smile as I open the door to the passenger side of my Mustang to let her out and she laughs, mentioning how I'm like the regency hero I'm named after because my Mustang is my trusty steed. I roll my eyes, but again, I'm taken with her. Hayden looks like glowing sun at midnight, and my heart might actually skip a beat.

"This isn't where we usually meet your business partners," she comments.

Placing my hand on the small of her back, I lead her to the entrance. After opening the glass door for her, I follow her inside and am instantly hit with sweet and sour smells. I chuckle when Hayden spins around, a million questions in her eyes as she takes in the empty building.

Well, empty save for the handful of servers and the teppanyaki chef.

"You don't normally close down famous restaurants for your meetings, either."

I kiss her briefly, wanting to linger but knowing we have all night. "No, I don't. Welcome to our first real date." I offer my arm, she loops hers through, and I escort her to the hibachi table.

"Wait," she says. "I need to make a restroom run."

I let her go, wondering why there was a twinge of sadness in her eyes. Did I do something wrong? Does she not actually want this?

No. That can't be true. She loves hibachi regardless of who takes her there. And she wants me. She's made that clear. Now is not the time for my insecurities to flare.

She's not going to leave me, I repeat in my head. Over and over. Forcing myself to believe it.

I'm into this woman.

I swore I'd never entertain the idea of love, but if this is what falling for someone feels like, then I've been an utter fool to block my heart from this blissful, albeit terrifying, state of existence. I can't call what I'm feeling love quite yet, but I can say it's headed in that direction. Though, I never would have gotten here without the ingrained trust that bonds Hayden and me.

Checking my watch, I rock back and forth on my feet, waiting for Hayden to come back from the bathroom. She's been in there for about five minutes now, and I hope everything is okay.

Is it acceptable to ask that when a lady comes back from using the facilities?

A young teppanyaki chef steps behind the grill in the middle of the u-shaped table arrangement, and attempts to ask me a question that I can't understand through his broken English. I ask him to repeat the question, but I ask him in Japanese and let him know that I can speak the language fluently. A smile lights up his face and he begins to repeat himself in his native tongue. We converse for a moment after the order is placed, and then he walks away in buoyant strides.

Hayden is suddenly behind me, speaking in Japanese a phrase that translates to "you've got to be kidding me" as she plops into the chair beside me. She lands so hard that she slightly bounces back up. I can't tell if it's a fire of passion or a fire of frustration in her eyes as she stares at me, her face mere inches away. Her glossy lips, slowly forming a pout, look tastier than anything this restaurant has to offer.

Hayden speaks slowly. "You could speak fluent Japanese this entire time?"

Frustration. Definitely frustration.

"My best friend is Japanese." It's an obvious connection, right? Ren plus me equals years of Japanese lessons.

"And? My best friend is southern. That doesn't mean I learned how to speak it."

I laugh, but I quickly disguise it as a stuttered cough when Hayden knits her brows together and narrows her eyes.

Clearing my throat and trying to stifle any amusement from showing through my face, I try again. "What I meant to say was, yes, I can speak Japanese. I chose it as my foreign language in school and stuck with it through college. And having Ren as my best friend helped tremendously."

Hayden's face softens, then she turns her body toward the table, places her elbows down, and lets her head collapse into her hands. "Oh my gosh, Darcy. This entire time. You've heard me when I've talked about you in Japanese, my conversations with Ren, and, OH MY GOSH..." She shoots up "You know what was written on your cup that day the coffee spilled all over me!"

A wicked grin consumes my face. I'll never forget it. "Namie."

"God's blessing," we say simultaneously, her with a deep groan and me through a broad smirk.

"I appreciated that one," I admit. "I didn't, however, appreciate all the times you called me a stubborn jack—"

"Okay, Darcy." She looks down at her fingers, her light laughter laced with embarrassment. I can't get enough of the pink coating her light brown cheeks. Finally, she looks at me in all seriousness. "I get it. I've called you some ugly names in the heat of my irritation with you. I'm sorry for that."

"Don't worry." I lower my voice to a murmur as I lean closer to her. She stiffens as I place my lips to her ear. "I promise to only remember that I am God's blessing to you."

Hayden shoves me away, but I don't miss the way her lips are pressing together, fighting hard to not let a smile break through.

The chef returns to the grill wearing his tall, black hat and apron. Hayden and I straighten in our seats as he begins cooking rice, veggies, and various meats tossed in sauces I can't wait to shove into my mouth. While he cooks, Hayden slips her hand into mine and weaves our fingers together.

"Thank you for tonight." She leans her head on my shoulder, and my heart beats harder than the spatula on the grill in front of us. "I thought we wouldn't get to go on a real date for a long time."

I remove her hand from mine and slip my arm around her waist, tucking her as close to my side as I can while we sit in these stools. "No matter where this campaign goes, no matter how busy our lives become, I will *always* make time for you, my Divine Princess."

Hayden

Always. I like that word. It's full of promise and hope and secured dreams.

"I like time with you." I lean my head against his shoulder, but just to mess with him, I add, "We'd have more time if I moved into your room, you know. I love my room, but it's kind of haunted and lonely despite the vibrant colors."

"It was Ophelia's room."

I shoot up, meeting Darcy's eyes. "What?"

He smiles reminiscently. "My parents—or I—never had the heart to renovate it after she passed. She loved yellow."

Tears push against my eyes, but now is not the time. I don't know how to feel. I'm shocked he allowed me to stay there all this time. "Darcy, I—" I'm at a loss for words.

"It's okay," he says, rubbing circles on my lower back. "When I saw you in that room after I brought you inside when I accidentally caused you to spill coffee on yourself—sorry for that, by the way—" His smile is sheepish, and it's adorable. "Anyway, you looked like you belonged in it. An outward manifestation of who you are." I don't have the nerve to tell him I'm not as happy on the inside as I pretend to be on the outside, so I continue to stare in disbelief.

Finally, I find some words. "Thank you, Darcy. I know that couldn't have been easy for you."

He shrugs, but I can see the weight visibly lifting off his broad shoulders. Instead of searching for more vocabulary, I grab his face and speak my unsorted feelings through a kiss.

T he humid June air kinks my curls and adds a sheen of sparkle to my skin as my bare feet sift through the damp, warm sand. But Darcy's fingers entwined with mine steady me.

"Are you sure you don't want me to hold my shoes?" I ask, reaching for the black strappy stilettos dangling from his free hand, but he holds them out of reach. I'm nervous, and I can't exactly pinpoint why. Dinner was fantastic; the food, the conversation (once I found my words after he dropped the news I was staying in his sister's former room), and the environment were all ten out of ten. We finished up, I threw my napkin on top of my plate, and complained about a food baby. I thought that was the end of the night, but Darcy said we needed to walk off the food, which is why we are currently strolling down his private beach under the twinkling summer stars.

The romanticism of the night is settling in, and as silence between us stretches on while the light waves lap against the shore, I'm left wondering how this is real life.

I've always been the woman who has held her own. I know my worth, and I inherently do not believe any human is superior to another. But Darcy Marshall feels out of my league. And the more I remember I'm not only married in name to him but am actively dating him with real-feelings building within me, the more anxiety nips at my heels and claws at my throat.

He doesn't know my full story. He doesn't know that I watched a girl die and did nothing to save her. He doesn't know all of the almosts that have happened in my life. He doesn't know all of the things missing from my life.

"What's going on in that brilliant brain of yours?" Darcy's voice breaks through the night.

Should I tell him? Is now a good time? I trust him, so I should, right?

I settle on small steps.

"I don't know when my birthday is."

His tone is infected with confusion. "It's January 18th, right?"

"I celebrate on January 18th, but if I'm being honest, I'm not sure when my birthday is. My parents only left a note saying my name was Hayden Bennett when they left me in the basket on the steps of the group home. My birthday could be in December, or it could be earlier in January." I squirm a little, uncomfortable with this wee bit of information I'm granting him. When he realizes he married a woman who had to pick her own birthday, will he bolt? "I chose January 18th to celebrate. It just seemed as good a date as any."

Surprisingly, he's quick to respond. "A winter birthday doesn't fit you. You are warm like summer. Should we celebrate this month instead?"

I stop in my tracks, struck by his statement. He meets my gaze, eyes widening as if asking what he did wrong. The innocence and sincerity painting his face throw me over the edge in laughter. "I appreciate the compliment, but I've spent twenty-nine years celebrating on January 18th, so I think I'll keep it." What is he thinking to suggest I change my birthday based on the season he associates me with?

"What's so funny?"

"You want to change my birthday," I choke out between laughs.

Darcy wraps his arms around me, dropping my shoes. As he draws me close to him, the sound of my laughter fades into the sea. He kisses me once on the forehead, and I realize I'll never tire of the warmth of his lips against my skin. "Well, at least your birth brings warm comfort to the longest winter."

I light up. I shine like the sun rays he believes I emit.

Terror rises as I fully understand one thing: I'm in love with my for-convenience husband.

I place my hands on either side of his face, standing on my tiptoes and dragging his lips down to mine, confessing all the things I don't have the nerve or boldness to say because I've never had something I so desperately wanted to keep.

For once since my childhood, I'm filled with fear.

But I let him press his lips to mine anyway.

"We should probably head home," I state between breathless kisses. "We have to get up early to head to Mississippi."

He groans, throwing his head back and running a hand through his tousled hair. He looks angelic under this moonlight. "I'm not ready for our night alone to end."

A thrill shoots through me. *There's so much we can do...*

But I need to get over my fear first. And I have to talk to him about my past.

"We can cuddle and watch a show together when we get back if you want." I hope he says yes because, if he's going to stay married to me for the long-haul, he will have to watch my favorite show with me at least once.

He eyes me warily. "What are we watching?"

"My favorite show."

CHAPTER TWENTY-TWO

HAYDEN

O nce again, I find myself awake at an unholy hour. And again, I'll be running on a few hours of sleep. But this time it's okay, because in less than ten hours, I will be face-to-face with my best friend.

And the reason for the immense lack of sleep?

Totally worth it.

We ended up devouring three episodes of *My Hero Academia* because Darcy kept asking me for details regarding what happens next. While he wasn't a fan of me comparing him to the explosive, grouchy, hot-headed Bakugou, he still seemed to enjoy the setup of the show. Maybe I'll get him to watch more.

It can become our show.

The thought consumes me: him and I rewatching the show for the umpteenth time, introducing it to our kids...

Oof. There's an image I shove away as I reach for a pair of linen pants.

After getting dressed, chowing down a protein bar for breakfast, and double checking our luggage, Darcy and I head out the door, into the transport car, and toward the airport. Once we arrive, we are escorted to the private plane that will take us to Mississippi. The flight is uneventful. Darcy is nose-deep in contracts and paperwork while I'm going over the event schedule and collaborating on plans with the other heads of the departments on the campaign team via a video call platform.

Finally, we land at the airport in Jackson and are escorted through the airport by the security team and into another transport car. After only minutes of driving, we arrive at the hotel and go straight to our room.

I unlock the door while Darcy takes a phone call behind me, and when I open the room, a smell I'm all too familiar with from my days escaping to the streets penetrates my airways. With my gag reflex triggered, I bolt from the open doorway and run down the hallway to find fresh air.

"Hayden, where are you..." Darcy doesn't finish his sentence, opting instead to join me at my gagging party down the hallway. "What the—" *Cough.* "Heck—" *Cough. Cough.* "Is that smell?"

"Weed."

I wave my hand in front of my nose, trying to clear every molecule of the stench. Darcy side-eyes me and raises an eyebrow.

"And how are you familiar with that smell?"

"Orphan, remember? I spent time walking the streets to escape the group home and the awful foster homes I ended up in. I tried weed once, but I swear I never did it again. I didn't like the effects, and I honestly couldn't stand the smell. It reminded me of people

peeing on the streets and injecting themselves with harder drugs."
I shudder, remembering *that* night when a needle fell into the
wrong hands.

But see? I'm opening up. Little by little.

Waiting for him to realize I might not be First Lady material.

Darcy doesn't respond, but his expression softens, almost as if
he understands. But how could he? He's been rich and protected
his entire life, which is why my status does not belong in the same
category as his, regardless of how I try to trick myself into believing
it does.

*No, Hayden. No human is better than another. Especially not
because of pasts.* It's as if I can hear the Lord's voice in my soul,
reminding me of that simple truth. I try my best to believe it.

"We will get a new room." He walks away, bringing his phone
back to his ear.

I slap my face. I really hope whoever was on the other end of
that call didn't hear a word I just said. It's not that I'm ashamed of
my past. In fact, I want to learn how to use it better, to advocate
for change and reform. I want to learn how to tell my story like so
many others do. I have to be ready, though.

And it has to wait until I secure the presidency for my candidate.
My husband. And he needs to know everything before the world
does.

Speaking of Darcy, he motions from the elevator for me to
follow him, so I plug my nose to walk past the weed room again and
join him right as the elevator dings open. After we step in, I have
the briefest thought of what an elevator kiss would be like. The
books and movies say it's exhilarating, wild, and passionate, but I

doubt I'll ever get to be alone with Darcy on an elevator because agents guard us 24-7 when we are away from Ophelia Estate. I bet it would be one hot kiss though...

Heat creeps up my face at the thought, and I turn away from Darcy so he won't notice. I fan myself lightly, which captures his attention.

Covering the microphone on his phone, he whispers, "Are you hot?"

I wink and mouth back, "Hot for you."

His pale skin turns a brilliant red as he eyes his agents standing in front of us before returning to finish his call.

We reach the lobby, and Darcy marches us to the front desk. He informs them of the situation and requests a new room. His tone is not unfriendly, but it's not what I would call warm, either. It's his stoicism that gets in the way. His autism. I bet he would make tons of friends if he simply learned to smile and inflect his voice when talking with people, but then again, who he is has grown on me like a thorn on a rose.

He does it well—the friendly masking—at rallies and dinner parties and during interviews. But away from cameras? The man acts like his life was made of lemons and sour candies.

Good thing I like sour. A grin stretches across my face as I fold my arms, looking my husband over. *What if?* What if we could really turn to the same page for once and crawl into the lines between the words that are black and white? What if he let me into the depths of his being, to a place he doesn't fully understand? The peeks I get have me on my knees begging for more.

Because the more I watch him and listen to what he isn't saying, the more I grow to appreciate him for who he is. Sour and all.

What if I open my cages and allowed him in to the dark undulating beneath the surfaces of my sunshine?

"Here." Darcy extends a room key card to me, effectively breaking me from my thought-trance. "It's not a nice suite like we had, but it will do."

I take the key. "Anything is better than that awful smell."

The receptionist profusely apologizes to me, but Darcy cuts her off. "It's okay. We will be on our way now."

"I plan to vote for you," she hollers after us in a southern accent.

"Thank you for your vote and support." I wave to her before Darcy grabs my arm and hauls me toward the elevator. The thought of the elevator brings back the former thoughts of kissing him, but security files in and I contemplate how to get him alone on this thing by the end of the night.

We take the elevator up to the new room, which isn't on the top floor like the other one. With hesitancy, I swipe the key card and nudge the door open.

Sweet, deliciously clean air.

Security stops me and says they should check the room out first and apologizes for not doing so before. I think it's a bit much, but whatever makes them feel better. Within seconds, they come back out and give us an all-clear.

I enter the room. Darcy follows behind me. And we both stop once we see the entirety of the room: one queen bed, a sofa chair, and a desk.

That's it.

Darcy swallows beside me, and I can't bring myself to look at him. My face must look sunburnt; it's blazing hot.

Because Darcy and I will be sharing a bed tonight.

It's the first time we've stayed in a hotel together since we've confessed to wanting to try this relationship out for real.

And since we've started dating, the images curated inside my head are not PG-13.

And since we're technically married, I wonder if I'll be able to control this wild desire like I desperately need to do.

Lord, give me strength not to jump my husband's bones.

"I can sleep on the floor," Darcy says. I finally look at him.

"No, you need to rest. You have the rally tomorrow. I'll take the floor."

He raises his dark blond eyebrows. "I can't let my wife sleep on the floor."

Simple words, but they wrap me in an electric hug. "And I can't let you sleep on the floor, Mr. Future President."

Darcy smiles. "Hmm. I like that nickname better than Killjoy."

"That was a one-time reprieve, Killjoy. But seriously, I can probably curl up on the sofa chair and wake up without a crick in my neck."

His blue eyes trace me from head to toe, and the electricity in the air hums. "You may be smaller than me, but you're still tall. Not to mention, you *are* a princess. A divine one, at that." He winks, and I get the feeling I am a mouse caught in a trap.

Darcy is toying with me. Flirting with me.

Like foreplay before a wild night of consummate passion.

I can't stop myself from eating this moment up, though I know I should douse the blue fire in his eyes with a bucket of water. "We are grown adults who can share a bed for a night. I'll build my own uncrossable thirty-eighth parallel line. You put so much as a finger across it, you will become a prisoner of the Republic of Hayden." I wrap my hands around his wrists.

He looks down at my hands holding his wrists, then snaps his eyes back to me. I swear, they are hungry.

"And if I want to be your prisoner?"

Oh. My. Goodness.

"Then cross the line." I bite my bottom lip, lifting my face to him in challenge.

Without hesitation, he takes back his hands and wraps one arm around my waist, tugging at my braid with the other. He angles me, claiming my mouth with a reverent passion that has me wanting to hit my knees in praise over this handsome, wonderful, delicious man of mine. He tastes like peppermint from the gum he was chewing earlier, and I want more. I deepen the kiss as I bring my hands to rest against his chest, shoving him to the bed.

I crawl on top of his lap, snaking my arms around his neck and gluing myself to him as I lose all my sensibilities at the trace of his tongue against my lips.

Darcy's phone rings out, and I have half the mind to pick it up and throw it against the wall. We part, breathless and heaving. His lips carry a faint trace of my pink gloss, and a smug joy blossoms at the sight of it. Never taking his smoldering gaze off of me, he answers the phone. "Darcy Marshall."

The man on the other end of the line is loud enough to know I've got to crawl off Darcy's lap to allow him to take this call. He stands in front of me, tucking a stray strand of hair behind my ear and kissing my forehead as he so often tenderly does before leaving the room.

In his absence, my head clears, and I feel remorse knowing that if he hadn't gotten that call, I don't think we would have stopped.

When he comes back, we have to draw a line for the night. There are still so many things we need to talk through before we decide to make our marriage real. All the things we didn't touch with a thirty-nine and a half foot pole prior to the signatures and the ceremony.

I take advantage of his absence to shower, make sure I'm completely presentable for the night, and to claim my side of the bed. After doing all that, I lay on the firm mattress and do some work on my laptop while I watch the hours tick by, waiting for Darcy to come back through that door. He never returned after his phone call, but I help make his schedules, so I know he is having a one-on-one dinner with the governor tonight.

But when he still hasn't returned by eleven p.m., I call his phone. It goes straight to voicemail. Worry begins to set in. I call Darcy's personal assistant, Bennie, and thankfully, he answers and tells me that Darcy is still at the governor's place.

Knowing he's safe, sleep tempts me, and I doze off, snuggled in my blankets and leaned against my pillow-made thirty-eighth parallel, imagining I'm wrapped in strong arms and tucked against a lean body I've come to love.

CHAPTER TWENTY-THREE

DARCY

A side-sleeper, I see.

She has one leg thrown over a pillow with her hands tucked underneath her face. The way her curls are loose and unkept, sprawled across the pillow, remind me of a lion. Her pink lips, illuminated by the moonlight pouring in through the window, are slightly parted. Her breaths even.

Hayden looks peaceful.

Beautiful.

I lightly touch her perfect lips. Soft and supple. Kissable.

Reminding me of that mind-blowing kiss earlier and tempting me to wake her up to try and reenact it.

Feeling more like a creeper than ever before, I yank my hand away from her lips. She stirs this time, and I freeze in place.

Hayden grumbles, then says, "Killjoy?"

"It's me, Divine Princess. Just getting ready for bed."

"What time is it?" Her sleepy voice has me going weak for some reason. No, it must just be the after-effect from touching her lips and reliving that kiss over and over all throughout dinner with the governor.

"It's midnight." My voice is deep and gruff. I've got to shove away the thought of kissing her. Especially since I'm going to crawl into this bed with her shortly and we aren't ready for *that*. She needs to know the truth about my past and accept me before I can go *there* with her. Because if she rejects me after *that*, I might die.

"Glad you're back safely." She yawns. "How was the meeting?"

"Close your eyes or look away." Hayden looks at me first—why do people do that?—but then turns to face the opposite side of the room. I unbutton my shirt and take it off, tossing it over the sofa chair. "He invited other state officials, so it went longer than planned, but overall, it was productive."

"Hmm." She already sounds like she's headed for sleep.

I finish tugging my pants off and quickly change into pajama pants and a t-shirt. "I'm decent." She turns around to face me again, and I'm awestruck by the gorgeous woman highlighted by the moon. But I'll never sleep if there's light in here. "Do you mind if I shut the curtains? I have a difficult time sleeping if it's not pitch black."

She nods her head, and I walk around the bed to pull the curtains closed then slide into bed, extra careful not to take down the pillows between us because as much as I want to hold her in my arms, that's a dangerous game to play while her kiss replays on a loop. It's a snug fit, but I'll manage.

"Darcy?"

The way she says my name...

I clench my fists and close my eyes before answering. "Yes?"

She swallows. "What if, for tonight only, we did what real married couples do?"

My eyes fly open as heat pools in my stomach, my body desiring hers but my mind knowing it's not time. "You want to do what?"

Hayden bolts upward and waves her hand. "No. NO! I didn't mean—not *that*. Gosh, no, Killjoy. I just meant... forget it." She collapses back down to the bed with a grunt, then grabs a pillow and holds it over her face.

I sit down on the side of the bed and take the pillow from her. Curiosity gets the best of me, and while my heart rate works on slowing from my initial perception—which scared me and excited me all at once—I ask her, "What did you mean?"

She groans in embarrassment and wrestles the pillow away from me. She shoves it back over her face, then says something that comes across as mumbles.

"I can't understand what you're saying."

Hayden removes the pillow then sighs. "I was wondering if we could cuddle tonight. I think I would sleep better knowing I wasn't alone in this hotel room. It's a logical next step when dating your spouse, right?"

"I'm right here. You're not alone."

She sighs again. "I know. It's different to feel you, though."

I desperately want to throw these pillows between us to high-heaven, but Hayden and I can't risk slipping up even though we're married. Not if there is still the question of her leaving after I tell her about my past.

But there's something else, too.

And it's embarrassing.

"Yes, it's a good next step, but, I, um—"

"Forget it," she interrupts.

"No. It's just that," I take a deep breath, preparing for the awkwardness of my next statement. "I've never cuddled with anyone before."

She sits up, and I assume she's looking at me, but I can't see anything in this blackness. "Wait, really?"

I let out my breath. "Besides with my mother when I was young, no."

"Have you ever been romantically involved with another woman at all?"

"I was engaged to Priscilla." I run my hand through my hair. "We held hands. Kissed on the cheek and small kisses on the lips. But we never cuddled, or kissed deeper, or slept in the same bed."

Hayden sits in the silence with me, and I continue to reflect over my relationship with Priscilla. I never felt anything toward her. She was a friend. I trusted her. Much like how I feel about Hayden.

Well, felt. There are much stronger emotions coursing through my veins these days.

"I can teach you," Hayden finally says. Her hand finds mine, and I decide it's now or never. A hand has never felt as good as hers feels resting on top of mine. She's not going to mock me for my lack of relationship knowledge. She's taught me about proper dating, and now she's going to teach me how to hug her body close so that she feels safe and secure in my arms.

"Okay." I lay down and turn to face her, but instead I face a wall of pillows. "We may need to move—"

"Yeah, on it," Hayden says, already in the process of knocking down the thirty-eighth parallel.

This feels right. Hayden is the warm, open South Korea and I'm the dark, closed-off North Korea. But somehow, despite our outward differences, we share the same language and are working on merging our regional dialects.

This is more than passionate kisses. It's more than dates that end in separate beds. This is falling asleep and waking up next to each other. It's seeing one another in our most vulnerable forms.

"Okay, lay on your back and put your arm out."

She lifts her head, and I tuck my arm underneath her. She curls her body against mine and lays a hand on my chest. Can she feel my heart beating? "This is the simplest form of cuddling for you. You get to lay there and let your arm go to sleep."

The smile that stretches across my face is one of pure, genuine happiness. I could stay like this forever.

I wish I could see her, but the darkness is just what I wanted—pitch black. If I could see her, I would lose myself in her dark brown eyes. I'd kiss her temple and then trail my lips down her high cheekbone. I'd kiss the corner of her mouth before parting her lips with my—

A shiver runs down my body, and I push those thoughts far, far away.

Hayden pulls herself closer to me. "Are you cold?"

My voice is dark as I answer with a coarse no.

She wiggles against me, and I bite my lip to stop from groaning while she replies, "Don't worry. I'm too tired to try to steal your virtue tonight."

I risk the question because my head is mush with her body flush against mine. "What if I want to give you my virtue?"

Silence stretches on long enough for me to doubt asking that, but finally, she says in a low whisper, "Darcy, I don't know if I'm truly what you need. My past... It's unpleasant."

I turn to face her, making sure my arm remains under her neck. We're now face to face, and her minty breath washes over me.

She smells divine...

I shake the thought of pressing my lips to hers. "What do you mean? I know you were an orphan and in the foster care system. I know you spent some time on the streets. I know you've tried weed."

"That's not everything, Killjoy." She laughs and pats my chest with the hand that is resting there. I bring my free hand and hold hers on top of my chest. "Trust me. You'd divorce me if you knew the whole story."

Small red flags begin to rise, but I don't want to ruin this like I have in the past. Instead of assuming what Hayden needs to say, assigning her motive, and running away, I will hear her out. "Try me."

She's quiet for a moment, and I squeeze her hand, reminding her that I'm here.

"Not tonight," she finally says. "We should get some sleep."

She uncurls from me and rolls to her side of the bed. I want desperately to reach out and pull her back in, but something in her voice—something raw and broken—stops me. I can't make her say things she isn't ready to say, but the curiosity is burning me alive.

What do I not know about her? I ran a background check. I know she went to juvie when she was a kid for getting into a physical altercation with another kid. I know she has had issues with anger management in the past.

But doesn't she realize it's all in the past?

That we all have dark blemishes? Including me?

"You aren't your past, Hayden."

No response. Maybe she's asleep already, but I doubt she is.

"In fact, it's because of your history that you are the bright, intelligent, hardworking, sweet, trustworthy, and passionate woman that you are today. Don't let the rotting corpses of the past steal the liveliness of your present."

Her shoulders move up and down, and I swear I hear a sniffle, but she still doesn't respond or make any motion to face me.

I continue to face her and close my eyes. Right as I am drifting off to sleep, I hear through her muffled cries, "But she died because of me."

Halfway out of consciousness, I tug Hayden to my chest and hold her close as I fall asleep, hoping she can feel how much she means to me.

CHAPTER TWENTY-FOUR

HAYDEN

I stare at my reflection in the mirror, and memories from last night come rushing back. The kind words he said to me as I pretended to sleep while tears ran down my cheeks at the thought of that long ago night where I watched a young girl die because of me. The way Darcy held me close felt like I was wrapped in a never-ending warm hug.

Memories resurface of not too long ago: waking up with his arms still wrapped around me, the way his face was centimeters from my own. He was the first thing I saw this morning, and I loved the sight of his tousled hair, relaxed features, and steady breaths more than I should have.

I pin a loose curl back into my bun before smoothing down my peplum shirt and exiting the bathroom of the campaign headquarters in Mississippi.

"Hey, bestie." Stella bounces to my side. "Did you have a good night in your weed-free hotel room? And are you reliving it? Because you have a wondrous blush tinting your face."

I cut my eyes to Stella, but I can't lie to her.

"We cuddled, and he said sweet things."

"Ugh, way to leave a woman wanting more," she jests. But then her tone grows serious. "I'm so glad the two of you are like a real thing now."

I can't fight the grin. "Me too." But then that malicious voice pops in my head, telling me I'm not enough for him.

"Stella." I grab Stella's arm and drag her outside the Jackson Campaign Headquarters. "Stella, I don't know how to tell him about *her*."

She knits her brown brows together. "Why don't you just start with the truth of that night? That it was not your fault."

Guilt consumes me regardless of her words, and my legs wobble. Stella catches me before I completely collapse to the ground.

She holds me tight. "You did not kill that girl, Hayden. It wasn't your fault. You didn't put the needle in her hand. You didn't tell her to inject herself."

Tears burst through my eyes as I lose all composure. "She died in front of me. I didn't do anything to help her. I distracted the man she was with. If I hadn't distracted the man and caused him to chase after me, she would have been okay. He would have been watching her and would have stopped her. I could have stopped her. I ran away."

Stella ushers me somewhere, but I can't see anything through the onslaught of tears. The heat dissipates, so I assume we are back inside. She ushers me down into a chair, and I rest my elbows on my knees and let my head fall into my open hands.

"I saw reporters," she says swiftly. "Now, look at me."

After a moment, I look up.

"You were a child. Only nine years old." Stella cups my face. "It's not the duty of a child to save the world from darkness. We've been over this, H."

"I know." I sniffle. "But the possibility of something real with Darcy? It scares me, Stella. I want it..." sniffle, "so bad. But it scares me. Once he knows what happened, will he look at me the same way anymore?"

"You're the only one who looks at you differently."

"But—"

"No more 'buts', Hayden." Stella pulls me to my feet. "Don't be scared. He will not look at you any differently." I wipe tears from my eyes. "What if he tells the world? What if I'm barred from ever becoming Secretary of State like I want?"

"Do you really think he is that kind of person?"

No. "I don't know."

Stella sighs, and I refuse to meet her eyes.

"Is everything okay?" Darcy's voice freezes me. Did he hear any of that?

Stella steps around me, and I keep my back turned to them. He doesn't need to see the mascara presumably running down my face and my blood-shot eyes.

After a few moments of exchanged whispers, Stella walks over to me, takes my arm, and says, "Let's go get you cleaned up."

Ten minutes in the bathroom with Stella and I emerge looking like I didn't have a meltdown over my past.

We all sit in a conference room discussing polling data with the locals who are in charge of running the campaign in Mississippi.

Stella sits on one side of me and Darcy sits on the other. Lucas ditched the meeting and went man-shopping at the Bass Pro Shop, which Stella tells me is like redneck heaven.

While my colleagues drone on, I can't keep my thoughts away from the man beside me. It's barely noticeable, but his chair and body are angled toward me. He keeps sneaking glances, and they are laced with concern, which drives my rumination cycle back to wondering if he overheard me crying to Stella. He is so close to me that if I wanted to, I could move my hand a couple of inches and I would be holding his hand underneath the conference table.

My hand twitches at the thought, and I relocate it to my lap, clasped with my other hand.

But then he grabs my hand and stands up. I involuntarily stand up with him.

"My wife and I have plans tonight. We are in need of a break from campaign talk." He chuckles, wearing that easy-going smile that makes the world fall in love with him. I think I prefer the one he reserves strictly for me when we are alone. The world would keel over if he showed it to them. It's magnificent.

I smile beside him and nod along, ready for our dinner plans with Stella and Lucas.

The core team (plus Stella) say our goodbyes and file into the transport car. The drive back to the hotel is filled with more campaign talk and plans, and I lose myself in the familiar rhythm of work.

Once we're back at the hotel, I feel more like myself. My thoughts are on track, and I'm focused on the task at hand: getting

Darcy elected as president. We can talk about where our relationship goes once he's sitting in the Oval Office.

And until then, I'll date the heck out of that man.

"Go ahead and head up to the room. I need to make a phone call, and I'll meet you there," Darcy says, already walking away and raising the phone to his ear. I allow myself to watch his hips sway in his dress pants for a millisecond before turning around and pressing the elevator button.

Once I'm inside, I throw myself down on the bed and just take a moment to breathe.

Minutes later, there's a knock at the door. "Are you decent?" Darcy asks through a crack in the door.

"Yes," I reply, sitting up on the bed. "Come in."

Darcy slips through the door and fiddles with his necktie as he asks, "Remember when Loveless leaked our arrangement in order to sabotage the campaign?"

"Yes?" I narrow my eyes. I thought we had taken care of that.

He pulls his tie from one end and it falls to the floor. "He's back at it again, but this time, he's airing my father's dirty laundry. Stuff the general population didn't already know." Darcy laughs without mirth. "This time he might actually do some real damage."

I grab my phone and search Darcy's dad's name, Gerald Marshall.

Articles pop up with sordid details of affairs from his past. Women claim Gerald took advantage of them and used his power and prestige to coerce them into bed.

"This isn't good, Darcy."

He's silent, and I continue to scroll, stopping when I see my name: IS DARCY A REPLICA OF HIS FATHER? DID HE BUY-OUT HIS CAMPAIGN MANAGER-TURNED-WIFE, HAYDEN BENNETT?

"Oh, Darcy. This is *really* bad." I show him the article, my stomach twisting into knots. "I can make a statement. Maybe we can come clean about how we began, and—" An idea forms, and I stand, grabbing my phone from Darcy's hand and maneuvering to my bank app. "The money you paid me the first couple of months before I asked you to stop because we started dating. It didn't go straight into my bank account. It went into a private account owned by me, yes, but if we add your name to it, we can say it's a savings account for our future children. I'll add some of my earnings to it too, to say we both contributed."

He remains silent, though I can tell by his pinched brows and the wrinkles around his eyes that he's deep in thought.

Finally, he says, "Yes. That could work. But only if we have to. Let's see what we can do to negate my father's image tainting mine, first. If we have to come clean about the initial arrangement, then we will. If we don't though, I'd rather not fight that battle. Politicians marry for convenience all of the time. This isn't something new."

I nod, onboard with his plan. The fear that's been building settles because I know Darcy's got this. His record is too clean, his ideas too good, and his character too solid for this accusation to hold any real weight. Plus, we've busted Loveless once, so hopefully public opinion will land on our side.

"People do believe us to be hopelessly in love. Let's continue to act like it."

Darcy digs through his luggage and grabs a yellow button-up shirt. "We'll figure it out. I've got the best team." He unbuttons the top two buttons of his shirt. "And the best campaign manager-slash-wife." Then the third...and fourth.

"Darcy!" I spin around and wonder where my breath went because it's obviously no longer in my body. The sight of his rippled chest, however, is burned into my brain... right alongside the image of him naked in the hospital, which is making a reappearance.

And kissing me until my bones turned to sludge on this bed yesterday.

"I'm only changing my shirt." I can hear the proud smirk he's donning. "Done."

I don't risk turning around. "Can I have some privacy to change, then?"

"I'll be back in...thirty-five minutes." The door opens then closes. But it cracks open once more, and his sharp face fills the doorway. "And Hayden, I don't have to act like I'm in love with you." The door clicks shut.

Words catch in my throat as he disappears. Was that—? Did he—? *Love?*

I forget about Loveless and accusations and Darcy's father.

Darcy Marshall basically said he loved me.

Taking in a huge breath, I plop back down on the bed and wonder where (and when) in the world Darcy Marshall found the audacity to take my breath away. How did we get here? How did he make me fall in love with him in the span of a few months?

He's so much more than the hard, cold exterior he presents to most people. He's more than the media mask he wears for interviews, rallies, events, and dinners. He's a bundle of juxtapositions: warm and cool, worried and confident, sensitive and dominant.

A perfectly imperfect man.

I change into a short, white dress with lace that I know he'll love.

He knocks on the door exactly when he said he would, and I invite him in like it isn't the room we are sharing.

Darcy opens the door, holding a bouquet of yellow roses. "For you," he says, and I take the flowers, sniff the pleasant smell once, and then place them on the bed.

My heart beats wildly, and I'm dying to ask him if he meant he loves me. I also want to scream that I love him, but the only words on my tongue are, "You should wear yellow more often." Because my word, the man looks like sunshine. The lemon-yellow shirt and his golden blond hair light up his blue eyes. He emanates light instead of his usual shades of gray.

"You look rather good in the dress." I stifle a laugh at his compliment. His flirting game may be strong when it's rolling off his tongue in the heat of the moment, but when he's trying to flirt, it's too controlled and stiff.

"Thank you."

He takes my hand, and we walk to the elevator. I look around, and his agents are nowhere to be seen.

"Where's security?"

"They're around. I asked for privacy."

The elevator door dings open, and I swallow the rising lump in my throat. We step on. His hand tightens around mine. Is he fighting the wicked tension I feel too? Thoughts of spicy elevator kisses speed through my mind, and in each of the scenarios, Darcy and I are the lead actors.

The door shuts.

Before I have the opportunity to ask him my burning question, Darcy pins me against the wall, where the feel of the cool metal seeps through the light silky fabric of my dress, the lace around the edges pressing into my skin. One large hand grabs both of my wrists, and he drags them above my head as my breaths become labored in anticipation. *Just like every fantasy...*

His fingers trail up my side as I wiggle against him because of the thrilling sensation. Our eyes lock. His blue irises are dark with desire just as his touch sets me aflame. He slips his hand behind my neck and peppers me with kisses along my jaw. Each press of his lips and slip of his tongue along my skin is like a crashing wave of need, and I want so much more. Giving myself over to the tingly sensation, my eyes flutter closed.

"Kiss me," I beg. *I love you.*

His body rumbles against me as his lips trail to the other side of my jaw. My ear. "Later, Princess."

Darcy nips at the lobe of my ear before releasing one of my hands and intertwining his fingers with my other hand, moving to stand by my side.

The elevator comes to a stop, the doors open, and the cool lobby air flows over us and washes away the passion as if nothing happened. His hand loosens around mine, but he doesn't let go.

We spot Stella and Lucas standing near a small, cherubim fountain in the middle of the lobby, and she waves us over.

"Ready for—" she trails off, taking in what I imagine to be the expression of a lovesick, thoroughly kissed woman. She laughs and arches her brow. "Should we postpone and you two head back up to the room?"

Darcy, to my surprise, shrugs, wearing an impish grin. *It makes me almost want to say yes...*

But I only have this little sliver of time with my bestie, and I want to take every moment I can get before we fly out tomorrow.

"Get your head out of the gutter, Stella."

Lucas chimes in, his twang thick. "I like her head in the gutter."

CHAPTER TWENTY-FIVE

DARCY

I love you.

I love you.

I am so freaking in love with you, Hayden.

Sweat trickles down my back, my legs, my unmentionables... It's almost enough to persuade me to trade my suit and tie in for shorts and a tank top.

Though I doubt anyone would want to see my pasty skin on full display like that. I'd outshine the Fourth of July fireworks display happening in a few hours here in D.C. On top of that, it's not socially acceptable to wear shorts and a tank top to a charity ball.

And I'd like to look nice when I tell my wife I'm enamored with her soul tonight.

"If you ever work up the courage," I mutter to myself. Because telling her I love her means telling her *everything*. Over the past two weeks, I've thought long and hard about fully committing to our marriage, and, well, I'm ready.

I want her to be mine in every single sense of the word. I could lose this campaign and my business could go under, but I wouldn't bat an eye as long as I have Hayden to shower sunshine on my dreariest days.

Every date, every lingering kiss, every shared little secret...

The woman carries her ghosts like weightless tethered beings whereas I carry mine like a bag of bricks. I want to take hers and cut the bond just as she's been unloading my bag one brick at a time.

"There you are." Hayden slides her arm around my waist, a gesture that simultaneously brings about feelings of peace and turmoil. Peace because she feels like home and turmoil because I was already burning alive, and her presence seems to raise the temperature a few more degrees.

I glance down at my beautiful wife and smile. She's wearing a long, fitted, red gown with a slit on one side that reaches just above her knee. Her long leg sticks out of the dress and her calf is accentuated by a strappy and sparkling silver stiletto heel.

"Eyes up here, Killjoy."

My eyes roam back up from her feet, her legs. I can't *not* notice the way the dress hugs her hips. It's sleeveless but completely covers her front and ties around her neck. Very classy.

Very sexy.

"I am unbelievably glad you are my wife," I say when I lock eyes with Hayden. Her smile is breathtaking.

"But we are only technically dating at this point." She winks. "So no handsy stuff or looking at me like you want to do married people stuff—and no, not the cuddling type. Too tempting."

I groan and clutch my chest, acting on dramatic tendencies that seem to come out when I'm with Hayden. "But we *are* legally married. And you look like, well, a divine princess tonight."

"You don't look too bad yourself." She slips her fingers through mine.

I roll my eyes. "What a compliment."

She chuckles and begins pulling me toward the entrance to the Fourth of July charity ball. The only reasons I agreed to make an appearance at this ball were because the donations will go to group homes, it will raise awareness for foster care reform, and many people are using my networking app, COFFEE, and I'd like to see how it plays out. I haven't gotten to interact with my app as much these days due to running for president, but it's doing as good as ever.

So here I am. Typically, I run far away from anything involving dancing.

And if I know Hayden, which I think I do by now, she will force me to dance.

It's not that I can't dance; it's that I don't like to dance.

But the gleam in her eyes as she turns to face me after we enter the ballroom says I'm not getting out of here tonight without at least one dance.

"Mr. Marshall, it's good to see you here. How's the campaign going?" An older man approaches me, and I faintly remember he is an oil tycoon.

Hayden whispers in my ear, "Harold Young."

"Mr. Young." I nod and shake his hand. Others approach Hayden and me, and we are immediately swept into a frenzy of introductions and small talk with familiar and unfamiliar faces. I ask about the app, people pull it up on their phones to show me their success rate with meeting new clients and discovering new partnerships for their businesses. My heart swells with pride, and I almost wish I could drop the race and dive back into my tech world and create more apps to connect people who are bad at connecting in real life like me.

Almost. I still believe this country needs me, and not because I'm me, but because I want to actually listen to the people and do what I can to help the weak, stimulate the economy, protect the country, and clean out the rats that have made D.C. their permanent home. I have the means, the status, and the power.

"Let's dance," Hayden demands as soon as we have a break in conversation with others. I groan, but I don't fight her.

"One. You get one dance."

Her eyes light up. "That's all I need."

I take her hand and lead her to the dance floor just as Art Galbraith's "4th of July Waltz" begins to play. Hayden places one hand on my shoulder as I set my hand on the small of her back. We clasp our other hands together, and I take the lead. Couples twirl around us, all moving in unison. It doesn't surprise me that Hayden dances this well, even with her background. She has fought hard to become the brilliant, classy woman that she is today. What is it that she always says? One can choose to be a victor or a victim...

"You are a great dancer," Hayden says.

"Would you expect anything less?"

"Who taught you how to dance?"

"My mother." I pause. "Do you make a habit of talking while you dance?"

Hayden smirks. "It would look odd if we stood together without speaking occasionally, don't you think? Especially since we are married."

"Hmm."

My hand is an ever-heating furnace against her back, and midway through the dance, I realize I have tugged her closer, and we are only inches apart. Her brown eyes bore into mine. *I love you... just say it.*

"You're supposed to look offset when waltzing," I say, swallowing a lump in my throat at her intense stare. The words are stuck; why can't I say it?

Hayden doesn't skip a beat with her response. "I have something much better to look at right now, so excuse me if I break the rules this once."

I pull her closer, our lips only breaths apart. Everyone in the room disappears except for the beautiful woman in my arms. We spin and glide across the floor, our eyes becoming doorways to our souls. I want to know absolutely everything there is to possibly know about this woman.

And then it dawns on me that I don't even know her middle name.

"What's your middle name?"

She gulps, shifting her eyes away from me and onto the red, white, and blue decorations. "I, uh... I don't have one."

I keep my facial expressions in check at her answer, though I'm not sure how someone ends up without a middle name.

"Mine is Fitzwilliam."

She laughs, then composes herself. So much for me keeping my reaction in check.

Rolling my eyes, I continue to lead her in the dance. "Yes, I know it is Darcy's first name from that ridiculous *Pride and Prejudice* story. My mother loved it."

"I know your middle name, Darcy, and I love it. I should make my middle name Elizabeth. Since she's the heroine. Then we could be all tied up in the story."

I try out the name on my tongue. "Hayden Elizabeth Bennett Marshall."

She sighs. "It's a mouthful."

"I like it," I say simply. "Elizabeth is a classy name, and the media would love it."

"I don't want to do something simply because the media will like it. It's a name. My name. It should mean something."

I contemplate for a moment. "Then what about the name Sarah?"

"Why Sarah?"

"It means 'princess.'"

The waltz comes to an end as I whisper against her ear, "Hayden Sarah Marshall. My divine princess."

We stop moving but remain standing in each other's arms. A small smile pulls at the corner of her lips. "I love it. And I'll keep it."

"Look at what the cat dragged in." My spine stiffens at Mr. Loveless's voice. Hayden's hand moves to rest gently on my lower back, grounding me.

I turn around and nod. "Mr. Loveless. Didn't expect to see you here tonight."

He chuckles. How can that menacing sound be considered a laugh? "Oh, I am swarmed with interviews, campaign stops, and events. But I could take one night off to attend a ball for such a... needy cause."

Needy? That's what raising awareness for foster care system reform and money for group homes means to him? Like he is a benefactor in aiding children he considers less than him? Though his words are innocent, it is his tone that implies the cause of this ball is a dirty plight of his existence.

My fists clench at my side. "Yes, well, I'm sure the parentless children will fall at your feet in gratitude over your presence and support here tonight."

His eyes widen, as if he is actually considering my words. "You think so?" He taps a man beside him on the shoulder. "That is a good photo opportunity, actually. Jot that down."

My stomach churns and blood boils at his selfish, narcissistic attitude. How could anyone in America vote for this cold-blooded reptile of a man?

Oh, yeah. Because he has the coveted "R" behind his name.

When will people learn Republican doesn't equal conservative?

"How is marriage treating you?" Mr. Loveless bounces his eyes from me to Hayden, his lips pulling to one side. I want to sucker punch his face. He's tried twice to disavow my marriage.

I grab my wife's waist and tuck her into my side, kissing her on the cheek, and a genuine smile sweeps my face. "It's the most wonderful thing to have happened to me."

Hayden uses her index and middle fingers to finger-walk up my chest. She rests her palm against my cheek. "This man is the world's best husband."

Mr. Loveless chuckles. "World's best, huh? I guess I better up my game."

"Love isn't a game," I whisper under my breath. Hayden isn't a game. She's real and intelligent and beautiful and I love her.

And I really need to tell her what she means to me. Even if I stumble all over the words.

I swallow, and then at a normal volume, say, "My wife and I need to make our rounds."

Mr. Loveless shakes my hand, pulls me toward him, and whispers loudly, "Yes, show off your Diversity Trophy."

Hayden stiffens at my side.

Evil incarnate leans away and lets go of my hand.

I use that hand to punch him square in the nose.

"We'll be lucky if he doesn't sue us, Darcy. There's no way we are getting out of this without the media twisting the event six different ways to Sunday!"

"Ow."

Hayden loosens the pressure she's applying to my own nose.

Turns out Mr. Loveless has a pretty mean right hook himself.

But I regret nothing.

"At least your man defended your honor, Hayden." Ren gives me two thumbs up, and I sigh.

"I didn't need him to defend my honor. I can do that myself, thank you very much. Plus, it doesn't matter what Loveless says. He doesn't know us. He only suspects our origins, which we've determined doesn't matter one bit because arranged marriages happen all the time in politics. We've done an excellent job at appearing in love to the public, right? Our ratings have never been higher."

"Right," Ren chimes in. "You have me fooled that the two of you aren't in love."

I glare at Ren, and then pull Hayden's hand off my nose. She looks like she needs to pace. As soon as I take over the process of stopping the bleeding, she kicks off her shoes and paces within the private bathroom she, Ren, and I are holed up in.

"We will tell the media what he said about us and all will be forgiven," I say, my voice muffled. I don't want to play the "racist" card, but what he said was uncalled for and disgusting.

Hayden laughs. "We would garnish enough support and attention that his career would be finished." She stops pacing at the far end of the bathroom and turns to face me and Ren. "But Darcy, I don't think I could do that to someone. No matter what they've done to me."

Now I laugh, and that action hurts my possibly-broken nose so badly that I want to cry. But I speak anyway. "Remember the dinner party where you almost beat up Priscilla?"

She rolls her eyes and then continues to pace. "Yes, well, that was an attack against you. Not against me and the color of my skin."

"So you will beat someone up for me, but you don't want me beating someone up for you?"

Hayden stops in front of me and drops to her knees, eye level with me. She places a hand on my shoulder, and I use my free hand to cover hers. Immediately, all pain seems to subside at the touching of our skin. I've enjoyed finding little ways to touch her since we officially started dating.

Hayden stares me in the eyes as she says, "You're important to me. I'm strong enough to defend you and support you."

I stare back and inch closer. "Hayden, I am strong enough to defend and support you, too. And while I appreciate the warrior on her knees in front of me, you have to know, my quiet exterior is only an exterior. No one will talk about my wife the way Loveless did tonight. The world will know that if they do, there will be consequences."

Hayden cups my cheeks, with tears forming in her eyes, and gently draws my lips to hers, avoiding any contact with my nose. Her lips are soft, sweet, and tender. She lingers as if she is unsure of what to do now, but for as long as I've known Hayden, she's never been unsure about a decision.

Coolness replaces the heat of her lips on mine when she pulls away, and I instinctively trace my lips with my thumb. That kiss was different than our quick hellos and goodbyes, than our passion-filled moments of aloneness. That kiss was tender and raw and full of love. I have to tell her. Tonight.

"Oh, shoot, your rag." Hayden picks up the bloody fabric from my lap, which I apparently dropped, and places it back on my nose with a bit too much pressure. I wince. "Oh, sorry."

"It's very much okay," I say, my mind still replaying her kiss. Her lips have become my new home, and I want to stay there every day for the rest of my existence.

A throat clears beside us, and we both slowly turn our heads to face Ren, who is standing with his arms crossed and a grin the size of Texas stretched across his face.

"Told you that you would fall in love with her," he mocks.

I'm silent because I can't agree to that right here with Hayden in front of me. I need her alone. I need to confess my demons and then confess my love if she still wants me.

Hayden stands up and smooths her dress down, her face transforming from concern to blankness. Her tone is all business. "I will let you get cleaned up. We will have to face the reporters outside at some point. Look presentable. Ren, will you help him?"

Ren nods and Hayden slips her shoes on and exits the bathroom.

Holding out his hand to help me up, Ren clicks his tongue. "Darcy-*kun*. What you just did will go down as the biggest mistake in history."

I grab his hand and hoist myself up. "I will not apologize for punching Mr. Loveless when he called my wife my diversity trophy."

Ren shakes his head. "No, I am not talking about that. I am talking about you remaining silent after I suggested you'd fall in love with her."

"I do love her, Ren. I've been working up the courage to tell her about Ophelia. If she doesn't bolt, I'll fall to my knees in relief and pour out my love. But I want the moment to be right."

Ren nods while a huge smile overtakes his face. He washes out the bloodied rag while I change into the new shirt he brought to the ball for me.

"I'm proud of you, Darcy-*kun*."

"For falling in love?"

"For letting someone in." Ren pauses, and then he says, "And there will never be a right time to tell her. Just do it."

POP CULTURE NOW!

FIREWORKS AREN'T THE ONLY THING POPPING OFF TONIGHT.
DARCY MARSHALL PUNCHES RICHARD LOVELESS OVER
COMMENT ABOUT HIS WIFE!

By Krissy Towers

Oh. My. Gosh. (Did you say that in Janice's voice like we did?) We have the tea for you tonight! I'm writing this article as I sit outside of the White House, reeling over what I witnessed between the Republican and Independent presidential candidates. When Darcy Marshall and Richard Loveless clashed tonight, it overshadowed the fireworks show put on in our nation's capital. Here's the scoop.

Darcy and Hayden were partaking in a beautifully executed waltz, and the heat they were emitting rivaled the heat of the balmy July night. We are talking touches and light kisses and a certain playfulness that can only be curated between two lovers (can you tell we are officially #TeamRealMarriage over here?). But then Richard Loveless approached the couple. You should have seen Darcy's shift in demeanor at his rival's company. The two exchanged words, ending with Darcy punching Richard in the nose.

Later, we found out the abhorrent words of Loveless. He had told Darcy to "show off his Diversity Trophy." We at *Pop Culture NOW!* condemn this type of speech and, quite frankly, understand exactly why Darcy stepped up to the plate in his wife's defense. We'd expect nothing less of our brooding-in-private, Austenian hero. As we all know, the two came clean that they arranged their marriage. They told us it's become very real, and by the looks of tonight, they meant every word. We are cheering them; are you? Let us know in the comments!

Check out the videos here, and remember to stay tuned for more cultural tea with a dash of politics.

CHAPTER TWENTY-SIX

DARCY

"I can't wait to be home and out of this wet heat." Hayden fans herself as we walk into the Waldorf Astoria in D. C. I only offer a grunt, my mind preoccupied by the sheer amount of homelessness and people hooked on drugs a few blocks over from this massive, expensive, luxurious place.

That's one of the reasons I need to win this election. I'm going to do everything in my power to aid the homeless and reform the system. I'm not naïve enough to think I can change every city, but I am going to do what I can and try to persuade those who have more localized authority to follow my lead.

I want to save all the little children of the world from picking up drug needles disguised as pens and accidentally sticking themselves with them like my sister did.

"Look, Darcy. It's Krissy Towers."

My head snaps in the direction that Hayden nudges me, and I see the blonde-haired woman dressed like a Barbie slinking toward us.

Hayden smiles and waves while I force my media mask into place. Hayden takes my hand and all is right in the world.

"Play nice," Hayden whispers in my ear.

"Mr. Marshall, Mrs. Marshall, it's so good to see you both. Last time we saw each other, you were telling the world you had found a woman. Little did we know it was your campaign manager. And the two of you arranged it." Krissy extends her hand, and I give it a brief shake before replying.

"Yes, well, we had kept it on the down-low due to not knowing how people would receive us, but once we knew it would be forever," I glance down at Hayden who is smiling up at me, "there was no reason to hide it. Political arrangements such as this happen all the time. Ours just happened to develop into so much more."

Krissy grins, but unlike last time all those months ago, it isn't forced and venomous. What is she after now?

"Since you two are here, do you have it in your schedule for a quick follow-up interview from March? Oh, the public would eat it up." True excitement lights her eyes, and I have to admit that she's right. It would be fantastic for my image, and with the election so close, it could be like a last-minute effort to persuade pop-culture fanatics to get out to vote for me.

But I also want to confess my love to my wife tonight.

And that's more important to me.

Hayden, however, speaks before I can deliver a kind dismissal. "You need to do this." She cuts her eyes to Krissy. "Give us an hour to prepare?"

Krissy nods. "Let's meet in the meeting room down the hallway from the lobby in an hour."

"Perfect," Hayden says, then she turns to me. "Let's go to our room first."

I bid Krissy farewell and follow my wife to the elevator.

Once we are inside the elevator, I press my back against the cold wall and cover my face with my hands. "Hayden. Talking to a snake wasn't on my to-do list tonight."

Hayden steps up beside me and kisses me on the cheek. Nerve endings explode as her lips touch my skin. "This will be good. Maybe it will secure a good opinion of our marriage from those who still have qualms from Loveless's attacks. Plus, she's written pretty decent things about us lately."

"She might ask me about punching him earlier tonight."

Hayden shrugs. "Just repeat our statement that we said at the ball before we left. You'll be fine." She leans in for a kiss, but the elevator dings and the doors open.

Hayden slips out of my embrace and stands close to my side as a few people enter the elevator, giving us looks—one younger guy is smirking, one older lady is scowling, and one kid giggles.

I release a breath and catch Hayden's movements from my peripheral vision. She covers her mouth with her hands, her shoulders slightly moving up and down like she's laughing.

We ride up in silence, stopping to let the others off, but the old lady remains with us until we get to the top floor.

Once we are inside our room, she begins styling me for the impromptu interview and peppering me with questions such as what is her favorite color, her favorite food, her favorite show, etc.

I shrug my black suit jacket on while she fiddles with my red tie. "Yellow, ramen, and *My Hero Academia*. Why do I need to prove I know these things about you?"

"Because," she exclaims, patting me on the chest. "This is a pop culture interview, and she will probably test our story. A married couple should know these things about each other."

"Those were easy," I reply, pulling her into a hug. "Try harder questions."

She hums. "Okay, what is my greatest fear?"

I give it some thought and think about her past: She was left in a basket on the steps of a group home in New York City, was in and out of foster homes until she was old enough to age out, and while she was in the system, she ran with the wrong crowds at times.

"Being on the street again?"

She shakes her head and looks up at me. Her eyes are warm like melted chocolate. "My biggest fear is being abandoned by people I love."

My heart cracks, and I squish her against my body. "I won't leave you. Mother won't leave you. Stella will never leave you. Heck, I'm pretty sure Ren will always stay by your side. You have so many people who care about you, Hayden. We will not abandon you. We will stay. I will stay."

She sniffles into my jacket, and I try not to think of snot getting on it. I love this woman, but I also *really* like my suits.

But, of course, she can blow her nose into it and I'd let her. Love does that to people, it seems.

"Thank you, Darcy. I–I never dreamed I would have so many people in my corner. Much less someone like you."

I squeeze her tighter, and she cries onto my shoulder.

I want to tell her everything right now, but I have to wait until after the interview because I'm fairly certain I will die a painful death if she leaves me after I tell her the truth of Ophelia.

After a moment, she straightens and pulls away. I don't let her go, but I do give her a little of the space she is clearly wanting. With one last sniffle, she says, "I need to tell you something, Darcy."

"What is it?"

"I—I think I was an unofficial accomplice in the death of a child."

My body stiffens at the statement, the words "death of a child" have my mind to spiral down memory holes involving Ophelia and dark streets and drug needles.

"I'm listening," I say, prompting her on. "Nothing will change my mind about you. Once I set my mind to something—to someone—I don't go back."

"You might retract that statement soon," she mumbles. Hayden wipes her eyes with the backs of her hands, black mascara smearing across her face. She takes a deep, steadying breath, and I rub circles on her biceps with my thumbs.

"When I was nine, I ran away from the group home I was living in. I was upset and furious with Director Hoggs, the man who managed the place, because he had beaten one of my best friends when she snuck a cookie from the kitchen. Anyway, I ran away because I didn't know what else to do. Kerri, my friend, was taken away in an ambulance. I found out later they told the medics that she had fallen down the stairs."

Hayden pauses, and something between raging anger and utter sadness passes across her features. She sighs again and looks down at her twiddling fingers. I give her arms a squeeze, reminding her that I am here.

She continues, "I was on a street in the middle of a classic dark and stormy night. I kept picking up rocks and throwing them at abandoned buildings, trying to sort through the big emotions I felt. That's when I saw her. A little girl who looked to be my age. She was wearing a pretty pink dress and her golden hair was tied in a matching pink ribbon. I only saw the colors with each flash of lightning. She was walking with a man, and as I sat and watched the two of them, the man caught sight of me. I ran away because I didn't know if he was dangerous or not. Growing up with the older boys in the group homes, I grew to have a healthy fear of guys who were bigger than me. Anyway, the man followed, which sounded alarms in my young brain, and I scaled the side of a building until I perched on the roof. He never saw me there. As I caught my breath, I saw the young girl pick something up off the street and then, a few moments later, the man heard her scream and ran back to her. He tried to calm her and figure out what was wrong, but it was too late. Minutes passed and she fell to the ground. She never stood back up."

With every little detail Hayden tells me, my stomach churns. Blood rushes from my face, and I'm left frozen as a stone-cold statue. Memories of cold, pouring rain soaking through my clothes as I hit my knees and tried to restart my sister's heart swirl in my head, making me dizzy. I kept looking back to see if the other girl was around, but she had disappeared. And because I chased her, simply trying to help her, my sister paid the price. Hayden's story is familiar.

Too familiar to be coincidental.

"She died. And I ran away," Hayden finishes in a blank tone.

My emotions roar as realization sinks in. *How twisted is fate! How intertwined our lives are! How God sees so much further into the future than we give Him credit for!*

Silence encompasses the room as my mind screams and spins. I swallow, sandpaper coating my throat. "Hayden, I have to tell you something."

"What is it?" She sniffles.

"That was me, Hayden."

She meets my eyes, tears already running down her cheeks.

I tug at my tie, needing to find room to breathe in the midst of the thickness of the reality I'm facing. "I'm him. I'm the man."

CHAPTER TWENTY-SEVEN

HAYDEN

"What do you mean you're him?" Panic builds and builds like rushing water pushing against a cracked dam. "If you're him, then that means the girl I watched die on the street that night is..."

"Ophelia," Darcy whispers her name. "My little sister."

The dam bursts, shattered to splintered pieces by the force of the water. If only he hadn't said the words aloud, maybe I could have spun the story in my head.

But he said them. And there's no going back.

I'm the reason his sister is dead.

"Darcy, I–" Words fail me as heaving sobs take control of my body. My knees crumble beneath me, but before I crash to the hardwood floor, Darcy catches me and lifts me to my feet. He doesn't let go, but instead, draws me into his arms, holding me tight and steady.

"The interview, Darcy."

"Shh," he whispers against my ear. "I'll send Bennie a text to get a hold of Ms. Towers."

I nod and lose myself in a wave of sobs. My heart has never felt more cracked and broken. The girl who haunts my dreams sometimes is my husband's dead sister. If I hadn't run away from the group home that night, he wouldn't have been distracted by me. He could have watched his sister more closely.

Moments pass. Or hours. I honestly don't know anymore. But at some point, the tears dry up, my body slumps in exhaustion, and Darcy carries me to the hotel bed.

After he tucks me in and makes his bed on the couch, the words I've been trying to say finally find their way out. "I'm sorry. You lost your sister because of me. That night has haunted me for as long as I can remember, but I can't begin to imagine how it must have been haunting you all this time. If I hadn't run away from the group home, then—"

"Hayden."

My name is a whispered plea on his lips. I sit up in bed so that I can see him. He's sitting on the couch, legs splayed and head down in his hands as his elbows rest on his knees. The stature of a man in deep thought. Maybe even anguish. Of course he would be in pain. He just found out his wife is the reason his sister is dead.

"My heart is breaking, Hayden," he finally says, and the admission cuts me. "I've blamed myself for that night for so long. My mother was in Tennessee visiting my grandparents. I had taken Ophelia to see a movie she'd been begging our father to see. When we got home, he was—" he blows out a breath, his leg bouncing,

"—having an affair right there in the middle anteroom. Thankfully, I'd walked in first, so I turned Ophelia right back around and took her out for a drive. I was seething with anger and pain, so I don't remember driving to the part of the city we ended up in. I ended up getting a flat tire, so while we waited for a driver to come pick us up, we went for a walk. She had begged me to take her for a walk, and I should have stuck to my no. It started pouring rain, and that's when I saw you."

Somehow, another tear forms in the corner of my eye before it rolls down my cheek. The salty taste is a bitter reminder of the tears I never shed for Ophelia Marshall. No, I ran away. I tried to forget that night happened. But every time I closed my eyes...

"I'm so sorry." My simple apology is a plea I can't bring myself to speak: *Don't leave me over this. I love you. Stay by my side. Please. Don't abandon me. I'll make it right somehow.*

Darcy goes silent again, and the ache in my chest rips open little by little with each passing heartbeat. If I thought Darcy and I would ever have a real marriage, well, that possibility was washed away with the broken dam pieces.

My biggest fear is coming true.

Through another sob, though I don't know how I can manage more tears, I whisper, "I'll sign the divorce papers as soon as you get them to me. I know you must hate me. Despise me. You did before we were married, and now you must want to see me burn in—"

"Hayden." He says my name with a forceful breath as he springs from the couch. In three long strides, he's hovering over me, standing beside the bed. "I've spent years thinking about Ophelia and that night. I've often wondered what happened to the young girl who ran away in thundering rain. I've prayed for her. And it was—it was you. All along." He kneels down and rubs my arms. "God answered my prayers. You survived. You're okay. Two young girls were not killed that night by drug needles disguised as pens, and that's a wonder to me. My sister lived a short but good life, Hayden." He pauses and laughs without a hint of mirth. "If this information had come out earlier, I would have found a way to blame you, yes. But now? I know your soul. You deserved to get to live, to experience a good life like my sister did."

I cower, looking anywhere but into his eyes. He doesn't mean that, right? It should have been me, not his sister. He *must* hate me. "Seriously, Darcy. Just tell me when and I—"

He stands abruptly, his hands sliding from my arms, and then he grabs my chin and tilts my face upward until my eyes are locked with his blue eyes, a darkened color that resembles a storm lingering above the ocean.

His next words pierce me to my core. "You are not to blame, and I need to reconcile with myself that I am not to blame either. Fentanyl and arsenic are to blame. Sin is to blame. Addiction is to blame. Crappy fathers are to blame." Then his gaze flicks to my mouth as he says, "I love you, Hayden *Sarah* Marshall. I thought trust and love were two separate notions, but they're not. They are intertwined, and you can't have one without the other. I trust and love you. You are not the sum of your past mistakes. You are not the reason I lost my sister. It was God's painful plan for us, and I see that clearly now."

Before I can respond, he drags my lips to his. Shocked, my eyes remain wide open as he presses his lips to mine. Then his mouth moves against mine, forcing my lips apart, and I note that he tastes like the misty rain on a sunny day. With a sigh, my eyes snap close and my arms snake around his neck, drawing him closer.

As he kisses me, his name plays like a broken record in my brain. *Darcy, Darcy, Darcy.* Every racing heartbeat sings his tune, my own song intertwining with his melody, creating something new and beautiful and chaotic.

Darkness and sunshine.

Quiet and loud.

Reserved and spontaneous.

Serious and playful.

Two opposites, though I can no longer tell who holds which label. On the inside, I'm just like Darcy. And he's just like my outside persona on the inside. Two people who never felt comfortable being honest about who they were finally opening up and letting the other see the real human behind the mask.

I *know* I love the man behind Darcy's mask.

He pulls away. The only sounds filling the silence between us are panting breaths. Unable to control the giddiness consuming the darkness I felt only moments ago, I burst into laughter. Darcy's laugh mingles with my own.

He wraps me in his arms, and I relax into his now familiar embrace. We've kissed quite a bit in the past couple of months when we've found time, but this kiss... "That kiss is dangerous within dating territory."

His chest rumbles with silent laughter. "Good thing your last name is Marshall."

"Then can we do that again?"

His hands cup my cheeks as he draws my face toward his. Our lips connect in an explosive moment of pent-up desire, longing, and passion. Time is lost as I swim in his kiss. I'm seen, heard, and cherished through this kiss.

When we finally pull apart again, we are gasping for air. And it feels like this night is about to start the next phase in our relationship... the start of a *real* marriage.

"What does this mean?" I ask.

"It means I am kissing my wife."

"Wife in name only," I correct, though everything inside of me wants him to counter the statement. He doesn't disappoint me.

"As soon as we get home, I am ripping the contract to shreds. You are my wife and now we will make it official. I love you. I've wanted to say that for weeks. I'm so in love with you, Hayden. The things that should drive us apart—our differences, our intertwined past—it brings us closer together. We said vows, and I meant them regardless of love. I promised to protect you, and I will... not only physically but also emotionally. I love you because you are outgoing, laugh loudly, and always have a smile on your face. I love how you are secretly sensitive, and I love that you only show that side to me. Hayden, I love you." He looks away shyly with a puff of air, then says, "I can't quit telling you that I love you."

Lost for words, I open and close my mouth like a fish. "I—I," I stop. Search for the appropriate response. But all I can say is, "I love you, too."

"Let's make this marriage official."

My heart flutters as Darcy tugs at the hem of his shirt while striding toward the light switch. He flicks it off, the room now only illuminated by the moonlight pouring through the hotel window, a spotlight for our unspoken confessions. My heart sings a tune of unadulterated bliss as his lips claim mine.

My husband.

In the eyes of the law, God, and my soul.

"I'm yours forever, Hayden. So help me God." His spoken oath is physically sealed over and over.

And over.

CHAPTER TWENTY-EIGHT

DARCY

Two wonderful months of genuine marriage.

Falling asleep in the same bed.

Saying "I love you" every chance we get.

Making love...

"Sir?" Bennie asks, holding a schedule in my face.

I shake the welcome images from my head and focus on my assistant. "What?"

"Remember we have the cross-party dinner tonight. You should probably start getting ready."

"Right, yes." I pinch the bridge of my nose and sigh. "I'm not looking forward to this. Why did they decide it was a good idea again?"

Bennie laughs. "To build repertoire."

I roll my eyes. "Whatever. I'll go get ready. Sucks they chose my birthday to host this fight club."

I make my way to my room to get ready, missing my wife. She's been gone all day dealing with campaign matters, and I say a little prayer that she'll make it back for this dinner. I'll need her presence to keep my sanity and not bite the heads off of establishment politicians.

An hour later, I'm in the car, Lionel driving, and Bennie clicking away on his tablet next to me.

No wife in sight.

We arrive at the Tower, and instead of going to the fourth floor for dinner, we take the elevator to the roof top. I ask Bennie what's going on, but he smirks as he opens the double-doors. "Happy Birthday, Mr. Marshall."

I step through, and the sound of the world's worst song floats through the air. A few hundred people stand in suits and dresses, smiling and singing along as if we have all been the best of friends since my birth forty years ago. I glance around the area, taking a deep breath of cool, autumn air. The lights strung from poles are pleasant, the fire in the middle of the floor is warm, throwing hues of blue and green in the mix, and the jazz band in the corner is playing a riveting rendition of "Happy Birthday."

I glare at my assistant, but then I find my wife standing by Mother's side, making their way to me pushing a cart with a giant ten-layered cake, and my frustration at a surprise party fades.

The crowd erupts in applause, and I shake my head at the two women approaching me. "Why?" I mouth to Hayden, but I can't stop the smile from spreading across my face at the joy she's radiating right now. It's infectious. I shift my eyes to Mother and nod once in appreciation.

"Blow out the candles, Killjoy," Hayden whispers against my ear before kissing me hello. I oblige, blowing out forty candles.

After smoke rises from the put-out candles, I make a self-effacing joke. "You're married to an old man, Divine Princess. How does that feel?"

"Like I won the lottery. Because it's you."

I wrap my arms around her and kiss her in a deep but appropriate-for-people way. Then I hug Mother. "I'm so glad this isn't a cross-party dinner."

We laugh, and then I'm swept into a frenzy of hellos and happy birthdays from the crowd of politicians, businessmen, and media personalities. If Mother and Hayden had to throw a party with a bunch of people I don't really care to celebrate with, at least they chose the rooftop location of the Tower and decorated it with black and gold colors. There's a Gatsby feel to the night, and oddly enough, I like it.

An hour later, I want to kick everyone else off the roof and keep the handful of people who I know, without a doubt, are joyful about my birth: Mother, Ren, and Hayden. The three of them stand together around me, and I look each of them in the eyes and try to portray my gratitude. But Hayden's tilt of the head and curls falling to one side—I love it when her hair is down like this—says my look portrays disdain.

Can someone out there teach me appropriate facial expressions to convey specific desires and emotions?

Ren approaches with a holler and claps me on the back.

"I know I called you old man at thirty, but now that I'm thirty-eight and you're forty, I'm going to redact the statement and say: *Now* you're an old man."

I laugh, pulling Ren into a typical man hug. If guests weren't around, I'd probably embrace him fully. "You'll change your mind in two years."

"Move, Ren. My turn." Hayden's arms form a wedge between me and Ren. She shimmies into the middle, and Ren steps away with his hands held high in surrender. "Hi," she says, looking up at me as she loops her arms around my waist.

"Hello again, my Divine Princess." I wrap my arms around her shoulders and tug her snug against my body, loving the way her lioness hair fills my face. It smells like yellow daisies and sunshine. This woman has become my warmth in the midst of this frigid world. "Thank you for this wonderful party."

Her eyebrow quirks. "You really like it? Ruth and I tried to throw something together that would fit your style but also be media-worthy of a future president."

"You did a great job." I kiss her forehead, then we reluctantly pull apart. The last couple of months of true marriage has been a beautiful learning curve. Our bickering hasn't changed, but now we sit down and talk through annoyances and issues instead of reacting to them. Hayden has taught me how to do that. She's also taught me that it's okay to enjoy life's nuances even if they are challenging to me.

"Happy birthday, my son," Mother says, placing a gentle hand on my arm. Tears form in her eyes, and I wrap her in a tight hug.

"Thank you, Mother. Thank you for all of this." I close my eyes, memories of hugs with this woman throughout my life flashing across my mind. "You've always been here for me. I should be the one throwing you a party today."

She sniffles. "Nonsense. You're the light of my world, the only gift I need." She steps away, and I let my eyes fully examine the three people in front of me—my wife in a stunning little black dress with painted red lips, my mother wearing an emerald-green dress that brings out the warmth in her brown eyes, and my best friend in his snazzy navy-blue Canali suit. Three people who love me and support me. Three people I love and support.

"Happy Birthday, Mr. Marshall," someone says from behind me. I turn around, pasting a smile on my face when I see Marcus Loveless and Priscilla, hand-in-hand. My smile falls and my stomach sinks, but I recover quickly when Hayden steps up to my side and loops her arm around my waist with a gentle squeeze. I pray a silent prayer that Hayden doesn't think my reaction has anything to do with me still wanting Priscilla. It doesn't. It has everything to do with the fact that she was seeing my opponent's son while we were engaged.

"Thank you," I say through a forced, gritted smile. "How nice of you two," I flick my eyes to Priscilla, "to come."

She softly smiles like this encounter is just as awkward for her. How does Marcus walk up to me nonchalantly, anyway? He knew I was engaged to his fiancée while he wooed her. He knew that I was going to marry the woman he now holds.

I'm glad I didn't, obviously, but pride is an easily wounded thing that doesn't forgive quickly.

"Could I steal a moment of your time, Mr. Marshall? My dad wouldn't approve, especially after having his face plastered everywhere with a bruised eye and broken nose a couple of months ago because of you. Oh, I don't blame you for what you did; it was justified because of what he said about your wife. I'm sure you know his polling has taken a hit because of it. But anyway, I want to run an idea by you. Your app has been extremely successful, and I have a plan for an app that you might want to invest in." Marcus's smile is hopeful, and as I look at his blond hair and blue eyes, his build, so similar to my own, I can't help but see a younger version of myself—a version that was just as hopeful when he started his own app endeavor. And maybe helping him out is a way to stick it to his father.

"Sure. Let's go grab drinks and chat by the fire."

He releases a breath and thanks me profusely. I kiss Hayden's cheek and she whispers, "You got this," before I walk away with Marcus already beginning to tell me about an app that will enhance COFFEE. I have to admit, I'm intrigued with the young man and his grit and passion.

I glance back while I sip scotch and listen to Marcus. Hayden and Ren are talking, Mother is chatting with a few political action committee donors, and Mr. Sato is talking animatedly on the phone off in a corner, his eyes constantly shifting to his son.

Everyone looks to be having a good time, and my heart swells.

Maybe a birthday party wasn't such a bad idea after all.

"Hi."

I stiffen, and Marcus stops talking. Slowly, I turn my head to acknowledge the voice beside me. "Hello."

Priscilla's eyes shift between Marcus and me, and after a moment of awkward silence, Marcus says, "I'm going to grab us a couple more drinks."

My glass is several sips from empty, but despite my protests, he walks away.

The fire blazes before my eyes as I focus on deep breaths.

"I'm sorry," Priscilla finally says. Even though I don't look in her direction, she continues. "I was seeing Marcus before I broke off the engagement with you. It was wrong of me, and I'm sorry."

I close my eyes, take a deep breath, and ask the only question that I can. "Why?"

"I love him." She pauses, and I think that's the only answer I'm going to receive, but then she says, "And more importantly, he loves me."

Opening my eyes, I turn toward her. Her head is tilted, her blue eyes watering. She truly is sorry. And can I fault her? She's right... I didn't love her. At least not in the capacity she deserved. "You didn't have to cheat like my father did on my—"

"I know, Darcy. I know. I want you to know that I never held his hand, hugged him, kissed him, or did anything physical with him while I was engaged to you. I simply met him and—"

"Fell in love," we say in unison.

"Yes. Fell in love." Priscilla folds her hands together as she turns to face the fire. I mimic her pose.

"Thank you for apologizing and telling me the truth. While I still believe emotional cheating is just as bad as physical cheating, I can't really complain. I didn't have much emotion to give you to start with. I'm sorry for that." I chuckle, a sad, distorted sound. While I have Hayden and I would never dream of anyone else, I still put Priscilla through the ringer, to say the least. She fought for me emotionally, but I was closed off to her tighter than a shoe three sizes too small.

"We ended up where we needed to be," she says, and I follow her gaze back to Hayden, who is still having the time of her life chatting in Japanese with my best friend. Her smile is absolutely radiant, lighting up this night brighter than the stars and the stringed lights.

"Yes, we did."

"Excellent. Everyone who needs to be here is here," a loud voice booms through a mic. We all turn our attention to see Richard Loveless, who is holding a champagne flute full to the brim and a manilla envelope, down the entire drink before speaking again. "I have some news to share. Reporters, you might want to record this."

I look to Priscilla as if to ask what's going on. She shrugs, though concern paints her face. Marcus runs over to us. "He's drunk."

I scoff. "Yeah, I can tell."

Hayden, Ren, Mother, and members of my campaign team gather around us while reporters drag out phones and notepads.

Whatever is happening, I'm only mildly concerned it will hurt my campaign. He's obviously drunk, and well, I'm sure people will be more occupied with that than whatever he thinks he has in that folder.

"We should stop him," Hayden says with more worry in her voice than I feel.

"Let him make a fool of himself," I state, crossing my arms and waiting.

Loveless continues, "I've got news to share with everyone. I think it's important for political candidates to be honest and up-front about their pasts, and Mr. Marshall's father left dirty secrets that the family attempted to cover up, as you all know." He pauses and takes a breath. "One of those dirty secrets involves my family. You all know my son, Marcus," he points to Marcus, whose face reddens with embarrassment, "and my wife, who is not present tonight."

My blood begins to run cold as I connect dots.

"Gerald Marshall had an affair with my wife, and Marcus is a result of said affair." Silence is loud as he opens the manila envelope. "And here are the DNA results for proof."

Questions rise from reporters as Marcus and I stare at one another.

I don't think we need to see the DNA results.

He is a younger replica of me. I've thought that since I've met him.

My breath catches in my throat, but I have to ask, "Did you know?"

He shakes his head, blond hair swishing. "I had no idea, I swear."

And we both turn our heads to Richard Loveless, who is holding the DNA results up while reporters snap pictures and ask questions.

Then they turn to us.

"Let's get out of here." I grab my—my *brother's* wrist and drag him to the elevator, Hayden and Priscilla following close behind, Ren holding Mother's hand as he leads her to us.

I press the close button until the doors firmly shut out the chaos ringing out, and we all stand in stunned silence as we go down, down, down.

POP CULTURE NOW!

LOVELESS IS HEARTLESS. SORRY, REPUBLICANS.
THE INDEPENDENT WINS THIS RACE IN OUR EYES.

By Krissy Towers

We might be a conservative platform here at *Pop Culture NOW!* but we are prepared to make an official endorsement for the Independent. In our eyes, he portrays conservative values in bucket-loads compared to the disgraceful Republican Richard Loveless.

In case you missed it, Loveless crashed Darcy Marshall's fortieth birthday party and sent shockwaves through the nation when he announced that Marcus Loveless, Richard's son, is a product of an affair between Darcy's late father, Gerald Marshall, and Loveless's wife. Did Richard really think we'd take his side on this one? While we despise infidelity, Darcy is not his father. We've watched and reported on Darcy this entire campaign, and while he has his faults, he is not his father. It's unfair for Richard to drop this October Surprise, and we think it will backfire tremendously. Rumor has it that Marcus plans to publicly endorse Darcy over his father. We are waiting for the official announcement and will report on it when it drops.

It looks like Marcus and Darcy are half-siblings and will have much to talk through in the coming days. We wish them the best of luck and conversations, and we want them to know we support them.

What a juicy, wild ride this election cycle has been! Stay tuned for night-of reporting on the cultural whisperings during election night.

Chapter Twenty-Nine

HAYDEN

D arcy paces outside of the conference room we normally use for campaign meetings here inside the estate. He runs his fingers through his hair before shoving his hands into his pockets, repeating the pattern over and over as his brown loafers shuffle against the wooden floor.

"Darcy," I say gently. He doesn't respond, so I stand and wait for him to think through whatever is running around his mind. After we made it outside of the Tower, Marcus and Darcy made plans to meet here later tonight after Marcus went home to talk to his mother. My heart breaks for everyone involved, especially my husband. We are one month out from the election, so he doesn't have the time to sit with this news and figure out the best way to navigate it. Time evades us, and we have to work through this and generate a statement by morning, or rumors will spread and spiral through the tabloids.

They already are.

"I have a brother," Darcy states, coming to an abrupt stop in front of me, eyes blank. "I lost a sister, and I have a brother." His voice is calm, factual.

Yeah, he hasn't processed this yet.

Continuing, "My father slept with Loveless's wife. He cheated on my mom before Ophelia died. We knew about his affairs after her death, but this?"

I search for words, knowing none could even begin to balm the hurt and confusion he's experiencing. But sometimes words are useless things. I wrap him in my arms, even though he doesn't return the hug.

Squeezing tighter and pressing my cheek against his chest, I say a silent prayer that the Lord will help him navigate this because I, quite frankly, don't know what to do other than be present.

As I end my unspoken prayer, Darcy crumbles.

His large body shakes with sobs as he crushes me in a hug that signals he's using me as his lifeline right now. I spread my legs to balance myself against the fullness of his weight, tightening my grip around his hunched back.

"I–I hate him," Darcy says between hitches in his breathing. "How dare he not tell me about my brother!"

I cling tighter to my husband as liquid soaks my black dress. My heart fractures for him, and if I could resurrect his father from the grave just to have unkind words with him, I would in the blink of an eye.

"Darcy." Ruth's voice sounds from behind us, and I feel Darcy's head lift from my shoulder.

He breaks free from my hold and folds into her arms as they cry together, the fractals of my heart breaking down even further.

I maneuver around them and walk down the hallway, around the corner, until I'm at the winding stairs. As I descend to the first floor, Darcy's cries haunt me, and I wish I could do something to ease his pain. But I know he needs to talk to his mom right now, and I should be downstairs to greet Marcus when he arrives.

As I wait, my mind whirs.

Darcy has a brother. I have a brother-in-law. Darcy's dad is dead. I have no idea who my father is or if he's even alive. Darcy's mom just had her life overhauled. I have no idea who my mother is, but I know she abandoned me. Darcy grew up in a controlled, pressured environment. I grew up as a floater with no one to hold me accountable, for the most part.

We are so different, yet we are the same.

And sometimes I think to myself that maybe it's a good thing I don't have parents to cut me and carve me up the way Darcy's father has done to him.

The door opens, and Marcus walks in, hand-in-hand with Priscilla. For the first time, I remember she's Darcy's ex. And now she's with his brother.

Maybe it's a good thing I don't have siblings, too.

I smile. "Hi, guys. Darcy's upstairs with Ruth. I can bring you to meet him after I make sure he's ready." I turn to go back up the stairs, but I pause and look back. "Priscilla, it might be best to let the guys talk alone."

She nods, her blonde curls bobbing. "I agree. We should probably talk ourselves."

With that, I take the stairs and let Darcy know Marcus is here.

Once the two guys and Ruth are situated, and Priscilla and I have brought them all water, the two of us head for the sitting room. She sits down, crossing one long leg over the other before smoothing the sparkly, silver dress she still wears from the party tonight.

"This is awkward," Priscilla says in a self-deprecating tone. "Please believe me when I say I had no idea Marcus was Darcy's half-brother. What Richard did tonight is inexcusable. He hurt the man he raised as his own, humiliated his wife publicly, and in the process, turned the lives of two important people to me upside down."

I clasp my hands together, fiddling with my wedding band with my thumb. "Yes, he's a foul man, that's for sure. Glad we can agree on that. How are Marcus and his mom holding up?"

"Marcus is, surprisingly, overjoyed to have a brother. Martha, however, is getting ready to announce she is divorcing Richard."

"What? After all these years? Why did she stay so long?"

Priscilla shrugs. "Your guess is as good as mine. Richard has known from the very beginning that Marcus wasn't actually his, but the birth certificate says otherwise. He made the decision to raise him as his own, so we were all dumbfounded tonight. I can only assume Richard's disdain for Darcy and his father, coupled with the fact that Darcy and Richard are neck-and-neck in early polling, drove him to try and drop an October Surprise to ruin Darcy's chances at the presidency."

"Well, it's going to backfire," I scoff. Priscilla purses her light pink lips and agrees. I continue, "I think Darcy is happy to have a younger brother, too. But it's going to take time for him to accept it. He's having a difficult time because of how Marcus came into existence, especially because of Ophelia."

"I figured as much," Priscilla says, and I remember that the woman sitting off to the side of me in the ornate brown chair knows my husband. Maybe even better than I do.

"How was Darcy as a boy?" I ask.

Priscilla smiles, and her blue eyes take on a faraway look. "After Ophelia died, Darcy wasn't the same. Yes, he was always prim, proper, and controlling, but he had this warmth about him. He always looked for the good in others and was always the first to step up and help. He cracked jokes and smiled and let people in. He knew how to balance work and play."

She trails off, and I nod along, unfolding my hands. "He's still that man underneath his icy exterior. He's got a genuine goodness that saturates his soul. It runs so much deeper than the media mask he wears." I don't mention how much I love the way he is because of his autism. It makes him all the more special to me. But I don't know if Priscilla knows that about him. I don't know who he has or hasn't told in his past.

"You're partly to blame, you know?" Priscilla asks rhetorically, arching an eyebrow. Not one to opt for false humility, I grin.

"Yeah, I do. He's melted for me, huh?"

Priscilla laughs. "Yes. He has." And then in all seriousness, she says, "I'm glad he has you, Hayden. I was never right for him. But his younger brother," she waggles her eyebrows, "is like my favorite pair of jeans."

"Christmas dinner is going to be awkward this year, isn't it?" I stand, chuckling. Priscilla mimics my actions, but then she hugs me.

"Not if we don't let it."

Darcy, Ruth, and Marcus walk into the room at that moment, and Priscilla and I break apart to join our guys. I grab Ruth's hand and give it a reassuring squeeze.

"Well?" Priscilla asks, and I'm glad she beat me to it.

Marcus and Darcy, with puffy red faces that so closely resemble one another, smile sadly. Marcus responds first, "I was shocked, but overall, I couldn't have asked for a better older brother. I've looked up to him for a long time."

Darcy, to my surprise, snickers. "I guess I should have known. You look like me when I was your age."

"Just hotter," Marcus jests, and we all laugh, though it doesn't quite lighten the somber mood. If anything, it's a reminder that the men have different mothers.

"I know you aren't my son," Ruth says, choking on the words, "but you are always welcome into my household." She shifts her eyes to Priscilla. "You too, missy."

My heart swells.

I know the next few months will be difficult.

I know there is going to be story after story circulating with misinformation.

I know we could lose this election and Richard could win.

But at the end of the day, I have a family to come home to.

I have Darcy. We have Ruth and Ren and Stella. And now we have Marcus and Priscilla, no matter how awkward things may get. And who knows. Maybe even Marcus's mother will join us, though that will ultimately be up to Ruth.

I slip my arm around Darcy, and he looks down at me. I smile, mouth the words, "I love you," and bump my hip into him.

He leans down and gives me the sweetest forehead kiss before saying, "I love you, Hayden."

Nothing else. I will never need anything else than this right here.

CHAPTER THIRTY

DARCY

With a gritted smile, I force myself through the gathered crowd to the front of the banquet room within Ophelia Estate, step onto the stage behind the podium, and adjust the microphone. At any moment, I could tumble over. My knees are spaghetti noodles and my arms are fifty pound dumbbells. My heart can't decide if it wants to panic or stop.

While applause erupts, I peruse the room, exquisitely decorated in a variety of red, white, and blue flowers, American flags, and dimmed lights. Mother had a team come in and decorate the room for election night. Hayden has spent the day managing the campaign team, checking polls, and doing wifely things such as stolen kisses in private and short squeezes of my hand for reassurance.

Marcus, my new brother (which I'm still trying to wrap my head around as it's only been a few weeks since we both found out), and Priscilla, opted to announce their support for my candidacy and are in attendance here at my election night watch party.

Richard did not drop out of the race like so many people were calling out for him to do, but the polls show he is the biggest loser of tonight. I just have to beat out the Democratic candidate at this point.

Taking in a deep breath—and trying not to salivate over hints of Italian spices wafting into the room from the kitchen—I lock eyes with my wife, who is wearing a dazzling smile and a long-sleeved, ribbed, button-up white dress that hits right below her knees. At the nod of her head and bounce of her curls, I begin my election night opening speech.

"Thank you all for coming out to my election watch party tonight. As you may know, early voting results are not necessarily in my favor, but those votes are just the tip of the iceberg. As the eastern states begin rolling in their voting day numbers, my team and I expect to see a dramatic increase in our favor. Thank you for your unwavering support throughout this campaign, and no matter what happens tonight, you all have been the best team and support group a person could ask for. Enjoy the night."

Hands clap together in a thunderous sound while I make my way down the few short steps and off the elevated platform, right into the loving arms of my wife.

"You did good," she whispers in my ear. I squeeze her tight, inhaling the scent of daisies and vanilla and sunlight. We break apart and make our way to the viewing room that the team set up. I take a seat while Paul and Hayden pull up the live electoral map on the big screen at the front of the room. Other computers are lined up alongside the walls with current voting trends, statistics broken down at local and state levels, and different news stations on mute with the captions on.

"The eastern polls close in thirty minutes," Paul says with a smile and two claps of his hands. "This is going to be a long night, as you already know, but it's going to be worth it when Mr. Marshall gets to stand in front of the nation and give his first presidential address." The team nods and shouts their agreements, and I'm swept up in the vitality of the night. It's going to be one of the longest nights I've ever encountered—second only to my sister's death—but I won't need coffee to stay awake; my nerves are wired enough for the job of ten espresso shots.

As the minutes tick by, I try not to look at the clock and instead focus on silent prayers asking God for His will to be done, and also selfishly asking that His will is for me to win the election. Bargaining thoughts begin to form, but I quickly shove them aside; it's not smart to try and bargain with God. I sit there, twiddling my thumbs, because at this point, there is nothing left I can do but pray and wait.

"Son, I'm so proud of you." Hands fold around my shoulders, and I look up to see my mom standing behind me, gazing lovingly down at me. I smile and place one of my hands over hers. Her admiration fills me with warmth and goodness—traits that could have only come from her.

The way she has handled the news about my father's affair, talking with Martha Loveless and allowing her into our space as she divorces Richard, has thoroughly winded me. I don't think I could have done it if I were her, but then again, I actively talk to Priscilla again. Mostly because of my brother, though.

"Thanks, Mom. But I should say that without you, I wouldn't be the man I am today. I owe every ounce of success I've had to you and your pure, kind heart."

"Oh," she cries and wraps her arms around my neck. I stand up and twist in her arms, wrapping my arms around her waist.

"Seriously, Mom, how did you put up with him for so long?"

She cries again and stutters out, "You called me 'Mom'. I haven't heard that word since you were nineteen and Ophelia passed away."

My body still stiffens at the mention of my sister's name, but I choose to overcome it and breathe, mandating each muscle in my body to relax. "It was hard to deal with her death, and then finding out about what Father did. Calling you 'Mother' instead of 'Mom' was a way to dissociate from reality, I think. It placed you at arm's length, though you never respected that subconscious decision of mine." I try to laugh, but instead, a dry cough releases.

She lets go of me and pinches my cheeks. "No son of mine is going to push me away," she says in a cooing voice before laughing.

"Goodness, Mom. Stop it." I laugh, stepping away from her. "It's election night for crying out loud. Do you know how many cameras are outside these doors?"

"It will only help your case if the nation sees how much you love and adore your mother."

"Ha, ha, ha." I roll my eyes. "But seriously, Mom. How did you overcome what he did? I heard you all those nights, sobbing in your room alone. I'd walk in and you'd wipe away the tears and smile like you had been smiling the entire night."

Mom smiles a sad smile, then she grabs my hands. "I had to be strong for us, Darcy. You were all I had left. Ophelia left us, and your father couldn't handle the pain. He found his way to escape it. At the time, it hurt, knowing he was with other women, but I felt I couldn't blame him because I was a shell of a human at the time. I had to find a way to escape the pain, too, and in all honesty, looking after you was my escape."

I squeeze her hands, and she looks away from my eyes. "I know I am not to blame for his infidelity—nor for his decision to be unfaithful. It was his decision. But I was not the wife, the partner, he needed to lean on through his own grief. Grief is deceptive like that, you know. People think trauma will bind souls together, but sometimes, it rips and snaps the bonds so intricately sewn together until there's nothing left but a gaping wound."

"I'm so sorry, Mom." I hear her. I see what she's saying, but I can't bring myself to make the same excuses for Father that she makes for him. He should have helped her through, as the man, no matter what.

He should have helped me instead of verbally beating me into emotionless submission.

"Don't be sorry. I've never been sorry for protecting you from the harshness of this world for as long as I could. I've never been sorry for choosing you or staying by your side. I love you, Darcy."

I blink tears away and hug her tightly one more time.

"Darcy! Darcy, look! Buzz News Network just called North and South Carolina for you." Hayden squeals, jumping and clapping while barreling toward me. Mom steps away and my arms catch Hayden just as she pounces in my direction. Claps surround us as

I spin my wife in a celebratory circle. She places her lips to my ear and a rippling shudder runs down my spine. "I have a good feeling about tonight."

"Mm, so do I," I whisper back, pressing my hand against her back as I set her on her feet. She looks at me, catches sight of my smirk and lazy eyes, and then blushes.

"Darcy, goodness. About the election, I mean."

I chuckle. "That's what I meant, too. And also *after* the election." I wink, then place a kiss on her forehead. She giggles and rolls her eyes before turning away and heading back to Paul and the computer screens.

The door to the viewing room swings open, and Stella Harper walks through wearing a red version of the dress my wife is wearing. Objectively, she looks great, but my wife definitely wears it better.

I can't quit thinking and saying those words: my wife. I knew I would get married someday, but I always thought it would be a union like the one we started out with—one of convenience. Never had I dreamed I would become a simp (that's what the kids at the group home say?) for my wife. As I watch Hayden and Stella embrace, the smile on Hayden's face growing wider with each passing moment, and her laughter ringing out through the room, I know I would do whatever it takes to keep that smile on her face.

I would be that morally gray hero who brought a city to ruins for her.

"Look, Darcy! Stella made it." Hayden yells from across the room. Stella waves, and I wave. Analyzing Stella for a moment, I conclude she looks happy. I often wondered if moving to Mississippi took a toll on her; she thrived in city life. She used to talk about how much she missed home but always had an excuse as to why she couldn't return.

Walking over to the women, and Paul, I ask Stella if Lucas came tonight.

"No, he needed to stay behind. His friend, Jared, went and broke his leg again in a wrestling match. His wife, Gracie, is about to pop out their baby, so he went to be of assistance. I tried, but Gracie told me that I needed to be here and that they have enough help to finish last-minute house things before the baby comes."

Hayden wraps an arm around Stella's waist, and Stella leans her head on Hayden's shoulder. I wish the two of them had more time to spend in person. They were inseparable when Stella lived here in New York, always sneaking around this house and whispering in corners. Speaking of...

"Where are you staying tonight?" I ask.

"I got a hotel not too far from here. I didn't have time to check in as I wanted to come straight here, though."

"Why don't you cancel the reservation and stay here tonight? I can give my wife up for a singular night." As I say the words, I remember that only moments ago I was teasing Hayden about *after the election,* and I instantly regret giving her up.

Stella raises her eyebrows, but then her red lips stretch into a smile. "I'd love to stay. I promise I'll only steal her away for a little while. I'll send her back to you for bedtime." She winks, and I feel heat creep up my neck. I'll never get over Stella's emboldened spirit to say whatever is on her mind regardless of propriety.

"Oh, I'm so happy," Hayden exclaims, hugging Stella and then dragging me to her side. Marcus and Priscilla join us, and Hayden's smile somehow grows as she says, "All of my favorite people are here. Oh," she waves my mom over. "Ruth! Come join."

Mom walks over, greets Stella, and then joins this little hug group. Every fiber of my being longs to get out of this, but again, I'd do anything to keep that smile on Hayden's face. Then again... this is nice. We are just missing—

"Ren!" Hayden shouts as if she was reading my mind. "You made it."

I slowly turn my head to see Ren, and his expression is nothing less than I'd expect. His cheeks are swollen with all the laughter he is holding, his face going red. One hand clutches his stomach while the other rises to cover his mouth as air shoots out followed by uncontained laughter. "This is a sight to behold," he says between cackles.

"Come join us," Hayden shouts.

"I'm coming in." Ren barrels toward us, his body slams into mine, causing the group hug to shift and teeter, on the verge of sending us all to the ground in a heap of limbs. Thankfully, we steady ourselves, and I take the opportunity to slide out of the huddle.

"Central time zone reports are rolling in," Paul announces, and we all turn our attention to the screens.

The news outlets begin making calls based on combined early votes and the majority of the votes from the onset of counting, and most states, to my surprise, lean toward me over the democratic candidate, but it's still too close for comfort. With each call for the democratic candidate in some of the swing states, my heart sinks. I never expected to win over the democratic vote since my Independent leanings are more conservative, but now that I've thoroughly secured most of the Republican vote simply because of Loveless's idiocy, I might stand a solid chance. The night started fantastic with North and South Carolina, who by this point are leading by double-digit percentages for me, but I'm going to need more than that to get the needed 270 electoral votes to win.

"Don't give up yet, Killjoy," Hayden says, patting my back. "The night's not even close to over."

Mountain time closes and then Pacific time. Finally, Alaska and Hawaii close, and all there is left to do is wait. I am ushered in and out of the viewing room, giving small interviews with the press I invited in tonight and joining in watch party activities with those who are not on my team but have given their endless support for my campaign over the past two years. States continue to slowly report, and the Midwest creates a surge in support for me. Emotions shift with every tick of the percentages from the states, rising when a state is called for me and collapsing when a state is called for the democratic candidate. I wish the country understood the stakes of this election; if the democrats win, then the budget will significantly inflate, we will continue to be involved in senseless wars across the world, immigration reform efforts will stall, and, most importantly to me and my team, the foster care system and pandemic of homelessness will not get the appropriate spotlight that they deserve because that party is too wrapped up in identity politics.

Two in the morning rolls around, and the entire team and I are chewing our nails. We are tied, waiting for Florida, Arizona, Minnesota, and Wyoming to report.

The dilemma?

Both of us would need all four states to successfully cross the 270 electoral votes threshold.

"I have never been this on edge," I say to Hayden, who is sitting beside me and constantly rubbing my back with one hand. At this point, she has shifted out of campaign manager mode and has stayed by my side as my amazing, supportive wife.

The woman who is hopefully about to adopt the title of First Lady of the United States.

"Hmm, I remember countless times of you being ridiculously on edge with me around." Hayden bumps my shoulder, and I smirk at her.

I clear my throat, feeling a little sentimental since it's the wee hours of the morning. I face my wife, gazing into her warm, brown eyes. She lifts an eyebrow, and I take her hands into mine.

"Mrs. Marshall, you are one of the most infuriating women I know, but I wouldn't change your spitfire attitude or the fact that you speak truth regardless of who it offends. You are sunshine and happiness and every color of yellow on the spectrum. Even when you place me on the edge of sanity, I know that I can trust your judgment and I love every part of who you are, *my wife*." I kiss her cheek and whisper against her ear, "My divine princess."

She moans softly and her body molds against mine.

Someone clears a throat, and Hayden pushes back from me, releasing my hands, her eyes widening with realization.

"Do you two need to take a break and grab some alone time?" Stella asks, humor seeping through her words. "Seriously, I can go back to the hotel..."

"No," Hayden says, interrupting her. "I need best friend time, too."

"Um, guys," Paul says. We all snap our attention to him, and he stands in front of the screen, blocking our view. "Florida is in, and..." Paul steps away from the screen, showing that Buzz News Network has officially called Florida for me.

My heart races as applause fills the room. The doors to the viewing room swing open, and I vaguely hear Micah, my social media coordinator, shouting to the crowd about our recent win.

With each passing moment, my brain repeats one phrase: *three more states.* My heart beats in time with the words. I feel Hayden's hands grasping mine like they are her lifeline, but I can't seem to hear what anyone around me is saying. My eyes are glued to the screen as another alert comes through.

Wyoming is in, and it's called for Darcy Marshall. For me.

Halfway there.

The world blurs around me as all I can focus on is the screen.

Minnesota is called for me.

Hayden says something, but I can't hear her. She pulls me from my seat and ushers me out of the viewing room, though the entire time I walk backward with my eyes on the screen.

An alert flashes across the screen just as the door closes.

Hayden turns me to face the crowd. Cameras flash and reporters shove their mics in my faces as Hayden whispers in my ear, "I love you, Mr. President."

"We did it," I whisper, and then reality catches up with me and a Cheshire Cat smile takes over my face. I turn to the one person I want to celebrate this moment with: my wife. "We did it!"

The room erupts with cheers and claps, and a chant begins, probably started by Ren.

President Darcy Fitzwilliam Marshall.

I look at my first lady, she smiles like everything is right in the world, and I pull her into a deep kiss, pressing my hands firmly against her back as she entwines her arms around my neck.

She pushes me away before the kiss gets too wild, covering her mouth and giggling. "Darcy, there are cameras everywhere. This is live across the nation, possibly the world!"

I smirk. "Good. Let the world know that the president of the United States is madly and irrevocably in love with his brilliant wife."

"Thanks for trusting me with your campaign...and with your heart," she says with stars in her eyes. I'll never tire of that admiring gaze, and I pray she knows that I admire her more.

"Thanks for staying by my side and loving the roughest, coldest parts of me."

"USA! USA! USA," echoes through the room.

I take Hayden by the hand and lead her up the short stairs to stand behind the podium. We wave to the crowd, and then I clear my throat.

"Before I begin, let me introduce you to the real winner tonight." I grab Hayden's hand, kiss it, raise it in the air, and catch her eyes. "My campaign manager, my wife, and your First Lady,

Hayden Sarah Marshall. I thank God every day that He gifted me with you."

POP CULTURE NOW!

*DAYS AFTER LOSING ELECTION, RICHARD LOVELESS
FOUND DEAD IN UPPER EAST SIDE ESTATE*

By Krissy Towers

While we cheered on Darcy Marshall to win the election, we never imagined we would enter into a mourning period for his rival, Richard Loveless. The exalted and well-loved Republican candidate who has led a long career in politics was found dead in his Upper East Side mansion three days after losing the election to President-Elect Darcy Marshall. Sources say his wife, who was filing for divorce after Mr. Loveless exposed their son's true genealogy (see report here), stumbled upon her husband lying unconscious in their bathtub. Official toxicology reports suggest Mr. Loveless had traces of OxyContin in his bloodstream, and the official cause of death is a suicidal overdose.

However, we at Pop Culture NOW! like to dig, and some reports are touting cyanide poisoning as the cause of Mr. Loveless's death. Conspirators believe the government is attempting to hide the real cause of death in an effort to cover a massive underground organization known as One Love Organization. Theorists suggest this organization is running the world by planting leaders one at a time.

Did Richard Loveless take his life, or was it taken from him because he failed to complete the mission? We are simply asking the questions others are too afraid to broach.

Stay tuned for more information as we unravel the threads one by one.

EPILOGUE

REN

"So help me God."

After adding his religious affirmation to the end of the oath, my best friend is now officially the president of the United States.

President Darcy Fitzwilliam Marshall.

I watch the scene unfold as "Hail to the Chief" plays. The crowd roars with applause as American flags wave in the chilly D.C. air, Darcy and Hayden walk to shake hands with the former administration, and then Darcy prepares for a speech with Hayden standing brilliantly at his side.

The young man who once hid in corners to escape the public eye because of the reputation of his father has taken the family name back while giving the United States their most handsome and intelligent president yet. Sorry, Reagan. You will have to take a backseat to my best friend. I have no doubt Darcy will lead this country well.

He found his purpose, his drive. More importantly, he found a woman who keeps him in check and calls him out on his grumpy moods. Hayden Sarah Marshall is going to fulfill her duty well—being the real brains behind the president.

I tug at the hairs flying out of my *chonmage* from the slight wind, and then I tuck the thin strands behind my ear futilely.

Like my hair that refuses to stay put, I wonder what's in store for me now? Will I be like the flying hairs around me, having no direction for my future? As Darcy begins his speech, I can't think of anything else other than everyone around me seems to have found their purpose in life.

I'm thirty-eight.

Darcy is president at forty.

My dad became the ambassador at thirty.

I'm... only a shadow of my dad.

Is this all there is to my existence? Am I only called to be the son of a wealthy businessman and Japanese ambassador to the U.S., the son of a sweet, gentle woman who only wishes to have grandchildren from her only child, and the best friend to the president of the United States?

Am I only good enough to complete side business ventures for my father while he tends to his ambassador duties? Am I not able to stand on my own outside of my father's shadow and create my own path?

"*Musuko*, what's wrong? You look like your friend lost the presidency instead of being inaugurated just now." My father, Chikara Sato, places a hand on my shoulder. I smile at the aging man, who is slightly shorter and pudgier than my five-nine, slim frame. His gray hair complements his olive skin, and his dark brown eyes, the same as my own, shine with concern.

While Darcy's father was a complete tool, my dad has always provided for me, had my back, and loved me fiercely. He's had his moments of being "too busy" like any politician, but ultimately, my mom always brought him back down to earth to focus on the most important things in life: family and responsibility to others. Mom grew up in Okinawa, a small island off the larger island of Japan. She often spoke of the concept of *ikigai*, which I roughly translated to life's purpose. Though when I told her I had purpose in life—I was their son and good at helping Dad with business—she would sigh and say, "You need to spend time in Okinawa."

"Ren?"

I shake my head in an attempt to clear my thoughts. "I'm fine. Just thinking about what's next for me."

Dad chuckles. "I have an idea."

"Hmm?"

He begins to talk, his words flowing quickly as if he has to get them all out at once. "There's an opening for an U.S. ambassador to Japan. I'm already in the process of getting you the job. You leave for Japan in March. The embassy is in Tokyo, but the appointment doesn't begin until August. Until then, you can explore Okinawa where your mother grew up. You know she's wanted you to spend time there for more than one week a year. This is the perfect opportunity. They are already readying themselves for your arrival."

When he finishes, my heart is beating double time, and Darcy's speech has effectively faded into the background. I stare at Dad;

his eyes are hopeful while I'm sure mine are screaming a very Americanized message, "What the heck, Dad?!"

"*Oto-san*, you can't just spring this on me without asking me about it." Panic ensues as I think of moving to Japan. Yes, I'm Japanese, but really, I'm nothing more than a few customs Mom has taught me, the language, and yearly visits to the embassy in Tokyo with the occasional week-long visit to Okinawa.

Dad swats a hand through the air. "*Baka ei.* I can and I have. You are too Americanized."

I start to interrupt, but he holds up a hand to stop me.

"I know it's my fault because I didn't spend adequate time teaching you our traditions and things of cultural importance. I should have had you spend more time in Japan growing up, but we can change that now." Dad reaches into the pocket of his dark gray suit jacket and pulls out a plane ticket. As he holds it out to me, I eye it as if it will bite my hand if I reach out.

If I take this ticket, my entire life as I know it changes. It's not so much the ambassador position that bothers me as it is the idea of moving to Japan. It may as well be a foreign country to me, even though I've spent a little time there every year. I never bothered to learn proper customs and adhere to cultural norms. After a week, I would be back in America, so what was the point?

Japanese may be my ethnic make-up, but I'm all American.

Dad sighs and pushes the ticket out farther towards me. "You can do this, *Musuko*. I wouldn't have arranged this if I didn't believe in you. Take the ticket."

My hand lifts without my permission. My fingers brush the top of the ticket before I pluck it from his hands.

"When you're in Japan and someone gives you a gift, be sure to receive it with two hands and a slight bow of your head."

My fingers loosen their grip on the ticket, but I clutch it tighter before it has the chance to fall like a feather to the ground. The slight wind in the air would carry it far away if I let it. All I have to do is let go...

But I don't.

It's as if something came over me, calmed my nerves, and boosted my confidence. I can only accredit the certain peace to God.

Only moments ago I questioned what my purpose was, and it seems God is giving me a nudging answer. I can do this, right? Japan is in my blood, after all. And becoming the U.S. ambassador to Japan is a career I know I could tackle, thanks to growing up under the Japanese ambassador to the U.S.

Who knows? Maybe this is my calling. I never thought I'd actually step into my dad's footsteps, but this could be good. At the very least, I can have a worthy career that would make my parents proud.

I've been content in life, always the cheerful, happy-go-lucky guy. But seeing Darcy run for president, to strive for something more in his life than business as his father did, well, it's inspiring and challenging to me.

I could have more in life; I could step out of my father's shadow.

"Okay, *Oto-san*. I'll give it a go."

The End

LOVED THE STORY?

C onsider leaving a review on Amazon and Goodreads!

ALSO BY

DREW TAYLOR

Scan the QR code or click on the link to learn more about Drew Taylor's books!
www.drewtaylorwrites.com

ACKNOWLEDGMENTS

(Original Version): This book was a labor of pain and love. When I set out to start the first draft, I cried. I kicked myself for making Darcy such a big, complex guy. I wanted to scream and throw the entire idea out of the window. But then, as I began draft two and later draft three, I fell in love with the story. When I began draft four, I had the story down, and then draft five was simply to change the formatting. I'm proud of myself for not giving up on this story, and I'm even prouder of myself for writing this story while deep in the trenches of my own heartbreak.

There are a handful of people who I need to thank because they simply wouldn't let me give up on this story: Jordan (#manreadsromance), thank you for pushing me to finish this and for loving my stories. Kaitlyn, thank you for marrying an amazing guy (and for being my bestie, of course). Aubrey, thanks for letting me use your middle name and for loving P&P so much that I generated this book idea. Seriously, this book is a result of you in a way, ha! Leah, you fixed Darcy. At least, you helped me fix Darcy. Thank you for your 17 page developmental edit. I TRULY needed it. Lastly, Callie, Abby, Latisha, and Whitney. Thanks for letting me bounce ideas off of you and rant about how difficult this book was to write. You are the real MVP. Dear Reader, you can thank these people alongside me because without them, this book probably wouldn't exist.

As always, I want to thank my Lord and Savior, Jesus Christ. I'm always left in awe at the end of every story I write simply because You take hold of the stories and direct them into places I never imagined I'd go. Thanks for being the Heart of every story. To my parents, my brothers, and my grandma who always support me; I love you. To my betas, thank you so much for helping me tighten this story to its final version. To Drew's Crew: THANK YOU so much for sticking around even in my lull period. It means the world to me that you waited for me and cheered me on. Finally, thank you, Dear Reader, for picking up this book. I pray you smiled, laughed, cried, and swooned. I also hope you learned that love and trust go hand-in-hand and that both are mighty important to relationships. Never settle for someone who can't give you both.

(Revised Edition): I want to say everything I said above, except I want to add one thing I experienced during this re-write.

I've grown so much as a writer. From 2023 to 2025, I can tell how much my craft has grown. I'm so thankful to the Lord for allowing me to steward this ability. This book is now something I am so very proud of.

Special thanks to Anna, Hannah, Kim, Latisha, Whitney, Lindsay, and so many others who I may have forgotten to name!

Ally, thanks for coordinating the relaunch of this book. You simply amazed me with your skills, and I genuinely hope we work together more in the future!

To the OGs who loved the original story: thanks for understanding that I absolutely had to re-write this novel. It brought closure to a part of my life that was painful. When I look upon this book, I now feel joy and peace instead of resentment and chaos. Thanks for sticking with me, friends!

ABOUT THE AUTHOR

Drew Taylor writes modern closed-door romance stories from a Christian worldview. She believes faith-based romance can be full of heart, humor, and hope while showcasing the reality of our fallen human condition. Her redemptive and engaging stories point to the One who embodies true love–Jesus Christ.

Drew is from south Mississippi but now resides in Alaska where she attempts to engage 15 and 16-year-olds in classic world litera-

ture. When not teaching or writing, she enjoys reading, Booksta-
gram, baking Christmas goodies (even in the middle of June), re-
searching random history facts, watching K-dramas, and spending
quality time with the people who mean the most to her. Sign up for
her newsletter for important updates in case Social Media decides
to kick her off one day: https://mailchi.mp/61fed5b940fb/drew
-taylor-author

Follow Drew:

Instagram: @authordrewtaylor

Facebook: Drew Taylor, Author

Pinterest: @authordrewtaylor

www.ingramcontent.com/pod-product-compliance
Lightning Source LLC
Chambersburg PA
CBHW050008120726
47903CB00006B/1681